AMBITION
& LOVE

Books by Ward Just

AMBITION & LOVE

WARD JUST

A RICHARD TODD BOOK

Houghton Mifflin Company

BOSTON   NEW YORK   1994

Library of Congress Cataloging-in-Publication Data
Just, Ward S.
Ambition and love / Ward Just.
p.   cm.
"A Richard Todd book."
ISBN 0-395-68196-0
1. Women artists — France — Paris — Fiction.   2. Americans — France —
Paris — Fiction.   3. Paris (France) — Fiction.   I. Title.
PS3560.U75A77   1994   93-33758
813'.54 — dc20   CIP

Printed in the United States of America

BP 10 9 8 7 6 5 4 3 2 1

To Sarah

AMBITION
& LOVE

HARRY

W HEN THE WEATHER CLEARED I left my apartment,
no destination in mind. I only wanted fresh air and
the mild morning commotion of a city street, and you
could find that anywhere in Paris. I bought a newspaper and read
it while I drank a coffee at the café around the corner. The café
was cheerful but the newspaper was as gray and lifeless as a
tombstone. Roll the dice, I thought, and ordered a marc to go
with the coffee, something I had not done in years. And when I
tasted the marc, I remembered why.

I walked through the market to the river, intending to look in
the bookstalls, always a specific for the blues. The city was coming alive as the seasons changed. It was March, too early for
brisk trade, but still the miserable tour buses were parked in
front of the Louvre, across the river, and I reflected again how
truly graceless the old palace was, a fine example of sixteenth-
century megalomania. A tour bus from Amsterdam had more tact
than the façade of the Louvre, and was much cleaner.

My friend Georges was back at his stall near the Pont du Car-
rousel, and I stopped a moment to chat with him. He had been

away, some unspecified medical problem, and I was glad to see him looking fit.

And how is your dear wife? he asked.

She is — fine, I said after a moment.

Hasn't it been a difficult winter?

Impossible, I said.

And business is terrible, he said.

Mine, too, I said. Horrible.

Plot? he asked. Or characters?

Everything, I said glumly.

With an amiable smile he reached into the small bin and brought out a used book, presenting it to me with a flourish. It was the French edition of my second novel. In pristine condition, the book had been priced at a hundred francs, up twenty-five from the last time I'd checked. So Harry Forrest was rising on the Bourse, a growth stock. My spirits improved immediately.

It came in the other day, Georges said.

If I sign it, you can ask another twenty-five francs.

Perhaps fifty, Georges said.

If I signed it *to my chère amie Edith Piaf* you could ask five hundred.

Alas, Georges said. Our noble little sparrow was dead long before your book was published.

An inconvenience, I said. Perhaps — *to Sartre?*

He is surely an immortal, Georges said. Did you ever meet him?

Once, at a reception, I said. A few years before he died.

Once was enough, he said.

We laughed together, I signed, and he put the book back in the bin.

Very many thanks, he said.

With pleasure, I said.

Will you remember me to your wife? A lovely woman.

Au revoir, Georges, I said.

À bientôt, Harry. Be of good cheer! The day is fine.

My wife and I had separated. She had departed for America in

January, and as I continued up the quay I remembered the many times we had walked this quay and other quays, watching the boats and the fishermen and the strollers. She had always helped me with my books, and now I found myself at a loss, though Georges had helped things; even the façade of the Louvre was improved. Up ahead was the Musée d'Orsay, another favorite morning rendezvous. It was unmistakably my destination; it had probably been in the back of my mind all along. Often when my work was stalled I would visit the Musée d'Orsay. Ellen and I had often gone together.

For a long time we would avoid the lower floors and go at once to the great Impressionist galleries higher up, and somehow I would be led back into my own work by Degas or Manet. I thought of the pictures as stories, not necessarily narratives but actions; often they were allegories. When the picture was done properly, you knew what came before and what was likely to come after, and what you saw was not uncompleted action but a kind of summing-up. Think of Degas's absinthe drinkers sitting stunned at a café table, the table top apparently suspended in midair; or the bar girl with the thousand-yard stare. Of course you had to return again and again to get it all, and even then there was something out of reach. This was true also of the early canvases of the Expressionists. They were few in number and relegated to a side gallery on the ground floor. The wintry northern sensibility was too close to our own time, our disheveled epoch, which can in a certain sense be called the German Century. Dix and Kirchner were at least as far from Manet as Manet was from Thomas Couture, perhaps much farther.

Couture was the nineteenth-century genre painter, a favorite of the Salon and my wife. *Les Romains de la Décadence* was his masterpiece, given pride of place in the great central gallery. It's hard to miss, the size of a billboard though less subtle, an example of the Romantic manner in which can be detected, dimly, the first intimations of realism. Half-naked women and their derelict male companions sprawl drunkenly on couches, overseen by a statue of a blank-faced Caesar set against a virtuous blue sky. Couture's Caesar bears a passing resemblance to the Ohio Republican Warren G. Harding.

Ellen made the count. There are thirty-one figures in various stages of corruption, remnants of the exhausted empire, observed stage right by two hard-faced courtiers looking like bailbondsmen or Wall Street mergers-and-acquisitions thugs. The picture is emblematic of everything the Impressionists were struggling against, in subject matter, technique, emotion, and politics. That is why it is the centerpiece of the central gallery — it was Ellen who reminded me that Luther hung a sketch of a sensual Pope on the wall of his study at Wittenberg to remind him of the true face of the enemy. The museum is deemed a repository of the art of the nineteenth century, in French time roughly the period from the failed revolutions of 1848 to the advent of the Great War. Thus, the century that begins with Thomas Couture ends with Edvard Munch.

When I went to the Musée d'Orsay I was working no less than a newspaper reporter on assignment, cultivating sources. I became intimate with the bar girl and the absinthe drinkers and Degas's bourgeois family on the balcony, along with Toulouse-Lautrec's blowsy whores and van Gogh's admirable country doctor. When I saw them arrayed on the long white wall, I thought of them as members of a single family, the dissolute and the upright, the conformist and the rebel, always torn, blinded by emotion, confused in their motives, and ambiguous in their reactions to things. They did not always know what they wanted or why they wanted it. They did not always see life's possibilities, because they did not know their own horizons, or knew them all too well.

I could place these Impressionist figures in my own past — the bourgeois family at dinner in Winnetka, the bar girl waiting table at the country club near the lake, the whores lounging in the railway hotel near the 12th Street station in Chicago. I found my father and my brother. I found friends. And I found myself — Lhermitte's harvester, a laboring man exhausted at the end of his day, a scythe resting heavily at his feet, his face drawn as if he were remembering something painful. You would say it was an interesting face, and perhaps that was not pain at all but pride. Anyone can see that Lhermitte's weary harvester is reliable, a man who gives a full day's work for a full day's pay.

Having the Impressionist galleries of the Musée d'Orsay nearby was a constant provocation — to see things differently, shapes that never appear in nature, colors that seem poured from the pot of God. Artists and writers borrow from each other all the time, often finding anomalies that cause them to revise their most deeply held beliefs — theories of narrative, theories of history, theories of modernism, theories of the moral life and the creative spirit generally. Imagine my surprise when I discovered that Edouard Manet had been a devoted student of Thomas Couture.

Along the quay men sat in the sun with their shirts off, watching the near-empty tourist boats glide past the Tuileries. I hurried along, my morale buoyed by Georges's news. So Harry Forrest was a growth stock after all, and like all growth stocks was subject to market correction. I had been stalled in the past and had always managed to work my way free, confident that material would turn up. It always had before.

This time I decided to visit the museum not as a reporter at an arraignment but as a spectator, wandering from gallery to gallery without plan. I began on the ground floor with barely a look at the wretched billboard, moving instead to the side rooms with their Whistlers and early Monets and restful Millets. I stopped for a long time in front of Monet's magpie, the simple picture of a bird on a wooden gate, a low farmhouse and a shallow snow-covered valley in the distance, the bird the only spot of life in the composition. It's a tiny bird but it has the force of an eagle. It is not well defined but your eye is immediately drawn to it. Without the magpie the picture is commonplace and with it a masterpiece.

At noon the museum was not crowded, so I was able to view the magpie in privacy, moving forward and backward, left and right, trying to discover how Monet did it and whether there was any application to my own work, something useful to be learned from this inconspicuous black bird nearly lost in its natural surroundings, overwhelmed by them, until you examined it carefully. Then the magpie seemed poised, prepared to fly away; it was alive and the surroundings were dead. Monet's picture seemed almost a statement of philosophical principle, as if Plato had taken brush in hand and decided to examine an avian life, one that had been lived in loneliness and introspection, in thrall to its own task, and lived heroically.

In the room next to the magpie were some nondescript Boudins and Millet's portrait of Madame Canoville, a somber likeness of a chaste bourgeoise. I had no particular reaction when looking at it, a pleasant enough piece that did not cry out or seize you; certainly I had no desire to put it on my own wall, except for the bold signature of the artist. Madame Canoville's eyes seemed to me dazed, and then I saw that the canvas had been placed in such a way that she was staring across the central gallery to *Les Romains de la Décadence*. Curators do nothing by chance, and I thought this placement especially droll. Madame Canoville was the housewife in the bungalow across the street, and the eyes that I thought were dazed were not dazed at all but stern and disapproving of the grotesque bacchanalia of the neighbors, riffraff from the indolent summer climates.

This discovery made me laugh out loud. I left the side gallery and stood in front of the billboard and let it shout at me. A young woman was there also, evidently with the same idea. She was glaring at the hard-faced courtiers with an astringent smile, the sort of knowing smile that invites inquiry.

It's amusing, isn't it, Madame? Even now La Canoville is dialing nine-one-one, complaining of a lewd disturbance . . .

We were standing close together, aware of each other but not uncomfortable about it. I could smell her perfume, this very attractive Frenchwoman, not tall, dressed in corduroy trousers and a blue cardigan sweater, a bright silk scarf around her throat and gold on her wrists, a woman alone at noontime. You notice them on every street in St.-Germain-des-Prés, forty- and forty-five-year-old women, mothers of teenagers. But they do not look motherly, and you cannot imagine them correcting homework or dusting little Pierre's bedroom. This Parisian had turned-down eyes and a lavish bow mouth with a prominent upper lip, better-looking than any of the suburban-faced girls in Couture's picture, and lithe and poised in a way that they were not. The half-naked debutantes of Imperial Rome could have done with more exercise and fewer pomegranates.

I looked at my wristwatch, and then again at the French-woman. I remembered that she had been in the gallery with Monet's magpie and had looked at it as carefully as I had, once I moved on to Millet. Couture's billboard was a cartoon, and standing together in front of it made us accomplices, voyeurs, witnesses to the ludicrous orgy.

I opened my mouth to say something, then didn't. I was hungry now and tired of looking at the Romans. I turned to leave, then unaccountably glanced back at the Parisian, who was smiling to herself, staring at the floor, extending her foot, drawing it slowly across the marble as if she were about to begin a waltz.

Without looking up, she said, "Do you miss Chicago, Harry?"

I did not know what to think or say. Her voice was straight from the North Side. She was no more French than I am. But I had no idea who she was, and that put me at a disadvantage. I looked closer but no name came to me. She stood staring at the floor, her face in profile; she still seemed to me a Parisian woman out for the afternoon.

I said, "No, I don't think I do."

"Sure?"

"Pretty sure," I said.

"I don't either," she said. "The hustle, the lake, the El, the wind. The godawful struggle to stay sane." She was silent a moment, then gestured at the decadent Romans. "The Art Institute has one of those. Not Couture. Maybe a Laurens or a Delaunay. Huge thing, big as the scoreboard at Wrigley. Remember now?" She turned to face me directly.

I said, "Georgia?"

She said, "Yep."

I said, "Georgia *Whyte?*"

She said, "Come off it, Harry. I don't look that old. I haven't changed that much. A pound or two here and there and some gray hair if you look carefully, and the worry lines that if you don't have make you wonder what you've been doing for forty years."

"I thought you were French."

"Really did?" She moved her hips and cocked her head. "Probably it's the clothes."

"It's the look," I said.

"And what did you think?"

"I was going to ask you to lunch."

"Why didn't you?"

"Probably thought I'd be turned down."

"You? Never."

"Maybe I didn't want to get into trouble."

"Harry," she said, grinning. "You've changed."

I said, "What are you doing here?"

She said, "Looking at the pictures."

"I mean *here*," I said. "Paris."

"I live here."

"You do?"

"I've lived here a while," she said.

"So have I."

"I know that," she said. I must have looked puzzled because she added, "I read all your books, even the dust jackets. 'Harry-Forrest-lives-in-Paris-with-his-wife-Uh.' I've forgotten her name."

"No need to remember it now."

"Split?"

"Six months ago."

"You were married a long time."

"Many years. I told her we were too old to split, but she didn't agree. She was tired of Paris and wanted to go home, and

I wasn't tired and didn't want to go home. So she went back to the United States."

"Well," Georgia said. "Even if she isn't married to you, she still has a name. When they give you a name you usually have it for life. So what is it?"

I said, "Ellen."

"That's right, Ellen. I remember now. She wasn't from Chicago. Where was it, the West Coast? The South?"

That amused me, as if Ellen had been born beyond the pale and we all had to make allowances. I said, "California."

She said, "That's bad. Not Los Angeles, I hope."

"Little town north of San Francisco, nobody's ever heard of it."

She looked at me skeptically with her sly half smile. "You'd be surprised at the places I've heard of. You'd be surprised at the places I've lived, and some of the people I've lived with. But I hate Los Angeles. I was there for a while. It's wretched. It's a garbage pail, though I have a couple of dear friends who live there now. Or used to. Who knows where they are now." She paused, smiling falsely. "But I don't miss L.A. The garbage pail." She waited for me to say something and when I didn't she looked away. "I've kept up with you," she said finally. "Read about you all the time. I remember an article in some magazine, a long time ago. A wonderful photograph of you in a café, drinking a glass of wine, smoking a cigarette, wearing a Borsalino hat, looking as if you owned the place. It made me laugh. It made me remember the old days. I thought, That's my Harry."

But I was never her Harry. I hadn't seen her in years. We had not known each other well, and I was much older. And then I wondered if she had mistaken me for my younger brother, somehow confused our identities, unlikely as that would be. She and Dean had gone out together one summer and for a while it looked permanent, although in the event the affair never survived August. But it had been a wonderful summer for Dean because Georgia Whyte was not of our crowd. In Dean's eyes she was an exotic, a sexy highbrow from the wrong side of the tracks.

She was certainly freer-spirited than the girls he knew, and provocative and humorous in a way that they weren't. She was precocious, an avid, ardent, endlessly curious girl who seemed a half step ahead of her sisters, hell-bent for some lofty destination; she made you believe she'd get there, too. Georgia was opinionated and extremely pretty and that set some of our girls against her, not that she minded. When Dean took her to a dance, she plunged right in, like an anthropologist visiting a primitive tribe. I had a vague recollection that her father worked for the archdiocese.

She said, "I've seen your books, and read a few. What's the name of that character?"

"Pease."

"Pease, yes. He's always being outsmarted."

"Sometimes in the beginning. But by the last chapter he gets his man."

"Inspector Pease," she said. "*Inspector Pease in the First Arrondissement.* And the Second. And the Third." She laughed. "How many have there been?"

"*Inspector Pease in the Tenth Arrondissement* will be published in the fall. At a bookstore near you."

"Pease reminds me of Maigret. Should he?"

I said, "No." This was a sore subject. A critic once accused me of being a second-rate Simenon, and Pease a Maigret knockoff.

She said, "I've only read a couple. But I like them. Really I do. They remind me of the old days. You never write about Chicago, but sometimes I come across a name or an expression that seems familiar, and it'll remind me of some — lurid event. Remember that ghastly dance?"

"I remember."

"That club."

"It was a coming-out party."

"Yes," she said. "Winnetka."

Something came to the edge of my memory and dropped back.

"A party for the Demming girls. Wasn't one of your characters a Colonel Demming?"

"What a memory," I said. "*Inspector Pease in the Fourth Arrondissement.*"

"A British colonel, awful little twit."

"That's him," I said.

"And in the same book you had a law firm, Whyte and Cody."

"That's right," I said.

"My father worked for Cardinal Cody."

"I never thought of the connection," I said slowly, though in truth I must have when I was writing the book. I felt my face beginning to color.

"Don't bother to deny it," she said. "I don't care. Makes no difference to me. It made me laugh. All those years, and you've been here a long time."

"Ages," I said. "And you?"

"Not nearly that long."

And I remembered then. Georgia Whyte was a painter, and a very good one. I remembered seeing a review of her work and thinking, condescendingly, Well, well, hell-bent Georgia Whyte, lofty at last.

I said, "And you're an artist."

"True," she said, nodding curtly at the billboard. "Not that kind, though."

"What kind, then?"

"You mean what school?" She fluttered her eyelids. "I belonged to a school once, but I was expelled."

I laughed at that.

"How did you know I was an artist?"

"Is it a secret?"

"I haven't had a show in a while."

"But I saw a review —"

"Yes, there were plenty of those. I never lacked attention. As they say, it's not the crime but the cover-up."

Her manner was suddenly distant, her voice sarcastic, and it was obvious she did not like to talk about her work. I said, "Have you stopped painting?"

"I've slowed down."

"I suppose you can get painter's block the way a writer gets writer's block."

"Is that what you have?"

"No."

"Me either. Ever."

"Then you're lucky," I said.

"Am I?" She smiled fleetingly, her eyes shining, and for a moment I saw the young girl my brother had loved for a summer. "Kollwitz said that she worked the way cows graze. She wrote in her diary that when she was in middle age she cared about nothing but grazing. All her private emotions left her and all day long she grazed, like a cow. She did wonderful work, too. It's like that for me, Harry. For a while I went through the pasture like a reaper. I cut everything in sight. And then I stopped. And now I graze."

She spoke with such intensity of feeling that I was taken aback. I said, "But you have to have emotions in order to — do what you do."

"You have them," she said. "But you block them."

"I suppose so," I said, not believing a word of it.

"There's more to it than appears on the surface," she said evenly.

"I read a fine review of your work years ago. It was a show in Chicago. Or maybe I didn't read it. Maybe Dean told me about it."

"Yes, Dean."

"I'm sure it was Dean."

"He was a nice boy," she said slowly, her voice dropping. "We had that fling that summer, but it didn't last. We weren't suited, and Dean was so young."

"You were the same age."

"Not quite," she said. "But there were no hard feelings."

"He had some hard feelings, Georgia."

"He did?" She thought a moment. "Well, I didn't. Of course you were the one I liked really. Remember the long talk we had at the country club that night? You seemed very mature and organized. You wanted to write a novel and couldn't wait to get out of Chicago and into the world to do it. And Paris was the place. 'Paris is where the material is,' you said. 'No one interferes with your work in Paris.' I didn't know what you meant — how could someone interfere with your work? — but it had an effect on me. Not a good one, I'm afraid. You were wicked, Harry. I didn't know my own mind and you knew yours very well. It wasn't a good combination. You probably don't remember. I was just a silly girl at a dance somewhere, your brother's date. There was plenty of other drama that evening. I remember we talked about destiny, whether you had it from your genes or if you made it up as you went along."

I had no recollection at all, and I was irritated by her tone. It seemed to me that I was being held responsible for mistakes she had made in her life, and I had no wish to acknowledge this or make amends for it, loose talk at a dance during the Johnson Administration. Everyone had gone on with their lives except my brother.

She said lightly, "How's Dean? Where is he? I heard he married someone from Chicago."

I looked at her hard. My brother was dead. He died of cancer three years before and it was inconceivable that she didn't know. Everyone knew. I thought, foolishly, that she had somehow confused our identities, but she obviously hadn't; she knew who I was. And she knew that Dean had married a Chicago girl. All this made me uneasy, and for a reason I cannot explain precisely, I did not want to tell Georgia Whyte about my brother. She seemed to me in disarray, with her work and her life. As we talked it was difficult for me to connect her to the avid girl I dimly remembered as my brother's twist; that was the word we used then. And of course she bore no resemblance at all to the woman I had been watching, the one I thought was French, the chic woman with the sly half smile looking at *Les Romains de la*

Décadence. But she had taken me into her confidence, wicked Harry so mature and organized, a man who knew where the material was. And suddenly I wanted to know more.

I said, "Would you like some lunch?"

"I don't know," she said. "I should get back."

"Your husband?"

"My work," she said. "My grazing."

"We can go up the street to the brasserie; it'll be quiet now, a light lunch and a glass of wine —"

"I like the idea of a glass of wine."

"It's settled then."

She took a last look at the Romans. She was scowling, and for a moment she looked like Madame Canoville.

I put my hand on her arm and we moved closer. "See those two?" I said.

She nodded glumly.

"I think they're bailbondsmen or La Salle Street hoods."

"No," she said bitterly. "No, they're not. They're garbage men. They're waiting to collect the garbage. They sift through the garbage and take what suits them and throw the rest away. Anything of value they take, anything at all. And the rest they dump."

I said, "What happened in Los Angeles?"

She said, "Fuck Los Angeles."

"It's just a city where they make movies."

"Have you ever been there? If you haven't, then you don't know what the fuck you're talking about." She took a step backward and then turned, facing me. "I asked you a question and you didn't answer it. How's Dean?"

"Dean is dead," I said.

She closed her eyes briefly and stood very still. "That's right," she said slowly. "How stupid of me. How stupid and thoughtless. I'm sorry, Harry. God, I am sorry." She put her hand to her mouth so that the next words were muffled. "Of course I knew that. I knew that very well. I saw the notice in the paper. It was cancer, wasn't it? And I was living in Chicago then. I'd just come back from Los Angeles. There was a time when nothing stuck to me, in my memory or anywhere else. I was a basket case. God, it was a wretched time."

I had assumed she was French, in her blue sweater with the bright scarf and the gold on her wrists, her tan corduroys and smart loafers, so trim and pulled together. And it wasn't only the clothing; it was the way she walked and held her head and the privacy of her attitude. I had looked at her the way you look at a fashion advertisement, and if anyone had asked, I could have given her biography. I could have named the arrondissement she lived in and where she bought her shoes and where her children went to school and the kind of car she drove and where she was likely to drive it.

And all wrong. And I was wrong, too, about her composure. This was evident when we sat at the table in the nearly empty restaurant and I was able to look at her closely. She was not the same woman I had admired in the Musée d'Orsay, the one who seemed so seductive. Georgia's eyes were infinitely tired. Her hair was lifeless and her skin pale, so pale that I felt that if I tried hard enough I could see the bones and sinew. She looked as if she had not had a full night's sleep in a year, and as we received our menus and she looked at hers I thought of Degas's melancholy girl, the one with the thousand-yard stare, waiting for satisfaction that would never arrive; and she knew that, but waited for the miracle anyway. For a moment I thought Georgia was ill, but when she began to drink wine I knew at once that she drank too much, and that would be one thing that would account for her pale complexion and the circles under her eyes and the deep commas around her mouth, and her bad memory.

She drank greedily, from conviction, her mood improving with each glass. And she was vivacious after her own fashion, describing her impulsive decision to quit the United States for France and her good luck in finding an apartment in a quiet neighborhood where the street characters were harmless. She lived in rue Blaise across from an elementary school. Her con-

cierge was a tyrant but the neighbors were quiet, private people.
She usually worked at night and slept during the day, rising
in late afternoon so that she could begin work in twilight. She
rarely went out. Today was an exception.

It's such a nice day.

I wanted to visit my favorite museum.

And there you were, a ghost from my past.

I've never seen anyone I know in Paris, and no one has ever
spoken to me.

That's the charm of Paris, isn't it?

The indifference.

Georgia drank quickly and gracefully, bringing the glass to
her mouth, sipping a little, smiling, and putting it down again,
centering the glass just so between the pot of paper flowers and
the carafe of red wine. She never let go of the glass and watched
it between sips. Of course she was attractive. Her hoarse voice
added to her allure. It had something of the whiskey timbre of
Piaf's combined with the hard vowels of Chicago *profond.* We
began to talk of her Chicago and mine, hers of the far North Side
and night classes at the Art Institute and learning to paint, and
mine of the North Shore and the Gold Coast and learning to
write.

We talked a little of Dean, his long illness and the fortitude
of his wife and teenaged children. And then we were drawn back
to the summer of 1968 and how strange it was for her, accom-
panying my brother to a country club dance. She had never been
to one before, and studied it as she would study a live model.
Georgia said that when she saw me in the museum the years fell
away and she was twenty again, dancing a waltz in her sister's
hand-me-down dress, wondering if this was the life that was in
store. Do you remember waltzing? she asked. Do you remember
that character who made a pass at me and then collapsed?

She said, "You probably don't know this. I'm sure you don't.
But Dean was talking of marriage. There would be big trouble
from his family but he would handle them. Will you handle
mine, too, I asked. But he wasn't listening. Listening was not

one of the things he was good at. Of course our marriage would mean that I would have to move to New Haven but U. Conn. was nearby and it was a good school, really an awfully good school, and I could go there. Storrs was a challenging environment, and probably they had an art department. We would have each other and that was what counted. And after college we would move to the near North Side, Astor Street or Schiller or one of those."

She related all this in a cool, ironic voice, with the usual sarcastic undertones. But as she spoke I did not see my brother as he was then, sweet-natured and humorous and naïve, but as he was later, so sick the simple act of drawing breath was excruciating. This was so painful I had to look away.

"He wanted to become an advertising man," she said. "And the idea was, we would set up our own agency. Forrest and Forrest. We'd be on our own. 'And I'd be free,' he said, and of course when he said that alarm bells went off."

I turned to look directly at her.

"I asked him, 'This wouldn't have anything to do with the draft, would it, Dean?' And he stared at me with the most open astonishment. As you're doing now, Harry. And he said no. No, it didn't have anything to do with the draft. How could I think such a thing? You should be ashamed of yourself, Georgia. You're way off base. Why do you always think the worst? You have a hard heart, Georgia." She poured wine from the carafe, taking her time about it. And when she spoke next her voice was softer. "He was right. I don't think he ever thought of our marriage as a way to dodge the draft, and naturally I was ashamed that I'd brought it up. But when the bell rang, I had to answer it. And he took his patriotism seriously, because from that moment he began to back away. There was one missed date and then another and I had to confess to myself that he found me lacking in — character. I felt bad because I liked him. I knew I had hurt him and I felt bad about that, too. He was sincere, but his sincerity was no reason to marry. Marriage was not my ambition. Not at that age, before I had drawn a single picture that I could love." She looked at me, soliciting some reply, but I said nothing. I thought she had told an ugly story.

"One thing, Harry. I've always wondered. Was Dean ever drafted?"

I said, "No."

"Did he avoid it?"

I said, "He went to graduate school."

"Law?" she said. "Medicine?"

"Business," I said.

She took out a cigarette, lit it, and we sat in silence.

She said at last, "I'm sorry."

I said, "So am I."

"Old war stories," she said. "No need to bring them up now."

"Then why did you?" I asked.

"Off base again, I guess."

"You remember that all this time," I said. "Some things are better forgotten. He was my *brother*."

"Nothing is better *forgotten*," she said.

"The remark of a cynic," I replied.

"The remark of an artist," she said. "I gained something from that summer. After Dean and I broke up I drew my experiences in an Expressionist mode. I thought I could make Chicago into Berlin, narrow dark streets, toadlike men, and lethal women as slender as a knife's blade. I drew North Shore debutantes, pillars of our decaying civilization; and their fathers also. My instructor and I quarreled every day after I declared that I had no regard for colors or abstractions or any of the post-this-or-that twaddle, the stuff that keeps critics employed. I was striving for a new objectivity — a quest, according to my instructor, not merely retrograde but proto-fascist. He seemed to think that I wanted to emulate Speer and urged me to study architecture. Thereafter I referred to the new objectivity by its proper German name, *die neue Sachlichkeit*, infuriating him further. I was going to lay bare Chicago's hypocrisy, the Alexanderplatz smack in the middle of the Loop. I was sincere, but that's about all you can say for it . . ."

She did love to talk. And listening was one of the things I

was good at. The carafes arrived full and departed empty, carafe after carafe. She did not speak again of Dean, but Chicago was still there in the shadows. After a while she wound down and thought to ask me of my work, how I went about it; and I said I had a friend at the préfecture who passed me police reports, and when I found a crime that was gaudy I used it for a plot. Then I researched the arrondissement and two years later I had a novel. Pease aged as I did, but otherwise we were not similar. His marriage, for example, was a model of stability. I could not break it up because Pease's wife was more attractive than he was. Pease alone was a boring cop. Pease with his wife was — *Pease.*

She laughed at that.

"Your friend at the préfecture," she said.

"He's a clerk," I said.

"Without influence?"

"Totally," I said, wondering what she was getting at. Whatever it was, she was not prepared to pursue, for she fell silent. "And you," I said. "What's next?"

Georgia moved her head from side to side as you do when you do not intend to answer directly. She confessed that she had begun a strange adventure, not one she had sought but one she had been pulled into. It was not unpleasant. No one had forced her. She had behaved like any unstable object in an irresistible gravitational field. For a time she had lost control of her life, but now she had it back. She was learning how to live in a new way, outside society's expectations, much as people had lived in the Middle Ages. If it was true, as people were saying, that Europe was returning to a region of provinces and city-states, then she wanted to be in synch with the new scheme of things. She was on the run from bigness, conformity, and materialism. In a sense she was on the run from American life, and she believed now that she would live forever in France — not Paris, more likely one of the remote central provinces. She was with a man whose health required him to live in mountain air, away from city soot and garbage and the many tensions of urban life.

Out of reach of the authorities, she said.

She added quickly, "Probably you think I'm retrograde. Or an old leftie come home to revolution's cradle, waiting for the rattle of the tumbrils. But it's only what I said it was, an attempt to live in a new way."

I said nothing but groaned inwardly. How many times I have heard that. Americans, women especially, had the idea that Europe was a great eraser that could clean the mistakes from life's blackboard. "Live in a new way" meant the old way without the familiar landmarks, spouses or children or neighborhoods or the authorities. But I gave her my full attention, trying to suspend my natural skepticism and not be so quick to judge. It was some time since I had heard anyone speak of the moral life, and I wondered what it was that had brought her to this point, her strange adventure. As a young man I believed that nothing much would ever happen to my Chicago friends, trapped as they were between the featureless prairie and the long shallow lake, imprisoned by Chicago's energy, an energy that discouraged backward glances, and it was only the backward glance that propelled one forward. I thought my Chicago friends would miss out on life, which I defined as something that happened elsewhere. Nothing interesting had ever happened to their parents, and it was well known that torpor ran in families. There would be the usual commercial rivalries and petty emotional and financial troubles. There would be marital disorder. There would be appalling illness. Among the religious there would be loss of faith or a sudden born-again conversion. But they would miss out because life was variety and foreignness and the unexpected and the unruly, and Chicago was all too familiar and predictable. That was why it was necessary to get out, though you couldn't expect to erase the blackboard.

Georgia laughed and said that when she was younger she'd had the same thoughts, and they were with her still, though she phrased them differently owing to *die neue Sachlichkeit* that had come to her again now that she had reached the dangerous age. And the knowledge was hard won. She'd paid full fare. But the truth was, it was difficult to know where and how to live. The moral life was a search for value, something genuine that was here today and here tomorrow and the day after. It was not the favor of God or the favor of man, either. It was a matter of your own concentration, your field of force. It was a matter of ambition. Well, ambition and love and which one gave way. Everything came down to that choice, and while it was simple defining ambition, plain as the gleam in a courtesan's eye, it was not so simple defining love or love's object. Was it not ambition for yourself in opposition to love for your work? Each was a dagger thrusting at the heart of the other. You could not have both; one would have to yield, or you — the artist — would live in eternal anxiety. Of course for some there would never be a struggle, and good luck to them.

I looked across the table at her. She lit a cigarette and blew a smoke ring at the ceiling, then muttered something I did not hear.

She said, In America you could be Madame Canoville, an exhausted voluptuary, or a Wall Street hood. If you were a man, you could aspire to Caesar. But you could never be a simple magpie poised on a wooden fence rail, a solitary flash of color in a pale wintry landscape. In America the scale of things was immense and you could lose yourself between the seas, especially when you were at the dangerous age. You lost your identity, and while you could tell yourself it was unavoidable, that did not help you retrieve it. Always there was the urge to stay competitive. God help you if you didn't.

She was silent then.

I said she had made the wrong equation.

No, I have not. She was almost shouting. Distraught, she poured wine into both our glasses. There was a sudden commotion at the door, a disheveled party of six arriving for dinner. Their hilarious voices filled the room, but Georgia never turned her head. Do you understand me? she demanded. Do you understand what I'm saying to you? Sometimes you have to uproot yourself absolutely, to disappear into another country, to become denationalized.

Then, after a long pause, she began to explain.

I settled in, attentive but unconvinced. I was not eager to be led back into her American past, and I knew that was where she was headed. That was what you got when you entertained new arrivals; first they wanted to tell you how sublime it was abroad, and then they wanted you to know how terrible it was at home, the irresponsibility, philistinism, and corruption. When I first arrived in Paris, an American expatriate had spelled it out. There were worse fates than living forever in France but one of the forfeitures was any appreciation or understanding of America. You'll believe that distance and the passage of time will give perspective and irony, and it surely will, especially irony. But that's all you'll have — irony. And because you are not French and will never be French, you will never be fully accepted here. That's the bargain. You will become a marginal character and you will be comfortable or not depending on your own temperament. But do realize this: your memories of America will be vivid and cast in iron, riveted to the last year you lived there. America will have moved on, but you will not have moved on with it. And everything you remember will be wrong, out of date, or beside the point. You will be tempted to complain, when some idiotic American blunder appears on the evening news, *What is wrong with that country? It used to be a swell country. What happened to it?* You will be embarrassed, the way anyone is with a clumsy relative; and you will turn away, because it has nothing to do with you now. You will become charmed by France, the worldly pace of life, the beauty, the museums, the women, the weather, the cuisine. La Belle France — so supple on the surface, and so glacial underneath. You will admire the bedrock. You will approve of it — because you've never stubbed your toe on it.

Let me tell you, Harry. It hurts like hell.

But because you're an absentee American, you're excused.

This is a fact you will come to appreciate, and cling to for dear life.

So remember this.

Avoid your countrymen.

And don't be so quick to judge.

I smiled at the memory of the old expatriate, gone many years now. When he died he was mourned in every arrondissement. His memorial service filled Saint Philippe du Roule. The *Herald Tribune* ran a thousand-word obit, and even *Le Monde* was respectful. The old man had known Cocteau and Pound and Ford Madox Ford and Gertrude and Alice and Clemenceau and Braque —

But she was talking about the North Shore, and I tried to listen with objectivity. I tried to listen as if I were hearing it from a disinterested third party.

AT HOME

1

Y EARS LATER she remembered long-stemmed yellow roses
in huge vases gallantly rising to attention left and right in
the wide corridor, their fragrance mingling with the perfume of the women and the tobacco of the men. The carpet was
yellow. On the walls were prints of English sporting scenes, long
golden afternoons of croquet or cricket, and muscular rallies of
men, horses, dogs, and guns. French doors were thrown open to
a candlelit lawn as green and glittering as an emerald, round
tables here and there, and a bar and a dance floor in the middle
distance. Yellow roses framed the bandstand and the dance floor,
a regiment of flowers mustered from as far away as Lake Forest.
The thick branches of a great oak formed a leafy canopy over
the dance floor, the leaves rippling in a light summer breeze rich
with the smell of freshly mown grass.

How perfect, people were saying. How absolutely perfect.

Someone was heard to observe that it would have been uniquely perfect if the moon had been full instead of a quarter, and in
the receiving line guests took this new information and craned
their necks to peer through the French doors to the quarter moon
rising in the southern sky, a bright yellow beret on the crown

of the great oak, and nod in agreement and sympathy. What a shame that nature had not cooperated completely, to make things uniquely perfect. If Josephine Demming had known, she would have fixed it. She would have made one of her famous calls and fixed it like *that*, ha-ha. She'd have insisted that Earl whistle up a full moon for the evening. But — of *course* Earl and Josephine would know the lunar situation and take it into account. They were sticklers for detail. Probably there had been a conflict of some kind, with the plans of out-of-town guests or Earl's court calendar, so they'd had to settle for the third Saturday in June, which decreed a quarter moon.

Remember that time at Mackinac —

The Barrimores insisted that everyone *pray*.

— for a perfect evening.

And it rained like hell!

Then Ted Hummel had too much to drink and —

He called the Pope, I remember.

He *wanted* to call the Pope.

But Louise stopped him.

Louise didn't stop him. I stopped him. I told him the Pope had no jurisdiction at Mackinac. The Pope's writ did not run in the U.P. He wanted help, I told him to call whatshisname, Ramsey, the Archbishop of Canterbury. Then Bobby said she'd have none of that, Ramsey was a Red. Freddie said he wasn't a Red, he was an Anglican. But John had it figured out. Only the Ojibway medicine man could stop the rain, so John gave the bartender a sawbuck and sent him off to fetch old Running Hat, to climb the blue spruce and rattle the bones. Boomlay-boom. Rain, rain, go away.

And did he?

They couldn't find him. They looked high and low, even the clink. He was off drunk with some squaw. They're never around when you need them, medicine men.

It just rained like hell all night long.

Not that anyone minded.

The lights went out, but the band played on.

It was a nigger band, I remember. A nigger band from Saint Louis. People were dancing in the rain.

It wasn't a nigger band. It was a jug band from Kentucky.

No, that was the summer of 'forty-nine. This was the summer of 'forty-six, the mischief summer. The summer everything went to hell in a hack. Maybe it was because the war was over. Maybe it was the nigger band putting a curse on, voodoo or some damn thing. That was the summer that poor Ted drowned and Frank and Louise were breaking up, fighting like wolverines. I thought they'd kill each other. And Harold Barrimore was up to his old tricks.

And still is!

God, what a summer.

Do you think it was the war, really?

It wasn't the war that caused Ted to try to swim the straits. Ted wasn't in the war. But Frank was, and Harold and John. Freddie, too. Me. You. So I think you'd have to say that the war had something to do with it in the sense that we'd been away and this was the first reunion since 'forty-one and probably everyone expected too much, and so things went haywire. Always do, when you want something too much.

Expectations that can't possibly be met.

I loved Mackinac in the old days.

Everyone loved Mackinac in the old days. But it's changed now, as you well know. There's a new crowd; they're not from around here.

It was then, too, in the summer of 'forty-six.

Mackinac hadn't changed. We had.

It had, too, Tom.

Everything's changed now. Every single thing. Except us.

And Harold Barrimore.

Georgia had no trouble eavesdropping; their voices were loud. Their conversation was a kind of performance. She wanted to know more about the mischief summer and the expectations that couldn't possibly be met and Harold Barrimore's tricks, but now the talk had moved away to what people were wearing on this, the absolutely perfect evening. And that reminded her that she was in Marge's hand-me-down, too tight across the chest and too full in the hips, too off-the-rack, too sheer, altogether too loose in this formal gathering, too *pink;* in a sharp light it would be see-through.

Georgia smiled to herself and looked through the French doors, a few couples already dancing, though the music could not be heard in the crowded corridor owing to the giddy hum of conversation. The dancers and the musicians looked as if they were performing a pantomime. From the look of it, the band — a band specially brought in from the East Coast, it was quickly pointed out — was playing a tango. An enthusiastic crowd was collecting around the bar. Groups of men stood off to one side, pointing to a distant green and moving their arms, laughing. They were replaying the morning round, this shot out of bounds, that one only inches from the cup, dandy shot. The men re-minded Georgia of her father, who loved describing his golf shots to Father Shea, letting the priest know where he had been the previous Sunday.

The receiving line began to move. Two men and their wives were in front of her, both men very tall and well turned out in their tuxedos. They were the ones who had been talking about the mischief summer, when things went haywire because they wanted something too much. The wife of the one called Tom had said nothing but at one point had taken his hand and twined her fingers through his, leaning against him, listening to him, her body rigid. The other woman had seemed frankly bored and at the first opportunity began to discuss clothes, who was wearing what, who was stylish and who wasn't. She seemed surprised that there were people in the line whom she didn't know. She played with the necklace at her throat while she talked, her eyes patrolling the crowd. Now the men were tête-à-tête, back in Mackinac, another haywire summer. The women were oblivi-ous, their voices rising, brittle as glass. Georgia could not hear what the men were saying, but whatever it was moved Tom to smile.

Ahead of them in the doorway were the host and hostess and their two teenaged daughters, the guests of honor. They were homely girls, dressed identically in white. They wore pearls and white orchids, and Georgia thought suddenly of Goya's portraits of the Spanish court. A photographer maneuvered discreetly nearby. Dean had told her the girls' names, but Georgia had forgotten them at once in the excitement of arrival, the winding drive to the clubhouse, their car directed to a roped-off area next to a perfectly round sand trap, doors slamming, people milling about, loud voices and laughter, a flurry of introductions. She recognized one name as belonging to a department store and another to a boulevard on the far North Side. She and Dean had been arguing, and now she saw that he was nervous.

He took her coat and left her in the receiving line, where she was able to eavesdrop and study faces, the bones beneath the skin, and observe the way people stood and what they did with their hands and how they wore their clothes. She wished she had her sketch pad, now that she was face to face with the ruling classes. The women wore precious stones. The men had suntans. They were triumphantly at ease — and then she noticed that for all the black suits there was not a single priest. There were always priests around at parties, anniversary dinners or fund-raising events, everyone making an effort to talk to them; and they always left early except for Father Shea. But these people were not R.C., and this was not an anniversary or fund-raising event or wake or christening, it was a com-ing-out-par-ty. Dean had described the custom, subtly letting her know that this was something different, something *special,* something outside her experience, and she should be grateful for the confidence he had in her. He meant, Behave yourself, Georgia. He was not at his best when he was nervous; but she needed a guide, and for better or worse Dean was it. Now she wanted a drink. She stared at the back of Tom's head and thought mischievously, What luck. What great good luck, Mr. Tom. Mr.-Tom-who-wanted-something-too-much. I know who you are but you don't know who I am.

And then Dean was at her elbow, brusquely apologizing for leaving her alone.

"What kept you?"

"A line at the cloakroom. My brother," he began and then was shaking hands with the two men in front, smiling at their wives, making introductions, Tom and Maggie Browne, Byron and Jane Nicholson. The women looked at her with appraisers' eyes and called her "Dear" and told her how pretty she was, while Tom and Byron nudged Dean, nodding approval. The photographer was only a few feet away now, moving behind them. Then she was greeting the host and hostess and the two teenaged girls, the girls looking miserable. Georgia heard the whirr of the camera behind her and smiled, complimenting the girls on their dresses. They were close to the same age, but Georgia felt years older. She wondered if the girls were virgins and decided that they weren't, and that the father knew and the mother didn't. Suddenly she and Dean were outside under the stars, standing at the bar, listening to music, and waiting for the bartender to serve them.

She said, "What's Mackinac?"

"An island up in Michigan."

"And who's Harold Barrimore?"

"I don't know," Dean said. "My father and mother know him."

"What are his tricks?" she asked.

"What do you mean?"

Dean stood with his head slightly turned from her, and she knew that the argument was not ended. It never was, with Dean, until the ground had been thoroughly surveyed and the distances measured and ownership assigned, errors meticulously enumerated. And then someone was supposed to give way. Until that happened, everything was in dispute. But she was no longer interested in the argument; she was interested in the glittering scene unfolding before her eyes on this dreamy night in June, a quarter moon rising and the ruling classes at ease and unaware that a spy was in their midst. It was too soon to call it a drama, but she was certain that something extraordinary would take place, something unprecedented. And it would be visual, something she would remember as she remembered the conversation about Mackinac. Perhaps these men would be for her what the saints were to Caravaggio, or the Nazis to George Grosz.

The band had switched to a waltz and the barman was looking their way. She ordered a gin and tonic. Dean took beer.

"It doesn't matter," he said.

She said, "During the summer of 'forty-six in Mackinac things went haywire and Harold Barrimore was up to his old tricks, and I'm wondering what they were. And if he's still up to them." Dean, tight-lipped, did not reply. She explained that she had been eavesdropping on Tom, Byron, Maggie, and Joan. Really, it was very interesting. They called 'forty-six the mischief summer. She was eavesdropping because she was bored and had nothing else to do. They were talking and she was listening. Or, rather, the men were talking. Everyone else was listening except Joan, who was counting jewels. No harm done. Their voices were loud as foghorns.

She watched the photographer maneuver into position in order to frame Earl and Josephine and their daughters as they emerged onto the lawn, receiving-line chores concluded. The girls stood anonymously between their parents, everyone backlit by the indoor lights. The women had greenish complexions from the light reflecting off their dresses. Earl's face was bone white. And then Georgia noticed that they were looking in different directions, as if each was seeking a different face in the crowd; each was experiencing a different emotion in the moments before the photographer captured them forever. He was taking his time framing the shot, and Georgia wondered if he would give her a print. But he had to be quick about it because they were drawing closer, almost touching —

"I don't know what his old tricks are," Dean said.

"Something to do with sex, I'll bet," Georgia said. The girls were impatient, asking the photographer to hurry. But the parents wanted everything just so, a perfect portrait, something to put in a silver frame on the Steinway.

"Well, you'd know all about that."

"Would I? Not in Winnetka." The family suddenly pulled together, holding hands and smiling gamely. The photographer missed his chance, she thought; he had it, and he let it slip away. She tried to remember exactly what she had seen. Then the flash popped and there was a scattering of applause and cries of "Hear, hear!" Earl and Josephine beamed and then laughed because the girls were no longer beside them; they had vanished into the crowd.

"You shouldn't listen to other people's conversations," he said.

"But I was bored," she said innocently, adding a pout.

"I was only gone a minute."

"And that's how you learn things," Georgia said. "That's how you learn what's on people's minds, and how they live. Listening and looking, and remembering what's beneath the skin. Then you know that things went haywire because the war was over and they wanted something too much. And they were disappointed. Not that they didn't get whatever it was that they wanted, but because they wanted it too much. Weird, don't you think? So what disappointed them? They didn't say. I think Harold Barrimore's tricks had something to do with it, but who knows? You tell me. They're your friends. You know the lingo." She finished her drink and handed the empty glass to the barman, thinking that the photograph might still be of some value; it was a posed shot, but posed shots were not always worthless.

"If you're so interested, why don't you ask Tom."

"Maybe I will. Where is he?" She took a fresh drink from the barman, who had held on to the glass a fraction of a second more than necessary.

"He's over there."

"And he's looking at us."

"He's looking at you," Dean said.

"Yes, he seems to be. He'd better watch out, though. His wife won't like it. She'll be all over his back."

"Here he comes."

"What's his business, anyway?"

"He runs an advertising agency."

"And who's that character with him?"

"My brother," Dean said.

She smiled brilliantly for the photographer, who was aiming at them, waiting for Dean to focus. He was still staring at his glass of beer when the photographer shot, and Tom Browne was asking her to dance while Harry Forrest leaned between them and handed her a yellow rose.

Tom was an athletic dancer, holding her close, whirling, telling her what a nice boy Dean was, a very popular boy at the club, good golfer, everybody's favorite. It was always a great thing watching kids you knew grow up, one minute they're toddlers at the shallow end of the pool, and the next thing they're college boys with beautiful women in their arms, and every man in the room jealous, ha-ha, because a beautiful woman brings everything to life. A sexy woman is like a melody. And what do you do, Georgia, when you're not hanging around with young Dean? When she said she was an art student, he stopped in the middle of a complicated reverse, a little winded now, chuckling — gosh, that was a coincidence, but the student he had hired for the summer, it was only a summer job but the pay was competitive and the opportunities fantastic if you were prepared to put in long hours, meaning a permanent position if everything worked out. Well, the student he had hired crumped out at the last minute, an unfortunate family situation, so the job was still open.

I'm in the advertising business, he said. Little shop on Michigan Avenue.

Summer's our busiest time.

How good an artist are you?

Pretty good, I'll bet.

Artists are the backbone of our business.

If the art isn't right. If the art isn't *perfect.*

The thing falls to pieces, just goes to hell in a hack.

So what do you say, Georgia?

You'd be doing me a favor. Come by on Monday, meet my partners.

We can have lunch, get acquainted.

And who knows what might develop.

We could become friends.

They were dancing again, his hand a little heavier on her back, his breath a hot breeze in her hair. He was almost a head taller than she was and graceful when he moved. The men she knew were not graceful dancers; waltzing was not in their bag of tricks. Now he was talking about the North Shore, a kind of paradise. You couldn't know this unless you lived there, day in and day out. It was such a quick commute to Michigan Avenue, and when you came out again in the evening it was as if the city never existed. Business was going great guns. God, he said, I love Winnetka.

She looked around for Dean but he was nowhere in sight. His brother was watching her from the edge of the dance floor, smoking a cigarette and holding the yellow rose he'd promised to save for her.

She said, "Can I ask you a question?"

"Anything," he said. "The thing you've got to know is, the hours're long and unpredictable. Highly unpredictable. You've got to be on call nights, weekends. The client's the boss, and if he wants a presentation on Saturday morning, that's what he gets."

"I heard you talking about Mackinac in the receiving line."

"Do you know Mackinac?"

"No," she said. "But I was curious. What was it you wanted so much, you and your friend?"

"Well," he said, and began to chuckle.

"I don't think it was that, Tom. Tell me what it was."

"We expected." He coughed over her shoulder, stumbling slightly, losing his rhythm. Then he stepped back, looking at her strangely. His face was very red. "We were just back from the war. We expected certain things. We expected that there wouldn't be any changes, prewar to postwar. We expected Mackinac to be the same and the people to be the same and they weren't. Our wives weren't. We weren't. I suppose we thought that would be our reward, a beautiful prewar Mackinac. Mackinac in an evergreen time warp. It was such a great place. I grew up there summers." Tom Browne seemed about to say more, then changed his mind, shrugging, looking at her intently. "But see, it was just that one summer, the summer of 'forty-six. It was way before your time. The next year, everything was back on an even keel, more or less."

"So you went haywire because of the war."

"*Things* went haywire. *Things.*"

"Whatever," she said.

"What do you care?"

"It's interesting to me."

"It's ancient history."

"You called it a mischief summer."

"Sometimes I talk too much."

"No, it's interesting."

"Why is it interesting? We were just having a private conversation among friends. It didn't mean anything. It's nothing for you to worry about. Your generation has this fantastic chance to go beyond all that, if you don't screw it up. I'm sure you won't, despite the crazies. The hotheads and the screamers. The flag burners. The god-damned bra burners. And the boys won't fight. I don't know what the hell has to happen before they grow some balls. Commies marching down Sheridan Road maybe. Commies on the back nine. Shit. *We* fought. Byron and I and Freddie and Harold. We fought so our sons wouldn't have to." He laughed harshly. "And now they're not, so I guess we succeeded. What the hell. I guess it's a great time to be young."

"Better than you can imagine," she said.

"As long as you're not in a rice paddy."

"Now," she said. "What about Harold Barrimore?"

"Forget about Harold Barrimore."

"Is he here tonight?"

"I suppose he's here somewhere. So what?"

"I'm interested," she said. "I'm interested in the mischief summer."

"You don't give up, do you?"

"I don't, Tom. I never do. There are things an artist has to know."

Tom Browne turned away, breathing heavily, loosening his tie. His starched shirt was soaked through with perspiration. Dancers moved around them in a continuous merry flow, the floor rocking like a ship's deck. This seemed to put him off balance, and he stumbled, gripping her arm. His fingers were weak and clammy. He was close to her, so close that she could smell his aftershave mixed with sour sweat. "What the hell do you have to know to draw a tube of toothpaste?"

"What's in the tube."

"Very clever," he said thickly. "You're a clever girl. But no one gives a shit what's in the tube."

"I do," Georgia said. "I care."

"No one gives a shit," he said again, pausing when the music stopped. There was loud applause and almost immediately the band began again, a Broadway show tune in fast time. He looked wildly around him, then directly at her. "God, you're a cold one. You're the coldest girl I've ever seen."

She was about to reply when she saw Harry Forrest making his way toward them through the dancers. She was happy he was coming to cut in; Tom Browne looked ready to collapse.

"Jesus, Harry," Tom said.

"It's all right," Harry said.

"Jesus Christ, give me a hand. I'm all in."

"You'll be fine, don't worry." Harry had his arm around the older man's waist, turning to guide him off the floor. Tom was having trouble with his balance. Dancers had formed a little circle around them but quickly moved to clear a path. A few of the younger ones smiled knowingly, gin and hard dancing on a warm June night could ruin an older gent. They always bit off more than they could chew. It looked as if the dishy blonde was too much for old Tom.

"Over here," Harry directed, and in a moment Tom was seated, heaving to catch his breath. "Get him some water," Harry said to Georgia and she hurried to the bar for a glass. When she returned, Tom was gone, and then she saw him inside with his wife. He was lying on a couch in his shirtsleeves, his bare arm across his forehead; there was a tattoo on his biceps. His wife had pulled up a chair. She bent down to remove his black tie, then deftly slipped off his shoes and began to slowly massage his feet. He seemed not to notice. Georgia stepped closer, drawn to them. She was fascinated by this domestic scene, in its wordless intimacy the essence of married life. They could have been conspirators. Now Tom tried to rise, but his wife put her hand on his chest and he sank back, apparently grateful. She continued to massage his feet. They sat like that for a while in a little zone of silence as the music outside beat on.

"What did you say to him?" Harry asked.

"Look at them," she said. "It's amazing."

"They're very close."

"It's fantastic," she said.

Harry said nothing to that.

"He looked really sick," she said.

"It's happened before. He'll be all right."

"What was it?"

"What did you say to him?" Harry asked again.

"I asked him about Mackinac. You know, the mischief summer."

"Christ," Harry said. "What do you know about Mackinac?"

"Not much. I heard him talking in the receiving line. He and his friend and their wives. They were talking about the summer after the war." She thought a moment. "When he began to make his moves on the dance floor I decided to ask him about it. See how far I'd get."

"Did Tom make some moves?"

"He did," she said. "Pretty clumsy, too."

Harry smiled. "And how far did you get?"

"Not very far." She watched Tom's wife put his shoes on. She patted his knee and then turned abruptly. When she saw Georgia, she stiffened, her features hardening. She reached down for the glass on the floor, feeling for it, and brought it to her mouth, staring at Georgia over the rim.

"You didn't see that you were on to something personal?"

"Of course," she said. "That was the point."

"You didn't guess that you were trespassing?"

"There was something I wanted to find out."

"You ought to be more subtle about how you go about it."

"It was his fault," she said.

"I think you're persona non grata over there," Harry said.

Tom's wife had locked eyes with Georgia over her gin and tonic, and when Georgia made a gesture of sympathy — she thought of it as an expression of female solidarity, an unlikely alliance but an alliance nonetheless — the other woman put down her drink and began to rise, clenching her fists, angrily saying something to her husband, then sitting down again when he took her hand and didn't let go. They were together in a cone of light from a table lamp, the room resembling any bland, impersonal, suburban living room except larger. She shook her head sharply when Tom began to speak, holding both her hands now. He seemed almost to be crooning at her. He sat up slowly, towering over her, whispering into her ear, his long arm around her shoulders, squeezing. He handed her a handkerchief, but she curtly waved it away. All this time she was staring at Georgia. They were motionless a moment and then Tom's wife began to nod grimly, grudging acknowledgment of the truth of whatever he was telling her; and then they embraced.

Georgia said, "Wow."

"Wow indeed," Harry said.

"What does all that mean?"

"It means it's time for us to get a drink," Harry said.

She needed to know the sense of what she had witnessed but believed she never would. What she had was a double portrait that she could call *The Conversation,* and while she had the surface, she would never have the bottom. She had a photograph and she would have to imagine what came before and what was likely to come after, and inevitably that would be her story, not their story. She had fixed the room in her mind, the pale green carpet, the beige couch in the cone of light, more English sporting scenes on the wall, the drink on the carpet, and of course the yellow roses in glass vases. Her inventory was no doubt incomplete or partial; what they saw was not what she saw. *God,* he had said, *you're a cold one,* and had come apart before her eyes. She had never seen anything like it before and did not know what was happening to him. That she could be the cause never occurred to her.

She and Harry Forrest were talking together at the bar. The band was taking a break and people were standing here and there on the dance floor under the great oak. The quarter moon had disappeared behind the clubhouse. They had one drink and then another and finally put the drinks aside when the music began, this one a slow dance. She asked him question after question about the Brownes, but he wouldn't give, except to say that Tom was highly strung, often a surprise to those who did not know him well because he didn't look highly strung. He looked like any prosperous Winnetka businessman with a wandering eye, a strapping Republican with a low handicap and an IQ to match; except that none of that was true. The façade was so convincing that no one bothered to look behind it. Last year he had attempted suicide and been confined at Hartford as a result; and there was no doubt that he would try again sometime soon. As for his wife, married life was mysterious and better left mysterious. Married life was better left to initiates; and they were the only ones who understood it anyway, its ethics and modes of conduct, its ritual deceptions and modes of negotiation, and petty terrorism. Miserable life, Harry said. Hollow victories, hollow defeats.

"You're always at the end of a string, and it's someone else's string."

She looked at him closely, wondering if this was his view of marriage generally or only the Brownes' marriage. It sounded to her like a unified theory.

"Maggie Browne is always described as long-suffering but it's obvious you can apply that to him, too. In a marriage there's always one who's long-suffering, the saint opposed to the devil."

"I didn't know," she said.

"You pushed the wrong button."

"How was I supposed to know?"

"Common sense," he said.

"I'm sorry," she said at last. "I had no idea. I didn't like his moves. He offered me a job with the usual warning that it would involve night work. Duh. What crap. Who does he think I am?"

Harry smiled broadly. "Dean's date. A new face, a pretty face at that. Maybe even someone who's willing. A bit of fluff from Chicago, Dean's twist."

"Yes, Dean," she said.

"Seen him?"

"Not for a while," she said slowly. She had not seen him for an hour or more and had not thought about him at all. She had forgotten him utterly.

"He's around somewhere," Harry said.

Harry was a terrible dancer, not nearly so graceful as Tom Browne; but he also kept his distance. He didn't seem to care, content to lumber around the floor. Fortunately there were only a few other couples dancing, everyone else having gone inside for the buffet. She wondered if the Brownes were still there, and if Tom's wife really held her responsible for her husband's break-down, if that's what it was. But of course she did. She had that wifely dagger look. Georgia searched for Dean and finally saw him on the lawn, talking earnestly to a pretty girl in a blue dress. He was looking at his shoes and nodding grimly, listening while she spoke. No need to wonder what they were talking about. Poor Dean, she thought. And looking at the girl, Georgia saw that she was very well built. She looked like an athletic kewpie doll. Miss Suburban Tits, Georgia said to herself.

She said, "I'm not a bit of fluff from Chicago."

"No, that's true. You're not."

"Or Dean's twist."

"You asked me what Tom thought, not what I thought."

"How do you know what Tom thought? Let's forget about Mr. Tom Browne. He's old enough to be my father."

"Okay," Harry said.

"Tom's wife, too."

"You asked," Harry said.

"Subject closed," Georgia said.

"There's Dean," Harry said. "On the lawn."

"Who's the kewpie doll?"

"A former girlfriend," Harry said. "One of the many formers."

"You have to wonder," Georgia said after a moment, gesturing at the band, the other dancers, the great oak, the flowers, Dean and the girl on the lawn, and the distant green beyond. "It looks like what you'd want. You're supposed to want it. Tom thought this was earthly paradise right here. The bull's eye. I don't know him well enough to know what he meant exactly. Maybe he meant a sweet, sunny, summer Sunday, eighteen holes in par." Harry nodded but did not reply; he was listening hard, no longer concentrating on his clumsy foxtrot. "Many people have lots less. There are people who are sick. There are people who are starving or who have lost their families or their faith. Whose children or lovers are dying, and no help in sight. In Vietnam people are being bombed every day. So what I don't get is why, if you have all this paradise, you'd want to kill yourself. Unless all this is surface, so thin you can see right through it. Unless it's without substance, just a pretty picture, an amateur's

Sunday watercolor." She was silent a moment, thinking, letting her eyes wander to the rolling lawn where Dean and the girl were; but the lawn was vacant and a feathery mist was beginning to rise. The tees and greens were obscured, and they could have been on any remote moor. She imagined Dean and the girl running with abandon, the mist closing around them so thickly that they were imprisoned, the only sound a clarinet playing a foxtrot. The lawn with its heavy trees was Corot's material, perhaps Constable's; of course they would have to take account of the flagstick.

Cézanne would ignore it.

She said, "But when you looked through the watercolor you'd see another picture altogether, the one the artist painted over. The oil the watercolor hid. And that would be the masterpiece. You'd have to want to look, though, wouldn't you? It wouldn't be consoling. You'd need the greatest desire. You'd have to want to see it. You'd have to *want* to know, and not be afraid to know."

They were turning in a circle, not exactly dancing. Her head was flat against his cheek, both arms around his neck. She had been talking into his ear in an urgent whisper. She could hear his breathing and feel his evening stubble. His clumsiness had ceased to bother her. It went with his offhand personality. He was simpatico. He was very unlike the others. He was so unlike his nervous, unhappy brother, taking charge at once when Tom Browne broke down, seeing to Tom, and then leading her away to the dance floor. Harry Forrest seemed to her a grownup. His easy authority was attractive, so when he kissed her lightly on the neck she did not mind. The soft air and the night sky had made her lightheaded, aroused in a dreamy way. She kissed him back, closing her eyes, swaying to the rhythm, feeling the night breeze in her hair. Her dress was flimsy against the thickness of his tuxedo. She kissed him again. She liked his arms around her and the comfortable pressure of his thighs and belly. She felt his wrists against her bare skin. They continued to turn in a slow circle, wound tightly together, unaware that the music had stopped.

Then they were standing at the bar, Harry reaching into the pocket of his jacket to withdraw the yellow rose, a little the worse for wear but still intact, still a perfect rose. When he handed it to her, she did not know what to do with it. She wanted to fix it above her ear but her hair was too short. She was not wearing a bra, so she carefully slipped the stem between her breasts, mindful of the thorns, scratching herself anyway, wincing, but satisfied with the result, the rose peeking comically over the lip of her bodice.

Harry ordered gin and tonics for them both and they retreated to the back side of the oak, leaning against the rough bark, drinking in silence. The party continued inside the clubhouse, a low hum of voices and laughter. He was looking at her softly, and she noticed now that he had some gray hair above his ears. His eyes were gray and they came with crow's feet. His hair was unkempt but that seemed to suit him. He wore it with dash. Dean had said he was thirty years old, the family black sheep if he wasn't careful. Harry couldn't seem to settle down, bouncing from one job to the next and from one girl to another and Dad was about to lay down the law, except how could you tell a thirty-year-old man to pull up his socks, get serious, get a job, play by the rules? Inside the family they called him Contrary Harry and wondered where he had swum from in the Forrest gene pool. Everybody liked Harry but worried about him constantly.

You'll like him, Dean had said. Women always do. Harry doesn't give a damn about anything, and that appeals to women. They love it.

Poor dim Dean. She knew she had charmed Harry. She had not set out to charm him but that was what happened when she got the idea of Winnetka's transparent paradise, the oil under the watercolor. And he had hooked her, too. In some way she could not fathom he had drawn the idea from her. Had he not been present to listen, she never would have spoken. Her words were for his ears only. She remembered his great stillness while he listened.

She kicked off her shoes and reached up to touch his gray hair, wiry where it fell over his ears. The grass was cool and damp under her feet. She wondered if there was some inconspicuous way they could disappear into the mist and be alone for a while, barefoot.

She said, "Is it true they call you Contrary Harry?"

"Only when I'm in the room."

"And that women fall all over you because you don't give a damn about anything?"

"Dean has many interesting theories," he said loyally.

"It sounded about right to me," she said.

"How did you and Dean ever get together?"

"Mutual friend," she said. "A student at the Art Institute. He took her to lunch and I came along. She said you were the interesting one in the family, though. Contrary Harry. So when Dean and I started going out, I wondered when we'd meet, and so here we are."

"Look," he said, but that was all he said.

"Let's take a walk with our shoes off," she said.

"Look," he said again. "Georgia."

"Naked feet," she said. "I'm game if you are."

He said, "I'm leaving next week."

"Oh," she said. "Where are you going next week?"

"Europe."

"Well." She gave a little strangled laugh. "Have a ball in Europe."

"It's not a vacation," he said sternly. "I'm moving to Paris."

"You mean, permanently?"

"I mean permanently."

"France," she said, saying it as if the word were unfamiliar. She could not imagine living in France or any foreign country. She did not know how you would go about it. What if you showed up and they refused to let you in? She had never thought of living anywhere but Chicago and wondered where he'd got the idea, and why now. She was deflated, half sad and half angry, believing that she had in some way been duped. But from the expression on his face, Harry wasn't any happier about it than she was. She stepped back from the oak and gave a last look at the mist rising from the lawn. If there were stars overhead, she knew they were crossed. Then she saw Dean on the dance floor looking for her. She ducked back behind the oak and said, "Harry. What are you going to do in Paris? And why Paris?"

"My book," he said. "I'm a writer."

"So?"

"Paris is where the material is."

"What material?"

He gestured at the lawn and the country club, then swept his arm in an arc as if to include all of Winnetka and the North Shore, Chicago even, and the stars in the sky. "This material," he said.

"If it's here," she said, "how can it be there?"

"It's not accessible here."

She looked at him doubtfully.

"Paris is where you can get your work done without interference."

"Who says so?"

"It's well known." He thought a moment, searching for the least obvious expatriate. There were so many, and they loomed so large. He said, "Alice B. Toklas."

"Who is Alice B. Toklas?"

"A writer. A very fine writer. And Gertrude Stein's companion. Former companion."

"Companion?"

"Lover," Harry said.

"That would be another reason," she said.

She was quick, too quick for her own good. But they had rapport and this was not a subject he could discuss with his family, who did not understand his great ambition. His father had laughed at him and called him Ernie. He said, "I'm going to Paris to write a great novel."

"That cannot be written in Winnetka."

"Clearly," he said. Then, with a smile, "There has never been a great novel written in Winnetka."

"Good luck then," Georgia said. "Thanks anyway for the rose."

"I don't belong here," he said suddenly. "You don't belong here either."

"And the dance, that was fun. Thanks for listening."

"Listen to me now," he said.

"But how do you know where I belong?" She drew the rose carefully from her dress and handed it to him.

He said, "You think it's all surface here. You think we're thin, thin as a pale watercolor. You think we're a curtain you can part or a woman's veil, lift it and see Medusa's face. Lift it and see the sewers of paradise. But we're not thin. We're hard as iron, always have been. You can break your pick on us. So if you're smart, you leave."

She looked around her. "It looks soft to me."

"Don't wait until you're thirty, is my advice. Let's take a walk."

But Dean was suddenly in front of them. He wanted to leave; the party was breaking up anyway. What are you doing behind this tree? Then he looked at his brother's face and said no more, standing to one side, waiting patiently for Georgia to put on her shoes and Harry to slip the yellow rose between her breasts, Harry not giving a damn, as usual. The band struck up "Goodnight, Ladies." They stood a moment in silence. His arms crossed, a cigarette between his teeth, Harry was leaning against the tree looking at Georgia. He reached for her hand, but she was already walking away toward the clubhouse with Dean, leaving Harry alone and small-seeming under the great oak.

"That's Harold Barrimore," Dean said. They were standing at the inside bar, Georgia having insisted on a drink for the road. Dean nodded at a white-haired man sitting alone at a table in the corner.

Georgia nodded. She had lost interest in the Brownes and the Barrimores and the mischief summer.

"What was going on back there?"

"You mean with Harry?"

"With Harry and before with Tom Browne. There was talk."

"Talk? What kind of talk?"

"The usual talk," Dean said.

"Tom got sick," she said curtly. To the bartender she said, "Scotch, ice no water."

"Nothing for me," Dean said. "He's a great guy, you know."

"So it seems. Highly strung, though."

"Tom? Tom's as solid as a brick."

She took her drink, jerking it rudely from the bartender's hand, and said, "That's not what your brother says."

"I guess you and Harry got along pretty well."

"I talked, he listened."

"That's his secret, all right."

Guests were milling about in the corridor. The host and hostess were outside under the porte-cochère. Everyone was kissing and waving good-bye amid shouts and laughter. Georgia felt out of place now in this room full of strangers. She had lost her anonymity and her protection; she was as conspicuous as a turtle without its shell. Probably they knew her all too well, a bit of fluff from Chicago in a hand-me-down dress. And she did not know them at all.

Dean said quietly, "Come on, Georgia, let's go."

Scotch was doing its work. She took another pull, the alcohol cold and tart and irreproachable as it slid down her throat; and she would have another when she got home. She looked bleakly at her glass, imagining Harry Forrest in Europe, Harry in a café drinking wine with a stylish woman wearing black stockings and a beret and a too-tight T-shirt. Harry grinning, Harry taking out his notebook to write something witty the woman had said, Harry bending across the table to kiss the woman on the mouth. She supposed that Harry's theory was correct. It sounded novel. You had to separate yourself from your "material" in order to re-create it, and that meant crossing an ocean. The material was in one country and you were in another and the great distance made it — what was the word he'd used? — "accessible." The farther away you were, the closer the material was; and then no one could "interfere." Georgia began to smile. She looked out the window to the great oak. She wanted to tell Harry that he shouldn't be so afraid, but Harry had vanished. No doubt he would discover that for himself. Dean said something conciliatory to her, but she wasn't listening.

2

G EORGIA never revisited the country club and never saw
Dean Forrest again, yet the summer dance remained in
her memory, vivid and complete. She thought of it as the
apprenticeship to her sentimental education, and on the whole
believed that she had passed her initiation. Harry was right about
one thing: they were hard people. Certainly she had gained from
the experience, though that was the case generally with artists.
The artist had the advantage because the artist could rearrange
things, could seize a moment like a photographer or deconstruct
it as Picasso deconstructed a human face. All the civilians could
do was think about it and brood or exult according to temperament. The artist could break it down any way she wanted. She
could leave herself in or take herself out and be a presence nonetheless.

For years bits and pieces of the evening in June would come
back to her, retrieved by a chance remark or something she saw
or read. She would glimpse a quarter moon through the trees or
a bouquet of yellow roses on a table and think *Winnetka*. She
never saw an English sporting print without remembering standing alone in her hand-me-down dress in the receiving line, and

the parade-ground timbre of men's voices as they recounted the mysterious mischief summer in Mackinac after the war. Watching television one night, she saw Richard Nixon at a Republican dinner at the Palmer House, the President shaking hands with Harold Barrimore, Harold as pink and plump as a cherub. And then the newspaper obit of Tom Browne killed in a freak hunting accident up in Michigan. She believed these Winnetka men and their women constituted a repertory company that would entertain her for the rest of her life, dancing in from the wings at odd times and places, a merry band led by the writless Pope himself. How lucky she was! What a cast of characters! Poor Tom.

Then one winter afternoon the clubhouse burned to the ground. She read the account in the *Tribune,* feeling bereft, as if someone had destroyed a much-loved canvas in a museum, slashed it with a knife or drenched it with acid. Georgia was having a hard time of it generally, living alone, her personal life barren. She had broken up with one man and taken up with another when she discovered that he was married and playing out a fantasy that had everything to do with art and nothing to do with life; he thought she could turn him into a Bohemian. In fact he thought he was a work of art that she could retouch and turn into an avant-garde masterpiece. She was living day to day, broke and broken down. Her work was going badly but her work was all she had, and she clung to it to keep from drowning.

Winnetka had been a touchstone to her, the stone worn smooth but still provocative, a knot in her handkerchief. Not two weeks after the summer dance her parents separated, a calamity that had been inconceivable, as inconceivable as Tom Browne and Harry Forrest had been; and while the dance and her parents were not linked in any formal way, she rarely thought of one without thinking of the other. Families like hers did not break up, strained though the allegiances might become, and she believed her mother and father superior to the sort of slovenly melodrama so common to the North Shore. Yet her best work had come from the country club that evening in June, so the fire brought out her natural paranoia, a conviction that she was being controlled by malevolent forces. They were sending her a bitter message. When she came to the phrase "suspected arson," she could not believe it. And when, a few days later, this turned out to be true —

"DISGRUNTLED" WORKER
HELD IN CLUB BLAZE

— she wondered if the arsonist was anyone she had met that night, perhaps the bartender who had leered at her and from whom she had snatched the Scotch on the rocks, wanting a stiff drink for the road, the bartender furious at her rich-bitch behavior, a workingman humiliated by a socialite. Naturally he would seek revenge. But he should have known she was no socialite. And she was not normally rude. What had got into her? She was convinced now that she was responsible. Responsible but not guilty, she told herself; she had not actually lit the torch.

When the newspaper identified the accused as a grounds-keeper who held a grudge, she was not dissuaded. Groundskeep-ers doubled as bartenders all the time; this was well known. No doubt he had been insubordinate because he was so very angry. *At me,* she said.

And as a matter of fact, she probably was guilty. If you're responsible, you're guilty. Thank God no one was killed.

Georgia brooded about it for weeks, remembering the work she had done; it was so long ago, but she saw all the pictures clearly in her mind's eye. *Arrangement in Black and White* was her portrait of the Brownes, so titled after she had discovered that *The Conversation* had been successfully appropriated by Henri Matisse. *Winnetka Boy* was a portrait of a supercilious Harry For-rest leaning against the great oak, his arms crossed and a ciga-rette in his mouth. *Coming Out* was the group portrait of the Demmings, Earl and Josephine and their two daughters, all look-ing in different directions. The four canvases took her six months to complete and she was elated with the results, yet when she took them to her instructor, he dismissed them with his usual comment — "retrograde" — and advised her to quit school and do what she was suited to do, illustrate. Perhaps she could become a society portraitist, except her color sense was nil and up on the North Shore they liked their portraits rainbowy, to go with the draperies. She eventually sold the pictures to a Marxist professor at Roosevelt, one thousand dollars a picture and cheap at the price. She believed she had gone far beyond herself, a revolutionary who had overthrown the tyrant and now had to learn to govern, meaning consolidate her gains. After she quit art school she began to draw various Chicago characters, and then a series on children of the South Side. A few of those she sold; many more she gave away to the children; one was stolen at knife point. And then her work took a turn that depressed her. She thought her hand was being guided by something from the underworld. Her pictures became ever more spare, abstract, and perverse; and she decided that she was breaking her pick in Chicago.

This was the state of affairs when the clubhouse burned down. The material was there, but she no longer had access to it. She could not discover its nature, and it held no delight. She could not see over the city's big shoulders to the horizon, and then she realized that the horizon was Iowa. She felt diminished by the size of things and deafened by the hum of money. She could not hear herself think, except when she was alone with her canvases and her cat; the canvases spoke in a whisper, and the cat was silent but presidential. She was working on angular cityscapes, believing that Chicago was only a noisier and less febrile version of Berlin, nowhere people living on a landlocked northern plain. But she knew in her heart that Chicago was not Berlin, whatever Berlin was; she had never been there. She knew it only through its artists. She played the symphonies of Gustav Mahler all day long, thinking that if she could not have Berlin, at least she could have Vienna. At night she drank, hoping she could transcend her environment. She meant, Paint a new one. *Create* one. At this time she was living on the West Side, a monotonous grid without exit.

Georgia was thirty years old.

She was waiting in her dentist's office. Her father was taking her to dinner that night and she was to choose the place. She was thinking about dinner because she didn't want to think about the dentist's drill. Turning the pages of a magazine, she started when she saw a familiar face, *Winnetka Boy* ten years older. "Author Harry Forrest" read the caption, and there he was, in a Borsalino hat sitting at a café table reading a newspaper. So he had got to Paris after all; somehow she'd doubted that he would. Some North Shore crisis would intervene and he would remain in Winnetka, "Ernie" for the rest of his days. His hair was longer, but otherwise he looked the same. The hat suited him, taming the gray hair that tumbled over his ears and collar. His novel was called *Inspector Pease in the Third Arrondissement*, a detective story "rescued by the author's sure sense of the sights, sounds, and smells of the City of Light." The reviewer thought this book inferior to its predecessors "but quite good enough for a Sunday afternoon at the beach." She gathered that was like saying that a picture was good enough for the spare room but unsuitable anywhere else. She skimmed the review, resolved to read the book, and looked again at the photograph, turning it this way and that in the dim light of the dentist's waiting room. Harry Forrest looked content, and boyish still. He had obviously posed for the photograph but seemed relaxed anyway, an espresso at his elbow and a cigarette burning in the Cinzano ashtray. His gray eyes were alive, yet the man himself looked settled, at ease in his surroundings. Whatever he was looking for he seemed to have found. She read the review thoroughly now, and laughed out loud when she came across the name of a minor character, an artist, George White.

Well, well, she thought.

Contrary Harry.

That night she did not sleep but stood looking out her third-floor window thinking about Harry Forrest, who had done what he'd set out to do; at any event, he was in the place he wanted to be. He had rolled the dice, and walked. *I don't belong here.*

You don't belong here either. You could admit defeat without being defeated. Artists did that all the time when a place closed in around them. You could go anywhere, a South Sea island, the south of France, Cape Cod, or Iowa. Or you could choose California, in every respect the opposite of the Windy City. She pressed her forehead against the window glass and looked into the empty street, where nothing moved. She wondered what Inspector Pease had to do with Winnetka, Harry Forrest's special "material."

Around about dawn she saw her exit. It was what any disgruntled worker would do. She called her father and asked to borrow two thousand dollars, no questions please. He agreed, as she knew he would. At dinner he had been sympathetic when she told him about the country club, and how discouraged she was. He offered the advice he always offered: Don't burn all your bridges, Georgie. But that was exactly what she must do.

Thanks, she said.

Call you in a week, when I get settled.

Then she packed her bags, her canvases, and her paints, put her cat, Liebermann, in a traveling cage, and loaded her van for the long drive west. She had no idea what she would find there, and on the way there would be hundreds of bridges. She crossed the frozen Mississippi at Galena. Half the continent lay before her.

In Los Angeles she rented the spacious top floor of a square stucco house on a nondescript street in the anonymous suburb of Southgate, on the glide path to LAX. The apartment was surprisingly cheap, though the noise was distracting. However, she was not in a mood to be annoyed. The neighborhood was pleasant and the people loose and friendly. Students from UCLA lived across the street. There were a number of military families, all of them with children and animals. At the end of the street was a hippie commune, and at night the air was ripe with the sweet smell of dope.

Georgia set up her easel in the living room, seeking a hard north light. But no light in Southern California was truly hard, not if you'd grown up in Chicago. There was seldom any wind, only a light breeze from the ocean. The air was fragrant. She threw open her window to the night air and slept fitfully. She set to work in a tentative fashion, not knowing exactly where she was headed but certain that she would know when she got there. Something new was forming in her mind. She knew that the Expressionist angles and monochromes of her ominous cityscapes were a past subject. Cityscapes no longer interested her. She saw strange colors wherever she looked. When someone asked her what she did, she said she did nothing; and no one seemed to care. She fell in with the students and on weekends they all went to Santa Monica for beach parties, cheerful disheveled affairs that lasted until the early morning. Georgia saw something new every day, and quickly lost her hesitation. She began to paint self-portraits.

In six weeks she had six self-portraits, and one night asked her landlady and her husband to join her for a drink. She set the portraits on the floor against the wall, saying nothing; she did not want to draw a reaction from them, but hoped that one might come naturally. Hard for them to miss six portraits in a room that measured twenty feet by ten. And Mrs. Clyde had what she called "an interest" in a gallery.

But they said nothing until the second drink was poured. Mr. Clyde nodded solemnly at the pictures.

"Who're the girls?"

"It's the same girl, dear," Mrs. Clyde said.

"No, they're not," he said.

"Mr. Art Connoisseur," Mrs. Clyde said.

"They're great," Mr. Clyde said. "Just great."

"They're lovely, Georgia," Mrs. Clyde said. She was looking at the pictures over the rim of her glasses. "I admire artists. My dear late father was a Sunday painter. I've been looking at them since we arrived, trying to decide which one I like best. But they're all so lovely. They're so good. You've worked so hard on them. They're so — nice!"

"Great," Mr. Clyde said.

"Thank you," Georgia said. Nice was not the word she was hoping for.

"Who are they?" Mr. Clyde said.

"It isn't 'they,' you dummy. It's one. It's one girl."

"It isn't those hippie kids down the street, the ones with the long hair who don't wear bras?"

"No," Georgia said.

"Whoever," he said. "It's six different portraits of six different girls. Anyone can see that. Isn't that right, Georgia?"

"You're blind as a bat," Mrs. Clyde said.

"Those girls ought to be locked up," he said.

"They're just lost souls," Mrs. Clyde said.

"It isn't only their souls that're lost," he said.

"I like the eyes on that one," Mrs. Clyde said, pointing. "The one on the end. The eyes are lovely, though aren't they sad? And she should do something about her hair."

"How about the lungs," Mr. Clyde said.

"He's impossible," Mrs. Clyde said.

"Well," he said. "Which is it, Georgia? One or many?"

"Whatever you like," Georgia said.

"Don't humor him," Mrs. Clyde said. "When he gets a bee in his bonnet you've got to swat the bee."

"I know what I know," he said. "What are you going to do with them now?"

"Sell them," Georgia said. "I'm going to walk them around tomorrow."

"Fix a fat price," Mr. Clyde said.

"What do you think?" Georgia asked.

"Not a penny under a hundred dollars," he said.

"More," Mrs. Clyde said.

"And you've got to have titles," he said.

Georgia smiled and did not reply.

"She's not saying," Mrs. Clyde said.

"People buy something, they want a title. Buy a car, you want it to be a Buick. Buy a TV, you want your Sony. So titles're essential."

Georgia said, "I'm calling them *One, Two, Three, Four, Five,* and *Six.*"

"See!" He said triumphantly.

Georgia said, "Actually, I was thinking of calling them *Georgia One, Georgia Two, Georgia Three, Georgia Four, Georgia Five,* and *Georgia Six.*"

There was a little strained silence while Mr. Clyde leaned forward to look more closely at the pictures. He sighed heavily and turned to look at his wife.

"They are self-portraits," Mrs. Clyde said. She looked at Georgia a long moment, as if she were measuring her for something, a shirt or a shroud. Then Mrs. Clyde set her glass carefully on the table and rose.

"Lambie," Mr. Clyde said.

"You're salable, Georgia. I don't know if the pictures are."

"Don't pay any attention to her, Georgia. They're swell pictures."

Mrs. Clyde had taken a card from her purse and was writing on it.

"You'll get there, Georgia," Mr. Clyde said.

"Get where?"

"Successville!" he said. "Just be patient. It always takes longer than you think, ha-ha."

Mrs. Clyde handed Georgia the card. "Give this to Carole Fox at Archer-Orion Gallery. The address is on the card. I've written a note. She'll look at your portraits. I don't know if she'll do anything with them. But this will get you in the door."

"Thank you," Georgia said.

"I don't like them very much, be truthful with you. They're naughty, Georgia. But perhaps Carole will like them. She often does. Like things that I don't."

"Let's hope so," Georgia said.

"It would be better, you'd cover up."

Georgia said nothing to that. She thought the pictures quite modest.

"See Carole," Mrs. Clyde said and closed her bag, nodding at her husband, who joined her at the door. She turned to face the self-portraits. "Just what is your objective, Georgia?"

Georgia thought a moment. "The illumination of character through the manipulation of paint," she said.

And that was how it came to be, a month later, that Georgia Whyte was in Carole Fox's BMW motoring to Coldwater Canyon and a meeting with Ed Smid, film producer and art connoisseur. Carole had arranged the meeting after sending Ed the six self-portraits on approval. These are *fantastic,* Carole had said. No wonder La Clyde didn't like them. But thank God she sent you to me. Georgia was thrilled. Who wouldn't be?

"Nervous?" Carole said, and when Georgia replied that she wasn't, Carole laughed. "That's a bad sign."

"I can be a little nervous if it'd help."

"You *look* dishy, and that's good. Ed likes it when people — make an appearance."

She heard something in Carole's voice and said, "Too much?"

"No, it's a nice outfit. Elegant, plain, and simple." Carole was wearing jeans; Georgia, a plain white shift.

"Not too much, then."

"Well," Carole said. "Noooo. Not really."

Liar, Georgia thought.

They arrived at Ed Smid's at ten thirty-five, waiting at the gate while the guard telephoned the housekeeper. The guard wore a pistol on his belt and stared at them while he spoke on the telephone, his free hand on the butt of his gun as if they were suspicious characters, possibly terrorists. Carole was giving Georgia a briefing, repeating the list of dos and don'ts with Ed Smid, who liked things a certain way. No smoking, no interruptions while he talked, no jokes of the did-you-hear-the-one-about-the-Jew-and-the-dog-who-walked-into-the-bar variety. Above all, don't flirt. He hates it. It offends him. Ed's touchy; he's very sensitive.

At last the guard nodded and pushed a button, causing the gate to unlatch and swing wide. A team of Asian gardeners was at work on the flowering slopes leading to the house. Georgia thought it looked like the house of any prosperous business-man, whitewashed brick and cedar shingles under two enormous shade trees. Carole sped up the driveway and parked in the cir-cle. The housekeeper was there to meet them. In her jeans and tank top and espadrilles she looked to Georgia more like a starlet than a housekeeper. Two peahens glared from a bed of roses.

The housekeeper said that Mr. Smid was not in. Mr. Smid was skating, a sport he had taken up recently to relieve stress. He would not be back from the rink before eleven, possibly sooner, more probably later. He was really into it, you know, the skating. Sometimes he skated all morning long.

Too bad, but it can't be helped.

You can wait by the swimming pool out back.

You know the way, she said.

Georgia followed Carole through the portico connecting the main house with the garage complex, which contained a small gym and a movie theater along with space for three cars, a mo-torcycle, and a van. The van was painted with tan and brown camouflage and at various levels had narrow reinforced openings a few inches high and a foot long. A fitted metal plate protected the windshield, that too with a long opening on the driver's side.

"What's with the war wagon?" Georgia asked.

Carole giggled. "Ed's a survivalist."

"So's everybody," Georgia said.

"Not in that way," Carole said. She explained that the day things blew — and that day was not far hence — Ed Smid did not intend to surrender but to fight his way out of Coldwater Canyon in the van. It was armor-plated and fully equipped with small arms and a machine gun. Ed had an underground redoubt near Adelanto in the Mojave with enough food and water to last a year. It was equipped with a transmitter, radio, and television; and of course the aviary. He was taking the Asian gardeners with him. They were all small-arms qualified and were charged with protection of the art collection. Ed had reliable informants who had evidence that the many proles in Greater Los Angeles intended to revolt, and that Coldwater Canyon was Numero Uno on their list of objectives. Ed wasn't giving up without a fight, but in the event of overwhelming force the war wagon was always gassed up, ready to go. And when they wanted him back, it would be on *his* terms.

"And you can go ahead and laugh, Georgia. A lot of people do. Ed Smid and his war wagon. But when the balloon goes up, Ed'll have the last laugh. We're talking casualties here of a hundred thou, maybe more. Ed isn't a fool, you know. Ed wouldn't be where he is if he was a fool." And when Georgia asked how long Ed had had his redoubt near Adelanto in the Mojave, Carole Fox replied that he had had it for years and years; circumstances changed and Ed changed with them, threatwise.

The pool was situated beside a wide flagstone terrace that gave off the glassed-in living room, where the housekeeper was watching television and drinking a 7-Up. Half the room was an aviary containing brightly colored birds, some loose and others in cages. Georgia and Carole pulled metal tables and two chairs from the sunlight into the shade of a palm tree. It was killing hot, the sky the color of mercury. They could hear birds chattering, but the pool area was pristine and lifeless, groomed. The surface of the water was flat and shiny as marble. Carole excused herself and went to the phone.

When Georgia stood, she could see Los Angeles shrouded in mist far below. Left and right were the red tile roofs and chimneys of the other villas in Coldwater Canyon; the effect was vaguely Tuscan, except for the obvious fact of Los Angeles. She heard Carole chattering and then a tinkle of laughter. Things were motionless in the heat and she began to sweat. She wondered how they stood it; the heat was worse than Chicago in

August, and there was no breeze at all. Thank God for the shade of the palm tree. Probably there was air conditioning everywhere; inside, the housekeeper was wearing a sweater.

At the far end of the pool, beyond the diving board, were two man-sized Ali Baba pots and between the pots a life-sized boy. She and the boy stared at each other a moment, until she thought he was a statue, a trick of the eye. Then the boy moved. Startled, she smiled at him, but he turned at once and disappeared into the house.

Then Carole was at her side, holding a piece of paper, her appointments for the day, calls and calls-back. She began to speak in a low voice, her impresario's voice, at once brittle and brutal. She wanted to explain how they should proceed with Ed Smid, who, like many successful producers, was often difficult. He was highly strung. And he was a control freak. He needed to control the moment, so on no account deviate from whatever agenda he chose to set. But his word was his bond, and that set him apart from some others she could name. The trouble with his word was that he so seldom gave it unconditionally. If Ed was in a risk-taking mood, and he sometimes was, they could have it wrapped up by noon. It was just a wonderful opportunity, a private meeting with Ed Smid. *At his house.* He's really put himself out, Georgia. It would mean a lot to both of us, a sale to Ed. He loved the pictures I sent him and now it's up to you. Your haircut's fine, by the way. Thing is, Georgia. Be modest. Be *nice.* Ed likes nice people. Just don't say much.

"Who does the talking?" Georgia asked.

"He does," Carole said.

"All of it?"

"As much as he wants," Carole said.

They heard a door slam and suddenly he was walking across the flagstones, a lithe figure in blue jeans and a polo shirt. He moved on the balls of his feet like a dancer, springy as a teenager. Only the lines in his face betrayed his age, which was closer to fifty than twenty. He was very tan, but the tan didn't conceal the lines. However, his neck was taut. His eyes glittered beneath sandy brows, but they were lost to view when he put on aviator sunglasses. He kissed them both and began to drag the chairs and the table out of the shade of the palm tree and into the sun. He looked at his hands, dirty from the surface of the table, and wiped them on the seat of his jeans. The smog, he said, fouled everything. Then he took off his shirt, revealing a welterweight's torso. Georgia thought him extraordinary, and wondered how he did it. Most of the men she knew were not fit. When she nervously lit a cigarette, he frowned.

"Wish you wouldn't," he said.

She looked around for an ashtray.

"It's so bad for everyone."

"Even outside?"

"More than ever outside. We all have to do our part. There's just." He shook his head and looked at the sky. "So much to contend with."

"What shall I do with it?"

"Trude? Truuuu-deee?" His voice was loud in the humid silence. He waited for the living room door to open and then he said, without turning around, "Can you come here and do something with this?"

The housekeeper hurried across the flagstones into the sunlight. "With what, Ed?"

"That," he said, pointing. "That woman's weed."

Georgia held out the cigarette and the housekeeper took it, holding it cautiously with two fingers, ash end down.

Georgia said, "Thanks."

Trude said, "No prob." She looked at Smid, apparently awaiting further instructions.

"Is Gary here?"

"He was, a minute ago."

"Find him."

Trude nodded and went away.

"Well!" Smid said, smiling brilliantly, rising from his chair. He was looking steadily at Georgia, his eyes concealed behind the aviator sunglasses. "So we have product."

"That's it, Ed," Carole said. "And Georgia —"

Ed shook his head, wagging his forefinger. He had not finished his thought. He stood at poolside and began to stretch, moving his torso from side to side, hands on his hips. "It's interesting product. It's — superb!" He did deep knee bends while he talked, but Georgia wasn't listening. She was charmed by Ed Smid's voice; it was as trim as his body. It was a lean forearm of a voice, supple and furry. Now he was talking about Georgia's antecedents, Botero and Munch. He began to sweat as he worked out, stretching and talking, and presently he stepped out of his jeans. Georgia looked at him in his wee bikini briefs and her eyes widened. He was *magnifique,* no question about it. Ed Smid had narrow shoulders and small ankles, and a flat stomach without too much hair. It was a while since she had seen a man in a bikini.

Carole said something then, and Georgia tuned back in. The sun was directly in her eyes, and she had to squint. They were talking about European artists.

Ed Smid said, "The trouble with European artists is that they've been fucking for money for so long they don't know how to fuck for love."

"Absolutely," Carole said.

"Do you see what I'm saying here? It isn't that they don't like love. They do. They're ardent. They don't know how to fuck for it, though. They *think* they do. They'll talk up a storm. They're bullshit artists." Ed Smid's body was glistening with sweat, but he was barely out of breath. Little beads of sweat had collected in the curly hair of his chest and abdomen. He stood facing them, his fingers beating a rapid tattoo on his rump. "So I don't like European product."

"It's so true," Carole said.

"Not even van Gogh?" Georgia asked. She was looking at the Ali Baba pots and saw the boy peek around one and then jerk his head back.

Ed Smid flexed his arm muscles and turned to Georgia, smiling thinly. "I'll buy your product, all six."

She said, "My goodness."

"And then I'll want you to paint me."

Georgia did not reply.

"Warts and all."

Carole said, "That's wonderful, Ed. Georgia, what an opportunity!"

"You've got to know what kind of man I am, Georgia."

"What kind of man are you, Mr. Smid?"

He swiveled his hips, an athletic bump-and-grind. Then he threw his arms over his head, poised on tiptoe, and executed a back flip into the pool, diving to the bottom, where he lingered.

"You're in," Carole said. "*Fantastic.*"

Georgia watched his shape, wavy beneath the blue surface. "Did he actually look at the portraits?"

"Maybe, maybe not. Hard to tell. He likes you, though."

"I'll bet he does that for all the girls."

"No, that was for you. You've had a whole bunch of luck today, Georgia."

Ed Smid surfaced and began a slow crawl to the deep end of the pool. He swam beautifully, with slow, measured strokes.

He called, "Gary?"

The boy suddenly appeared from behind one of the Ali Baba pots.

Ed Smid turned. "This is my son, Gary. Gary, say hello to Carole and Georgia."

"Hello," the boy said.

"Hello Carole, hello Georgia," Ed Smid said.

"Hello Carole, hello Georgia," the boy said.

"Come here, Gary," Smid said.

"I don't want to," the boy said.

"It's time for a swim," Smid said.

"You'll throw me in," the boy said.

"No promises, Gary."

"You always do."

"I've got a secret. It's about Trude."

"But you're going to throw me in."

"No promises, Gary. No promises."

"I'll go in by myself."

"Come here, and I'll tell you the secret."

The boy approached slowly. He was just out of reach, standing awkwardly with his hands folded in front of him. Ed Smid's chin rested on the pool's gutter, and when he spoke his furry voice echoed.

"Let me go in by myself," the boy said.

"You've got to get closer so I can tell you the secret."

"Do you promise?"

"No promises, Gary. No promises."

The boy looked shyly at the women sitting in the sun. He moved a few steps closer to the edge of the pool, and Georgia saw suddenly the family resemblance, except that the boy had none of his father's sleek grace or his temerity. Georgia thought he was eight, perhaps nine. He was soft as butter. It was hard to say what the physical resemblance was, only that the boy was the shadow of the man. Georgia pulled her chair back into the shade of the palm tree and lit a cigarette. She wanted to close her eyes as she habitually did at excruciating moments in a film, but did not. She came to play, as they liked to say in Los Angeles, so she might as well play to the end, watching this vicious little duel in the sun whose outcome was not in doubt.

In a single explosive motion, Ed Smid threw himself upward and caught the boy's legs, sweeping him head first into the water.

When Gary came to the surface, he was crying.

"Boy, you never learn, do you?"

The boy paddled to the edge of the pool and hung there, heaving.

"Gary, Gary, Gary, Gary, Gary," Ed Smid said. "All promises are false." His words carried easily across the water. "False. All of them. Every single one." Then he pushed off, floating a moment on his back before he commenced his slow crawl back to the shallow end of the pool, where the women were. Gary disappeared behind one of the Ali Baba pots. Ed Smid climbed out of the pool and toweled himself off, taking his time. His bikini briefs were transparent now.

He looked at Georgia sitting in the shade smoking her cigarette.

"So when can we start?"

"We don't start. And I want my self-portraits back."

"But I've bought them. They're mine. Six faces of Georgia, all mine."

Georgia turned to Carole. "Have you cashed the check?"

"Ed's good for the check, Georgia. The pictures are *sold*."

"My work —" she began.

"Sorry, honey," Smid said. "They belong to me now. Always will."

She turned to Carole Fox. "I hope to God you got a good price."

Carole looked at Ed Smid. "The price will be good," she said. "For an unknown."

"She won't be unknown much longer," Ed Smid said. "When you finish my portrait, you'll own L.A. *Own* it." He shook his head vigorously, little drops of water flying here and there. "I like your tits, Georgia."

"Mr. Smid? You are an asshole." And, dropping her cigarette in the pool, Georgia left. She hurried through the portico and down the driveway to the gate. She thought she heard laughter behind her. The guard was on the telephone and when he saw her his hand went to the pistol on his belt. For a moment she had the fantastic idea that he was preparing to shoot her, on orders from Ed Smid via the telephone. Nothing was out of bounds for producer Smid. She would be shot as an intruder; it happened all the time in Los Angeles. People were armed as a matter of course. Smid had a war wagon and Asian mercenaries; and now he had six of her self-portraits. And she had insulted him. Suddenly she was quite certain she would be shot dead. The guard made a brusque motion with his hand and she stepped back, terrified. There was no place to run in the blinding sun-light, bees buzzing in the exotic flowers.

The gate swung open and the guard motioned her through, eyes hard on her breasts and then her hips, eyes up and down, a thin wiseguy expression on his face. She heard someone call her name. Then, "Close the gate, Carl."

A hand was on her arm and she turned, roughly disengaging herself. A young man stood looking at her, hands on his hips, smiling broadly. "Ed sent me."

"Tell this gorilla to open the gate."

"Ed says you've got spirit. Ed wants you to reconsider his portrait."

"Ed can go fuck himself."

"Yeah, well," the man said. "That's not hard for him to do. He does it daily."

She smiled at that. The man nodded at the guard and the gate swung open again and she walked through it. He followed.

He said, "I'll walk with you. Cabs are hard to find."

"I'll find my own cab."

But he insisted in an affable way and she assented, glad for the company because she was unnerved by the guard and sick-ened by Ed Smid. It looked as if her career in California was over before it began. There was no cab in sight, and scant chance of locating one in Coldwater Canyon. They walked the deserted suburban streets, so unfamiliar to her. The houses were charm-ing, but each street looked like the last and for a moment she thought she was in an absurd, lifeless maze of cul-de-sacs and false turnings and circles without landmarks, a municipal version of Ed Smid's pool area; except there were no Ali Baba pots and no small boys to humiliate. From time to time a car whispered by, a woman at the wheel. The stillness of it unsettled her and she began to walk more quickly, the man keeping pace with awkward strides. He was breathing heavily and asked her to slow down. After a few blocks he began to describe the birds they saw. To her they looked like ordinary city birds and not very many of them at that. She thought perhaps the birds were discouraged by the heat, and perhaps the stillness also. The man continued to talk, but she was only half listening. She was lulled by his soft voice.

She said to herself, You screwed up, Georgia.

You made a fool of yourself.

"Slow down," he said.

She turned to face him, staring at him hard. He was obviously out of shape, sweating heavily, his body ripe. He looked to be about thirty, but it was hard to tell. He had a little pot belly, incongruous because the rest of him was lean. His hair curled down over his shirt collar, leaving a smudge on the fabric. He sported the beginnings of a mustache under the shapeliest nose she had ever seen on a man. He wore it with pride, too. Above the nose were large black eyes with very long lashes. Somehow you knew before he opened his mouth that he was intelligent, his head tilted slightly backward so that his eyes sighted down that wonderful nose; and the eyes missed nothing. When he smiled at her, she was surprised at the brilliance of his teeth, movie star teeth as even as a piano keyboard. With all that, he was by no means handsome. His crooked smile was conspiratorial, inviting, sardonic, almost apologetic — strange, because he did not look to be the sort of man who spent his time on regrets. Then she saw it was not apology but its opposite.

She said, "Who are you, anyway?"

He said, "I work for Ed."

"I guessed that," she said. "What are you for Ed, bagman, chauffeur, valet, what?"

He fluttered his hands, remarkably small and well formed. "I'm Ed's bird man."

She said nothing to that, disappointed because it seemed a clumsy approach.

"I look after Ed's birds. You must've noticed them, around the yard and in the house where tricky Trude was watching television."

"That's what you do for a living?"

"He has a dozen species, some of them quite rare. There're two zoo-quality birds. He's provided for them in his will. Ed's very proud of them. To Ed, they spell Big Bucks. He has one friend who keeps giant carp and another with an aardvark. They like to keep things, Ed's friends."

"I'll bet they do."

"Ed likes things in cages."

At that, she smiled.

They had passed under a shade tree at an intersection. An empty boulevard stretched before them, and she looked left and right, searching for a cab. The bird man was at her elbow, closer than she liked.

"So you're an artist," he said conversationally.

"Not today," she said. "Today I'm an idiot."

"Ed said you were good, the genuine article."

Georgia glanced at him but made no comment.

"Look," he said, "Ed was just being a shit."

The bird man was staring at a common robin as it flitted from sidewalk to grass and back again. He stood motionless, watching the bird, and then began to describe its parts, the bones, the elegance of the feet and feathers, the nervous system and the bird-brain. Excellent eyesight, terrible sense of smell. In that way birds resembled reptiles — from which they were descended — yet human beings saw reptiles as symbols of evil and birds as symbols of freedom. Perhaps that was not so great a contradiction as it seemed. Still, hard to get inside a bird. Hard to know about the bird's instincts. Hard to know why birds behaved the way that they did. Granted, "behavior" was a human notion. Everyone knew that what was interesting was not what human beings thought about birds but what birds thought about one another. Georgia leaned against the shade tree, watching him. He was looking at the bird while he talked to her.

"Ed's just an ordinary shit. He thinks he's special but he's just a robin in the shit scheme of things. He's not distinctive. He's not a Baja oceanic bird, for example. You can't take him seriously; he's a movie man out to control the moment. He's not a research project, Georgia-the-genuine-article. You're not writing his biography. He's not your *life,* and to think otherwise is silly and stupid. Worse, it's sentimental. Know the definition of sentimentality? Paying more attention to a thing than God pays to it. God's not working overtime on Ed Smid. God's indifferent to Ed, and you should be, too." He stepped back, grinning, looking at her down his nose. "Ed offers money for honest work, you take it. It's as if a cash register offered it. You going to look at the cash register and say, No way, José? You're not fancy enough for me. You're not a brand name. You haven't got the requisite bells and whistles. You're ugly. You're plastic. You're vulgar. You smell. You're mean. You give the correct change but you don't give it *nicely,* with a friendly smile and a have-a-nice-day-come-again-soon, hear? And you're thinking right now, if the expression on your face is any clue, that the bird man's offering you Faustian bargain. The dweadful bird man's trying to cowwupt me. But it's not a bargain. And Ed Smid's no Mephisto. Don't dignify Ed Smid. Don't make more of Ed Smid than he is. And what he is, is only a tiny turd in the shit scheme of things. So let's get on back to Ed's," he said.

"Did you hear me?"

He looked at her blankly and shook his head.

"I know you," she said. "You're one of those men who don't *listen.* You don't hear the call, bird man."

"And aren't we lucky!" he cried. "Here's a cab to take us."

"You," she said. "Not me." And she walked away.

No wonder she was attracted to him. No wonder she thought she could learn a thing or two. She knew no scientists, and had the idea they worked in a realm of pure inspiration, ordering things to suit themselves. In that way they resembled artists. Scientists were obsessed with exactitude, yet the greatest discoveries were often reached through error and miscalculation. Scientists were acutely aware of the effects of their own observations. In the laboratory they led a double life, concerned both with the experiment and with themselves. In a certain sense they stood on the shoulders of their predecessors, and in that way they also resembled artists. They were never far away from the physical world. She was charmed when Richard Swallow described his ecstatic birds, their bone structure and musculature, the miracle of flight, their migrations, the way they hopped and soared and sang, and their place in the world. It was evident that Richard was a little mad, the way scientists were supposed to be, and she liked that. She was delighted by it. Who wouldn't be?

He was a god-sent distraction because she was having trouble with her work, entering a new phase, painting triptychs, religious pictures that were developing very slowly. She did not know precisely what she was getting at. She thought she was exploring temptation in the lives of the saints but wasn't sure; it might have been desire. She believed she did not know enough; her life had been narrow. She worked hard on her pictures but the material refused to yield. To paint a saint you must also understand the devil, and perhaps in Richard she saw a connection to the Lower World. And in her, Richard no doubt saw a disciple. It's enough to say that Richard Swallow believed that no man was an island and this was a fortunate circumstance for the fleet of foot.

He began arriving in the evenings with Chinese takeout, regaling her with tales *chez* Smid. Hollywood personalities came to drinks and dinner, furnishing useful facts, malicious gossip, or a tip on a horse. Ed Smid showed movies on the weekend, always the latest release sent over from Columbia or Fox. Sometimes the director or producer was there to supply inside stories about the erratic behavior of the stars, or strange line items in the budget. And if the birds did not require his attention, Richard was asked to join them in the theater. Often he took the personalities on a tour of the birds, occasionally inventing lurid stories about their mating skills. Of course the hours were long and Ed unforgiving generally, but the pay was excellent and there were other, more subtle benefits. Ed Smid was a valuable man to know. He had contacts in high places and liked to favor his friends, dispensing patronage. But like any ward boss, he demanded absolute loyalty in return.

You can't believe the money, Georgia.

I can live for a year on what he spends in a day.

He *mints* it. God, it's exciting.

And he has a new project. He's written his birds into a film. The birds're on salary and I am, too. I'll get a credit line: Ornithologist.

"Ed wants bygones to be bygones," he said.

Georgia said, "Forget it."

"You insulted him and he didn't like it."

"Meant to," she said.

"Yes, well," Richard said, smiling.

"Well, what?" she said.

"More here than meets the eye." Richard explained that she had gotten under Ed Smid's skin. She turned him on. Ed couldn't get her out of his mind. He frequently asked about her, what she was like, where she was from and what her "background" was, and what she was working on. Why does such a great-lookin' gal have such a nasty temper? Ed wanted another chance and he promised exemplary behavior. He wanted to apologize and that was a major concession because he never apologized to anyone, except occasionally to a studio head and once to Barbra Streisand. "He wants the portrait, Georgie."

Richard was at the phonograph selecting a record, Brian Wilson and the other Beach Boys singing about California. He claimed the record put him in a good mood, reminding him of the durability of the American dream. He put the record on and went to the triptych and examined it, humming off key.

"Make amends with Ed," he said. Richard was looking at Saint John this way and that, first one panel and then another. "What do you care? What does it matter to you?"

She said, "It doesn't matter anything to me."

"Exactly," Richard said softly, "Exactly, exactly. I'm talking misdemeanor and you're making it a federal case. You ought to lighten up, Georgia. Not take things so seriously. Get some fun out of life."

"Think so?"

"The color isn't right in this picture," he said after a moment. "The colors're pale."

"It isn't finished," she said.

He nodded and said he could see that. Unfinished work was always misleading.

"They're not done in an afternoon," Georgia said.

"It's too — straight."

"It's the portrait of a saint."

"Which one?"

Georgia did not answer. She had a question but did not know how to put it.

"You sure this is a saint you're painting? He looks familiar. You sure he's not the devil?"

"Stick to birds," she said.

"Wouldn't it be a scream if you started out to paint a saint and you got the devil instead? It's mind-blowing. And explain *that*," he said, pointing to a wooden shed in the background of the picture.

"That's where my saint keeps his conscience," she said. "He tries not to use it every day, and when it's idle, that's where he keeps it. It's dark in there, cool in the daytime and warm at night." She looked hard at him and asked her question. "How much does Ed Smid know about us?"

"That we see each other."

Georgia said, "That we see each other here?"

He said, indifferently, "Wherever."

She suddenly had the fantastic notion that Richard talked about them in bed, what they did and how they did it, what it was like, and how she "was." She saw them sitting around the swimming pool in the sun, Richard talking rapidly and Ed Smid listening carefully and asking questions. The questions would be crude and the answers would suit the questions. She held her breath.

Richard did not turn from the picture but chuckled as if he had read her mind.

He said, "I tell him lies."

She said, "Lies?"

"White lies," he said.

She said, "What kind of lies? What's the subject of these lies? I don't want you talking to him about me, lies or the truth or anything."

"It's nothing personal," he said.

"What do you mean, nothing personal? Anything you say about me is personal. What do you think I am, some kind of conversation piece? A new bird from Chicago, a conversation piece of ass, I suppose that's it, you and that pig giggling like a pair of adolescent boys in the locker room —"

"It's nothing like that," he said.

She was watching his back. Late afternoon sun spilled through the window. A sliver of brilliant sunlight cut the lower left-hand corner of the picture. The light hurt her eyes; so he was wrong about the colors being too pale. Richard moved then, and his shadow replaced the sliver of sunlight, which now rested on his hips. Brian Wilson was singing about California girls and Richard was moving slowly to the beat, his tiny hands on his hips.

He said, "You don't understand anything."

She watched him shimmy in the sunlight. He seemed filled with energy, as if at any moment he would sail aloft like one of his migrating birds. He had spoken as if he were talking to himself. Georgia said, "I understand that you talk about me with him and I don't like it. I hate it. I don't want to have anything to do with him, ever, and you know it. I'm disgusted with you. Why would you do such a thing?"

He said sharply, "Because I felt like it."

And she replied, "Fuck you."

"Because he asked me," Richard said. He still had not turned from the picture, and now he shook his head and muttered something inaudible.

She said, "Why don't you look at me when you're talking to me?"

He said, "You don't know anything."

She said, "Get out of here."

He said, "Ed Smid isn't interested in you. He's interested in me."

She began to laugh; it was so unexpected. So that was it. She said, "It figures."

He said softly, "That's not what it's about, either."

She said, "What is it about, then?"

Richard sighed and spoke slowly, as if she were slow-witted or someone underage. "He's fascinated that someone as ugly as I am is seeing someone as beautiful as you are. He's excited by it. What could gorgeous Georgia see in Dick? It's not the way things happen in Ed's experience, and he thinks I've got some secret and he wants to know what it is. It isn't as if I'm rich, and it isn't as if I can offer you a contract in the motion picture industry as the starlet *du jour.* So naturally he assumes that I'm Superman in bed, but knows also that there's more to it than that. Has to be. Always is. Am I your candyman? Are you a junkie? He's curious about this great secret of mine. So that's what we talk about when we talk about us. We talk about me."

He turned, the sliver of sunlight moving around him like a girdle. He gave her a wide smile, disclosing his pearly teeth and exaggerating the droop of his nose. His face was out of proportion, its asymmetry unsettling. It was then that Georgia conceived the notion that he was from a mysterious lost civilization, Carthage or Atlantis or Philistia. Richard grunted and made a baboon motion with his hands, and then he laughed.

"Ed gets it when it's one of those across-a-crowded-room-you-will-see-a-stran*jor* kind of things, the thunderclap where everything's settled in a few seconds. He knows all about those because he's in the dream business, movies. But he doesn't understand about us. And he's impressed. He's impressed by *you.* He thinks you have a mind of your own. So he wants to make amends, prove to you that he's not a shit. That he had an off day. That he has a heart and's as sensitive as the next man. And he's sincere. Did he or did he not pay top dollar for your self-portraits? He did, and you know it. And you loved it, admit it."

Her expression did not change.

"Also," Richard said, "he doesn't understand why you won't paint *him*. That's what he wants, Georgia. And he thinks he's owed."

She said, "So what's your great secret?"

"You can't tell Ed."

"You're the one who talks to Ed, not me."

"It's simple enough," he said. "Immodesty. It throws them off."

"Women?"

"Women, too."

"What a secret," she said.

"Unchaste," he said. "The sense that you're just a bit — unclean."

"Contaminated," she said.

"Adventure," he said. "I offer a dangerous expedition. You're in the Amazon with the piranha fish. You're in the Nile with the crocs. It's a simple fact that everyone, once or twice in their sorry lives, wants to put a hand in the fire to confirm that Mommy wasn't lying. Flesh burns. And hurts when it burns. Gee. Ouch." Richard listened to the last of Brian Wilson's harmonies, the record ending with a whisper. In the sudden silence he said, "Life's a challenge."

She said, "Women do not look at men the way men look at women. Physically."

He laughed. "Is that a promise?"

"It's just a stupid power game you're playing."

"Not stupid," he said. "Not a game. Mrs. Swallow didn't raise her little boy to play games. Mrs. Swallow was a great beauty. She knew every trick and taught them all to me. Mrs. Swallow played for keeps and so do I."

"Your father," she began.

"He left," Richard said. "He couldn't stand the heat."

"From your beautiful mother?"

Richard nodded but did not speak.

"Everyone always told me I was beautiful," she said. "From the time I was a child. People would stare at me in restaurants. In the school play I was always the Virgin Mary. Later, I was the princess. I was popular at school because I was popular with boys. My parents were terrified. It was as if I were Mozart or a child evangelist who had seen Jesus. And I didn't need anyone to tell me, I had only to look in the mirror. I could see it in the way men looked at me, even friends of my father. Jailbait, one of them said when he thought I wasn't around. I realized I had a kind of power over men and some women and it mattered a lot to me for a while, and then it didn't."

He said, "What happened?"

She said, "Nothing happened."

"Something must have happened for it not to matter. It always matters."

"Not to me," she said.

"That's hard to believe."

"I'd rather not have it."

"That's all anybody wants. Otherwise, what's the point?"

"And I thought I did, too. But I don't. And I've never doubted for a single minute that if I put my hand in fire, it'd burn."

"How come I never heard this from you before?"

"I never talk about it because people don't believe it. They think you're playing with them or lying to them, or lying to yourself. It's what you're supposed to want and if you don't want it it means either that you're lying or too stupid to see the truth. But when beauty begins to matter to you, then you can't do anything else. That's what you do, be beautiful. You're beautiful all day long and into the night and pretty soon that's all you are and all you can be and it's not the worst thing. It's not a crime; many women love it and make a career of it because there are advantages. It's the edge you have in life's challenge, and if you're not careful you become a bully. On the whole, women cope better than men. Men have such a flying start naturally that beauty tends to push them over the edge. It overloads their circuits. They begin to live in a dream world where everything's effortless. If Picasso had looked like John F. Kennedy, could he have seen what he had to see and felt what he had to feel to paint *Les Demoiselles d'Avignon?* Not a chance. To paint such a picture you have to stand in a certain relation to women, not when you're twenty-six and half rich and almost famous and a certified genius, but when you're fourteen and unknown and look like a toad. The fourteen-year-old boy is father to the twenty-six-year-old man. The boy lights the fuse, the man throws the bomb. The boy understood at once that he could get what he wanted through his *art*. So the art came first. It came first, second, and third. And with it, everything was possible. So you try not to make too much of looking good because if it was worth anything, why were you chosen to have it instead of Señor Picasso or Mother Teresa?"

Richard had turned back to the picture, looking at it this way and that. His shoulders began to tremble.

She thought, Oh, Christ. She said, "My saints aren't beautiful. Look at that one? Jug ears, a lantern jaw, and a long nose, and the chin's anything but forceful. He looks a little like you, darling. Bad complexion, weak eyes. My saint's myopic. Look at his body. Spot him on the beach at Malibu and you'd look the other way. Something about him that's sort of divine, though."

Still he did not reply and she knew she had offended him.

Her mother always said that she talked too much.

Try to enjoy things more, dear.

You're too serious.

You pick, pick, pick all the time, Georgia.

Why don't you take things easy?

Pretty girl like you.

You can have anything you want.

She was not angry with him anymore. Life was too short. She said, "Richard —"

And he turned, a huge smile on his mischievous face. He began to laugh, great gusts of laughter. "Georgia, Georgia, Georgia, Georgie. Mother *Teresa?* You're so full of shit. You're the billionaire who claims he hates money, that he only has money because it sticks to him, a feature of his life, a fact of nature, like lying in the sun and getting a nice, even tan, and he'd really rather not have it, he'd rather be white as a baby's ass but, gosh, sigh, there it is, God's on my side. What can I do about it?" He began to shed his clothes, throwing them around the room, his shirt parachuting to the sofa, his trousers draped over her easel, giving it the aspect of a surreal montage, socks popped like little basketballs into the wastepaper basket, shorts hanging from the lamp shade. Richard executed a comic pirouette. "Come to the devil!" he cried.

But by then she was already laughing, drawn into the spirit of things.

3

ONE MORNING a few days after Thanksgiving Richard
arrived at her apartment in a state of high excitement.
Georgia was still in bed and half asleep so he joined
her with a pot of coffee and some Danish from the delicatessen
on the corner, saying nothing but looking at her with a wide
smile.

She said, "Give."

He said, "I've been invited to Chicago."

"Chicago?"

"The Field Museum's having a symposium and I've been invited to read a paper."

"Congratulations," she said. "That's wonderful."

"It's the usual bullshit. But they're paying money."

"Lucrative bullshit," she said. "But it's an honor —"

"One Large," he said.

She looked at him. "What's One Large?"

"That's what Ed calls a thousand dollars."

"One Large," she said, and yawned.

"It's gangster talk. Ed likes to use mob slang. He thinks it
puts him in the picture, and it does." He leaned close to her,

whispering in her ear. "But that's not the point. Point's this. Do you want to come with?"

"To Chicago?"

"You can see your sister. You can listen to me talk about the Baja oceanic birds. You can show me Chicago, and we can blow the One Large."

"How long?" she said doubtfully.

"Three days," he said.

"Deal," she said.

Richard rented a suite at the Palmer House and the first night they took Marge and her husband, Jack, to dinner, the meal an agony of thrust and counterthrust, Marge's sarcasm in combat with Richard's irony, Richard as contemptuous of her as she was of him. Their mutual dislike was immediate. Georgia and Jack watched them like spectators at a tennis match until Jack said the hell with it, took his wife by the arm, and departed, pointedly declining to split the bill.

"She's a jerk," Richard said as he watched them go.

"So are you, sometimes," Georgia said.

Neither Jack nor Marge would understand Richard's appeal before an audience, his earring glittering, an ascot tied around his neck, French-style. The next day Georgia watched him from the third row of the museum auditorium; no one knew what to make of him. At the lectern Richard was more composed and intelligent and witty than he was in a room full of friends, where his manner was abrupt. As he delivered the dry-as-dust lecture on his sexy Baja oceanic birds, his voice acquired a lilt and his language became rich and nuanced and almost gentle. Richard seemed to find his creatures more purely interesting than human beings, more mysterious and, of course and foremost, less inhibited, disenthralled as they were from that bastard Voltaire. Richard called his birds morally sound. At the conclusion of a digression on nestedness, he made a pun, then paused to see if anyone got it; when it was plain that nobody did, he continued and made a pun on the pun, silencing the groans with a sardonic smile and a lyrical flight of avian fantasy. Not serious, the scientist next to her whispered to a colleague. Lacking gravitas, wouldn't you say? Damned show-off.

But the applause at the end was hearty and appeared to be genuine.

Don't kid yourself, Richard said afterward. They *hated* it.

They're envious, she said.

Envious that you're with me, 'cause you got great-lookin' legs.

Richard, she said. You're a fine scientist.

That's true, he said. I cook a damned fine steak, and they know it. I'm a master chef. But they hate the sizzle. This business, like any other, the sizzle's the thing. No sizzle, no grant. It's the main thing, Georgie, and don't you ever forget it.

Later, sitting in Marge's kitchen in Evanston, Georgia described Richard's bearing at the microphone and the ecstatic applause at the end, distinguished scientists rushing to the podium to shake his hand, congratulate him on his brilliant insights. I really enjoyed it, Marge, and I didn't expect to.

Then she apologized for the disaster the night before at the Palmer House, explaining that Richard was not himself, worried and nervous over his presentation. Still, he had behaved badly and knew that and wanted to make amends.

Marge could not wait to pounce.

He's quite a character, isn't he, Georgie? He'll take some getting used to. He'll lead you a merry chase, all right. A reserved little laugh: I hope Richard doesn't swallow you up. My goodness, he comes on strong, it must be thrilling. He has such confidence! And a *scientist*. I'd've never guessed *that*. Never in a million years.

Her sister told her: He's an arrogant tyrant and you never should've gotten within ten miles of him. He's not suitable. When he's finished with you, he'll throw you away like Kleenex. Listen to me, Georgia. With such men there's a constant, an iron law, no exceptions. Count on it: their mothers loved them to death. For such men nothing is beyond reach. Nothing is unthinkable. Nothing is forbidden. And it is the same in every country and in any language, rich man, poor man, black white yellow and brown man, Jew, Gentile, Moslem, Buddhist. Have I left anyone out?

Believe me, Georgia, Marge said to her sister.

I know what I'm talking about.

You walk into that country, you're walking into a nursery. Her little boy's immortal. Isn't he adorable? Look at his eyes. Watch his smile. Feel his grip. Isn't he strong? Isn't he intelligent? With hands like those he could be Rodin. See his patience and tenacity, his calm, his imperturbability, his restlessness, and his *vision* — he has the qualities of Mao Tse-tung. He'll sculpt the Burghers of Calais while leading his people on the Long March. Mom knows where all these sterling qualities come from, too. She's seen them before. The eyes? The set of the shoulders and head, the jaw line and the cleft chin — well, it's obvious he takes after *my* side of the family, his maternal grandfather, my dear father, who was a great man, one of the greatest men who ever lived, though he was scorned and cheated and traduced and misunderstood generally by his worthless associates.

And then she'll say,

What a lady killer he'll be!

And she'll be on the money with that *aperçu*. That prediction. That *expectation*. She'll make sure it comes true, too. So that no one can injure her precious little man she'll give him an arsenal of pig weapons and teach him to conceal them behind a heart of granite.

Georgia listened with growing fascination. Marge had never been a subtle woman, but this tirade was exceptional even by her standards. It was not difficult to provoke Marge Whyte.

"But you hardly know him," Georgia said. "You met him once, last night, admittedly —"

"Listen to me, Georgia," Marge said. "I've known him all my life. Richard Swallows are a dime a dozen. He's a type. And he's poison."

"That's a little strong, Marge."

"Not half strong enough," Marge said grimly. "And what

you're going to say to me now is that I've gotten bitter because of my own experience. That I can't recognize a good man when I see one. That he's the most exciting man you've ever met because he's unpredictable and fantastic and never takes no for an answer and seems to control events rather than be controlled by them and every day's a holiday, la-di-da-di-da. And he's doing *really important work* that you help him with and that half the world will recognize one day, and that's why he doesn't give one damn what the world thinks today. And why should he? The world's an inconvenience. Nothing is out of reach. Nothing is unthinkable. Nothing is forbidden. But when the time comes to settle accounts, you're the one who'll pay."

Georgia said, "He makes me laugh."

And Marge replied, "I'll just bet he does."

"Only the other day —"

"I don't want to hear it," Marge said. Then, "Naturally he's funny. And that's exactly what his mother would say. Richard — always Richard, by the way, never Dick — was the cutest thing. Richard and his pranks. Pranks in the neighborhood, pranks at school. The cutest thing about Richard was that as a boy, as a little child even, he'd make me laugh. He was a natural comedian, great with impersonations. He could've gone on stage. A devil, of course. Into everything and never understood the word No, as his teachers told me more than once. Rather emphatically. Oh, those report cards! What a caution! And so funny. Everyone loved Richard, underneath."

"Come off it, Marge," Georgia said. She was laughing.

"Have you met her?"

"No," Georgia said.

"Just wait," Marge said.

"It'll take a while, Marge. She's dead."

"That's the worst news yet," Marge said. "That means she's martyred."

Georgia laughed again. But her sister had a point.

Marge looked at the clock and sighed. It was midafternoon

and Marge had made tea. Her children were due home from school and had been promised a visit from Auntie Georgia.

"He won't be a scientist for long," Marge said.

Georgia looked up in surprise.

"Count on it. His type isn't suited for solitary work. He wants a crowd, and he's not indifferent to money, either. What do you suppose he'll do, Georgia, when science isn't enough?"

"He consults," Georgia said.

"That figures."

"But he'll never give up science."

"So who does he consult for?"

But Georgia waved the question away.

"The Vatican, probably. That would appeal to his taste for misrule."

"Marge," Georgia said. "You're so full of shit."

And then, slyly: "What happens to your career while you're attending to Richard Swallow's needs? I'd like it if you'd give me a hint, seeing as how we're sisters and we've known each other all our lives, and so forth and so on, and I've tried to be on your side of things always. What is it about him? You tell me. And you can forget about the bedroom athletics. I know all about them or can guess. Other than his ability to make each day a holiday. Other than his ability to make you go ha-ha. What's so wonderful about him that's worth ruining your life?"

"Lay off, Marge."

"Just asking. In my stupid suburban way."

Her voice sounded like their mother's, so prim it reminded you of a plastic flower. Nightshade, she thought, smiling, thinking about Richard Swallow. She had no intention of describing him to nosy Marge, so snug and smug in Evanston. Marge ran her life along different lines. Richard was outside her ken.

But she was right about one thing. His mother had loved him to death.

"So where does he consult?" Marge asked again.

Just then her two boys burst into the kitchen, yelled hello, and ran out again. In a moment the women heard high-pitched voices and electronic explosions. Georgia looked at her sister, but Marge was fussing with the teapot. Georgia went into the living room, kissed both boys, asked them about school, listened to their monosyllabic replies, and returned to the kitchen. She stood in the doorway, watching Marge fuss with the teapot.

"My work's going well," she said after a moment. "I have a gallery."

Marge nodded.

"In Los Angeles."

"That's good," Marge said softly.

"And maybe a show in the spring."

"They come in," Marge said, "they can't be bothered to say hello —"

"They said hello," Georgia said.

"— drop their books on the floor, go into the television room, and that's where they'll be until dinner. Welcome to Evanston."

"Boys," Georgia said.

"Shits," Marge said.

Georgia began to laugh.

"It's not funny," Marge said.

"That age," Georgia said.

"Any age. Any age at all."

"They're nice boys," Georgia said.

"No, they're not. And I don't think they'll be nice men, either."

"Maybe Jack —"

"*Jack.*" Marge snorted. "Jack has his precious business. I have the boys."

"Maybe you should —" Georgia began.

"I don't want to talk about it."

They stood stiffly in the kitchen listening to the muted racket from the television set, more gunfire and shouts. Marge leaned against the counter, smoking, the cigarette pack and lighter in her fist. Outside, the emerald lawn sparkled in the afternoon sun.

"I always liked that other boy," Marge said.

"Which one?"

"The one you went to the dances with. The one who brought you flowers. The one you were laying in the living room on Friday nights when Mom was at her bridge game."

"Dean," Georgia said quickly. She didn't want to talk about the bridge game.

"And Dad was at the Knights of Columbus."

"Dad was drinking in his study," she said.

"Nice boy," Marge said. "Handsome. Polite. He had beautiful manners."

"Yes." Georgia sighed. "A nice boy."

"What happened to him?"

"I don't know what happened to him. Probably he got married."

"Well," Marge said. "Whose fault was that?"

"Genetics," Georgia said.

"That's an excuse after the fact," Marge said.

"Marge, I was twenty."

"I was thirty when I married Jack." Marge blew a smoke ring, looking out the window at the lawn. The boys were bickering in the next room. She said, "Dad was at the K of C and Mom was with her bridge group and I made it my business to go to the movies so that you could have some privacy. Remember the time I came home early? What a riot. I admired you so, Georgia. All those great boys. Living it up. Everyone was living it up except me."

"Marge? Let's have a glass of wine."

"Too early," Marge said curtly. "So who does he consult for, Georgia?"

"A glass of wine brightens things up," she said. "As a matter of fact, he consults in Hollywood."

"Hollywood?"

"That's right," Georgia said. "Hollywood, California."

"What on earth would he consult about in Hollywood? What does Richard Swallow have that Hollywood wants?"

"You'd be surprised," Georgia said.

"No doubt," Marge said. "No doubt of that."

"There's a character called Ed Smid."

"That name means nothing to me."

"He's a producer."

"And Richard —"

"Works for him," Georgia said. "Red wine, white wine, I don't care."

"And you won't tell me about it," Marge said.

"No, Margie. I won't."

"I knew it," Marge said.

Georgia waited for Marge to disclose what she knew.

"Your Richard. Your *scientist*. Is just a cruddy little entertainer."

Georgia opened her mouth to say something, but one of the boys ran in, crying. His brother had hit him and it wasn't fair and what are you going to do about it, *Mother?*

That night she and Richard prowled Rush Street until two, ending at a neighborhood tavern. Richard was in fine humor, and it took her a while to catch up, and when she did she told him she would never ever live in the suburbs. She did not believe that marriage was in her future, either. It hadn't worked out for those women she knew well. It hadn't worked out for her mother and it hadn't worked out for Marge, although admittedly Marge was a special case. Marge and Jack. Marge and her children. God, what a life. Poor Margie.

Richard said, "Dealt bad cards, was she?"

Georgia said, "Promise me one thing."

"What's that?" Richard said.

"Promise me you'll never quit science."

He looked at her a long moment but did not reply.

She said, "Probably you don't make promises."

And then he smiled his brilliant wide-open smile, the one she knew would melt a mother's heart.

"I promise," Richard said.

* * *

Richard Swallow continued to work away at his doctorate, but by and by Ed Smid claimed his best efforts. Georgia thought it a waste. She had watched him at the lectern and in the laboratory and thought that was his natural element; science was his element as paint was her element. She said Smid was a fool and if Richard stayed with him he'd become a fool, too.

It's all right for you, he said.

You vant to be a-lone.

I don't want to be alone.

And you like it here, admit it.

He was right about that. Georgia found the relaxed atmosphere of Southern California productive. You were left alone in Southern California so long as you didn't want to make your presence felt in the Industry. In the unhappy event that you did, you had to play by their rules, which were as stylized as a bullfight and as complicated as mah-jongg. It was entirely normal for a film producer to employ a biologist to look after his zoo-quality birds and normal for the biologist to see the birds as his ticket into the Industry, for the film producer to grasp this at once, and to expect reciprocity, a payment. The payment was a portrait of his own sweet self. And naturally this was not gratis. Smid offered a very large fee, insisting to Richard that there was no free déjuner in Southern California. Of course Georgia declined.

The issue did not go away, but in the meantime Richard had made himself indispensable to Ed Smid and to Georgia as well. When he wasn't finding rare birds for Smid (there was traffic in them from South America, as furtive, thriving, and businesslike as the drug trade), he was tending to her quotidian needs. There were Navy-style swabbings of the kitchen on Saturday mornings while she slept in. He emptied the cat litter and took out the trash and did the marketing. He brought her hot croissants in the morning and Chinese or Mexican takeout in the evening. He often arrived unannounced, staying for a few days and then returning to his own place or Smid's. She was distracted much of the time, having become possessed by her saints, working all day long and into the evening; and when she put down her brushes and wandered into the bedroom to see what was up with Richard, he would be there, reading a book or watching television, reminding her that she had not eaten since noon and suggesting the restaurant around the corner, where they could buy a fat pizza and drink beer. Her treat, of course, since she had gotten so much accomplished that day.

When he was not there, she wished that he was.

When her cat died, he was superb. At the end, Liebermann was so old and frail she barely moved and one night simply passed away in her sleep. Georgia was desolate. Liebermann had been with her so long, her last link to Chicago. They had crossed the Mississippi together and climbed the Rocky Mountains and watched the sun set over the Pacific their first night in California.

Richard went downstairs to ask the Clydes if he could bury the cat in the back yard and when they indignantly refused he tried another approach, reaching into his great reservoir of charm, explaining how broken up Georgia was, a shy girl so far from home. Liebermann had meant so much and her corpse was smaller than a loaf of bread. And while he was at it, it would be no trouble at all for him to tidy up the flower beds, plant a nice rose bush in Liebermann's honor. Perhaps a Betty Prior or a rambling rose.

Thank you so much.

It's a real kindness.

Georgia will be so grateful.

After the burial they went for a walk on the beach at Santa Monica, looking at the birds. Richard identified cinnamon teal and coot, both fairly rare. He thought they had wandered over from the valley, interested in how the rich lived. They're upscale birds, he said. Cinnamon teal were always restless, never satisfied. They're on their way to Cuernavaca, probably. Or Acapulco.

There were groups of surfers here and there along the shore and out to sea. Georgia gave a little involuntary shiver watching them, so fleet and defiant, slicing the blue-green surface of the bulging waves. They were thrilling to see, moving like acrobats, beautifully balanced on the slippery surface of the Pacific. She was suddenly sorry that they hadn't buried Liebermann at sea, set her adrift on the outgoing tide like a fallen seaman. She turned to Richard to thank him again.

She said, "You're a good man, Swallow. I can't thank you enough."

"We can take the money and go to Egypt," he replied.

She looked sideways at him. "What money?"

"The money you get from painting Ed. Wouldn't it make a great change from Southern California? The museum at Cairo. The Great Mosque. The monuments at Aswan. What's the name of that other one?"

She said, "Luxor. But I won't paint Ed Smid."

"But you want to go to Egypt?"

"I hadn't thought about Egypt, but yes. Egypt would be lovely."

"Such a small price to pay," he said.

"But too high for me," she replied.

"And Ed would make a good subject, wouldn't he?"

"Yes," she said.

"And not merely good. *Excellent.*"

She agreed with that also.

"How many times in your life will you get a chance to paint an absolute prick?"

"Not very many," she said. "But maybe more than you think."

"Then why won't you do it?"

"*Because he wants me to,*" she said.

Richard laughed. Child's view of the world, Georgie. Paint Ed and you get a different side of things. You get another slice of humanity's cake. Ed's been baked in a hot oven. You'll get a wedge you've never seen before; you'll be like Picasso discovering blue. You'll have your own blue period in museums all over the world, except that the cognoscenti will call it your Smid period. Ed Smid will be to you what Madame de Canals was to

Picasso. And I'll wager that Pablo Picasso saw Señora Canals as just another rich bitch from one of the big haciendas on the hill, with pesetas in her purse and idle time to sit for a portrait. It wasn't who she was; it was what she represented, the character under the lace mantilla. And you can paint Ed Smid any way you want! He doesn't care if you make him look like Clint Eastwood or Wallace Beery or Bela Lugosi. Ed doesn't give a shit. Ed wants a portrait because he thinks you're great. Ed's betting that you'll discover something — wonderful. Ed being Ed, the more unflattering the work, the better he'll like it. He's willing to take a chance, a fat fee up front and you can take all the time you need. And the clincher's this, Georgie. He doesn't have final cut. You do.

She listened to this blizzard of words while she looked out to sea.

"It would help *me*," he said finally. And when she sighed he added, "It would help me a lot."

"That's the wrong kind of help," she said. "A man like that, he's poison. He kills everything he touches. He's cyanide."

Richard said, "You give too little. And if the shoe were on the other foot —"

She said, "I would never ask such a thing."

He said harshly, "Yes, you would. You bet you would. You would in a minute. You would if it mattered. You'd ask me to do something I didn't want to do if my doing it made a difference to your *life*. If your wanting mattered more than my not wanting. You'd be in the position I am now, pleading. And you wouldn't hear any lectures from me about how it's the wrong kind of help. I'd do it. I'd say, all right, Georgie. You win, Georgie. If it means that much to you I'll do it right away, no delays. And then I'd say: But you owe me a big one. And then I'd laugh. But I'd do it. And you wouldn't have to go down on your knees to make me."

She looked up. How much could such a thing be worth if you had to beg for it? She watched two terns fall like stones to the surface of the water. They came up with minnows and flew off in ragged lines. Two overweight men jogged by, music crackling in their tiny earphones.

"You've never wanted anything badly enough," he said.

"How do you know what I've wanted and what I haven't wanted?"

"Christ," he said. "Christ, Georgia. You're an open book. You're burning up with ambition, but you won't admit it. You want fame. You want money. You want honor. And the day's not far off, you'll need someone to help you get it. Wanting it's not enough. Not sufficient, baby. You think you can live on your own terms, and you can't. And nobody can."

She said, "You have no idea what I want."

"We all want the same things," he said.

She smiled broadly, knowing that would infuriate him. Richard Swallow believed in the field theory of human ambition, meaning that his magnetism was such that all filings in his vicinity were attracted to it. He spoke the simple truth. And if you were not attracted to it, you were willfully denying it or too thick to see it or simply lying about it, or you had bad character. You were contradicting universal physical laws. She sneaked a look at her watch now. Dusk was falling and she was tired of the argument, and sick at heart about Liebermann. Mostly, she wanted to get back to her work.

Richard said, "You have a cold heart."

She said, "I've been told that before."

"And you will be again."

"Not by you," she said.

"You won't *compromise*," Richard said.

Again she smiled and did not reply. She thought, What was there to compromise? Either she painted the portrait or she didn't.

He said, "And I thought you were different. I really did. I thought you were special. But you're just like every other goddamned woman. It's your way or no way at all. It doesn't matter what's gone before, what there's been between us, what I've given, and what you've given. And what you've taken. You don't recognize debts; you never have. Debts are for other people. Debts are for men. But there's always an accounting, and you're in default."

Richard raised his arms and let them fall. He was staring out to sea, watching a gull ride a wind current, the gull perfectly motionless, then leaning, sliding away effortlessly.

She said, "Bully."

He said grimly, "Always at your service."

She said, "Go back to your birds, Richard. That's what you're good at. You've spent most of your life with them. Until recently you said you loved them. You said they meant more to you than anything, and you'd devote your life to them. Until recently you had a dissertation. And you had your laboratory and your grant, and the promise of more support when you needed it. And it's important work. But it's not Smid work. It's not work in your precious Industry. Your problem is that your bird work isn't *conspicuous* work."

He said mildly, "Birds don't interest me anymore."

"But don't you have a debt to them?"

He looked at her and grinned.

"I'm ready to go," she said.

"But it's so nice here." He picked up a stone and pitched it at the gull.

"It's getting dark."

"So what?"

"It's time to go," she said.

"Only a few minutes more," he said. "Do you have something else to do? Someplace you have to be?"

"I have my work," she said.

"Lucky you," he said.

She turned, but he caught her arm.

"You owe me."

"I owe you nothing," she said.

She turned again but he would not release her arm. He was not looking at her but was staring off into the bluff back of the beach, squinting as if he were trying to locate something there. They were standing almost at the waterline.

She said, "What's he promised you?"

"A job on the next film. But he won't do it unless I can deliver you. That's my end. And that's Ed's vigorish, his interest on the loan."

"And I'm the loan."

"That's the deal, Georgia."

She pulled to get away, but he had her arm in a vise grip.

He said, "You'll pay."

The beach was almost deserted. Behind them people were having drinks on the deck of a beach house. The house was built on the edge of a bluff, cantilevered for stability. It had the look of the Bauhaus, severe right angles and a brooding presence. She raised her arm to wave, a signal of distress. The people were watching the sunset. Richard, too, was staring back at the house on the bluff. The sea was quiet, allowing little splashes of laughter to reach them, though the house appeared quite far away. Lights inside gave off a rosy glow and seemed to beckon anyone within eyesight, the glow a kind of summit of aspiration. Looking at it, she understood that was Richard's desire, a beach house at Malibu, drinks on the deck, violins playing Mozart on the stereo inside, and Industry personalities on reconnaissance in the rosy glow. Allowing for local taste and the maritime setting, and the evolution of construction techniques, this house could be — Giverny. The people were attractive in the garish sunset, the women in white and the men in black. All the women seemed to be blond and the men slender. Eighteenth-century music would be about right, any Mozart concerto a sound track for the Enlightenment. Georgia imagined the Porsches and BMWs in the drive; probably there would be a Harley-Davidson or two as well. Champagne would be cooling in a crystal bucket and later they would dine on cold soup, followed by fist-sized birds and wee raw vegetables; and just then she noticed wire cages hanging from the eaves over the deck, the cages swinging in the breeze. Rare parrots, no doubt, parrots that could recite the morals clause in an Industry contract or squawk the "Marseillaise." This was what Richard wanted in his heart and needed as badly as she needed — whatever it was that she needed. A drink would do nicely, a drink at home in the company of her saints, although the house on the bluff was a mighty improvement over the anonymous apartment in Southgate, with its tatty furniture and scarred walls and view of the overgrown garden where Liebermann rested, jumbo jets thundering into LAX every few moments. This house was beautiful in the way that a giant ruby was beautiful. The only question was, Could you wear it? Or would it wear you? She tried to picture herself on the deck of the beach house, a flute of Champagne in her hand, attractive men in attendance, parrots chattering — but she could not. She could not imagine her easel lit by a rosy glow. She could not imagine working with the restless Pacific at her back, the sky so high and pale blue in all directions. A bar of Vivaldi drifted down from the deck, along with the laughter. Someone waved and Richard waved back.

She said, "I'm going home."

He said, "You'll be sorry."

She said, "I'm going back to work."

"Afraid you'll get seduced?"

"Not by you," she said.

"Not me," he said, pointing at the beach house. "Them."

"Not them either," she said.

He said, "Let's crash the party."

She said, "Forget it."

He said, "I bet we'd like them."

"You'd like them," she said.

"God damn you, Georgia. *Look,* will you? *Look,* for once," he said, pointing at the house.

"Go on up there," she said. "Ask them nicely, they'll probably give you a big hello and a glass of Champagne. They've probably never met a bird man before." She turned away, but when he looked at her, smiling sourly, not replying, she shouted at him: "Do you want it that badly? How badly do you want it,

Richard? Bad enough to kill for it? Steal for it? Bad enough to crawl on your hands and knees for it? And when you get it, is that all you'll need? Will it be enough — the beach house with deck in the sunset and the cars in the driveway, and the music and the wine and the personalities? The parrots in cages?"

"It's a beginning," he said.

"Take it then," she said.

"You're such a prig, Georgia."

And she thought that in that, as in many things, Richard was close to the mark; not on it, but close to it.

"Richard," she said. "Fuck off."

Richard growled and pushed her roughly, causing her to stumble in the soft sand. From the deck she heard more laughter. They were lined up along the rail like passengers aboard a cruise ship watching the antics of the porpoises below. One of the slender men was moving left and right, his legs wide apart and his arms flared. Georgia thought he was dancing until she saw the brilliant reflection of the camera's lens as it caught the sun's rays. He was filming while the others watched. Richard caught her arm and whirled her around. She ceased to struggle and stood very still, knowing now that he would do nothing stupid. The eye of the Industry was upon them.

Suddenly they began to clap.

Richard said, "Take a bow."

But she was dizzy and off balance. The cameraman continued to film, leaning over the deck railing, rotating the lens. There was something familiar in the way that he moved, but she could not place it.

Richard released her, spread his arms, and took a deep bow, and then stepped off a few paces and pointed at her, grinning and clapping. Someone threw a bouquet from the deck. They raised their glasses in a toast, as people do at the end of a banquet. Ed Smid — of course that was who it was; she could see him clearly now — continued to film, moving nimbly up and down the rail, his camera raised to catch the dying sunset and the gulls floating on the shore breeze.

The people on the deck pitched their wine glasses over the side, the crystal glittering in the last rays of the sun. The falling glass looked like the work of a special effects man, crystal tumbling in slow motion; it hurt her eyes to look at it. Besides Smid, she recognized a starlet, a politician, and Carole Fox and Trude. Carole waved and jumped up and down, pointing. A tiny figure moved in the doorway — Gary, brought in to meet the company. Georgia was disoriented and did not know what to think.

There were cries of "Bravo!" and more laughter.

Ed Smid continued to film.

Richard clapped harder. Glass continued to fall from the deck, a merry blizzard of lethal confetti. A Champagne flute shattered on a rock and exploded into tiny fragments, glass flying every which way around them. She took a step backward, not so disoriented now but thinking that she was so far out of her element that she might as well have been on the far side of the moon, a sandy terrain of fantastic shapes in a murderously thin atmosphere, permanent twilight.

Fresh glasses were produced, and Trude poured more Champagne.

Richard moved up close.

"That's Ed's place," he said.

He added, "Ed has a beach house. They all do."

"Of course," she said. "The parrots."

He said, "I thought you'd pick up on them. I thought you'd see what was cooking, that we weren't here by accident. I always thought you had second sight, paranoia's shadow. And now I see that you don't."

Georgia continued to move backward, out of range. But Richard kept up with her, talking all the while. She kept her eyes on the deck, as you would observe an armed and unpredictable enemy. She had no idea what they were planning, but whatever it was it had not yet ended. Richard stayed with her, and she noticed now that the beach was deserted except for two surfers, far offshore. She could see their blond hair in the dying light as they paddled along, bouncing like playful seals.

Richard said, "You were set up, Georgie. Ed's idea, a Candid Camera type of deal. He'll find a way to use it in a movie, though you won't be recognizable. Your face won't be seen. It's your body and your way of moving that Ed's interested in. He likes your tits. Ed was shooting into the sun so it could be any girl on a beach arguing with her boyfriend. It's a little cameo of two lovers having it out at Santa Monica, splitting up. It's the moment of truth in a love affair that's broken down beyond repair. Two attractive young people who can't communicate because of the love of one and the selfishness of the other. Ed said you were a downer, and Ed was right. He said you had an ego the size of Coldwater Canyon. He has us miked, too. See the gizmo under the parrot cage? It's a directional microphone. The authorities use it to eavesdrop. And aren't we lucky that the ocean's quiet today, so he has good sound. Ed won't miss a word."

She said, "If I had a gun I'd kill him."

"What he wants is for me to give you a good slap in the face."

She swung around, shocked. Richard would never do that. But when she looked into his face she decided that he would. There was nothing Richard Swallow wouldn't do.

"He can hear you," Richard said. "Everything you've said so far, he's picked up."

"You'd hit me?"

"It's only for the film, Georgie."

Ed Smid was motioning from the deck. Two men were hurrying across the sand toward them, but when she stepped forward to speak to them — help me out, this man is annoying me — she saw they were Smid's friends, unmistakably of the Industry, beautifully turned out in smart slacks and bush shirts and smiling to beat the band. With their long curls and rosebud mouths they reminded her of Sandro Botticelli's slender boys, the ones with the frank looks and sexy intentions — so far from God, so close to Florence — and thrilled with the gift they were about to bestow. These languid boys swung when they walked.

When Richard raised his hand she took off running, and when he yelled she ran faster. She heard him behind her, and then the

Florentines began to shout. She picked up speed, running in the hard sand where the water had receded. Ahead of her was nothing but beach and the other houses strung along the bluff like jewels in a crown. All the swimmers and sunbathers had gone home, though the surfers were still around somewhere. Probably they were paddling in now because it was almost dark, the sun gone at last and stars visible in the pale sky. Overhead she could hear the chop-chop of a helicopter and truck noise from the highway, and Richard's steps behind her and his heavy breathing. He was cursing under his breath and she knew he could not maintain the pace. She was flying, running with abandon, and soon Richard began to fall behind.

She dared not look back but thought the two boys were way behind, no doubt anxious not to ruin the creases in their doeskin slacks. She was enjoying herself, running in the soft salty air. She began to lope in wide curves, to the shore and up again to the soft sand, her arms outstretched and her mouth open, thinking that she had not run so long and so hard since she was a child on the playground or with her father at North Beach and how much fun it had been, running all-out, no clear objective in mind — and then, on impulse, she turned into the water and dove in the surf, staying under as long as she was able, fighting the air trapped in her clothes, the air forcing her up at last. She ballooned to the surface, her body chilled and tingling. Her hair was in her eyes and for a moment she lost the shore. She drifted; and then she saw the bright lights of the houses on the bluff. She was beyond the point where the waves broke. The water was phosphorescent. She imagined small fish gathering around her; something touched her leg, and her skin began to crawl.

They were waiting for her. They had not seen her enter the water and they did not see her now. The Florentines and Richard Swallow stood uncertainly, looking this way and that, and then at their watches. One of the boys detached himself and walked to the waterline. She gulped air and submerged, holding her breath in the thick silence. But they could do nothing to her now; she was in her element. When she surfaced, she came up an inch at a time, believing she was invisible to them; there was nothing new in that, of course. She was fifty feet from shore and it was dark, and she began to think about what she would do. She was no longer frightened, but she had no plan either. It was easy floating in the Pacific without plans, feeling dreamy, the water so buoyant and safe. In her dreams she had often found herself on the surface of a great ocean, drifting, carried along by the current. This was not passive; she was always thinking of the future and her destination when the current went slack.

The boy was opposite her, his hands on his hips, staring up the beach toward Smid's house. He ran a slow hand through his curls. He called her name and when there was no answer he turned and walked back to his friend and Richard Swallow. They stood there together, conferring, something in their postures reminding her of movie gangsters. She could read the body language.

I can't see her.

Where to God has she gone?

The bitch.

Probably she went up the bluff.

That's all she is, bluff.

What a bitch she is. She wanted to kill Ed.

Where did you ever find her, Professor?

Ed's going to be pissed.

Maybe she decided to swim.

And if she did, good luck to her.

Good luck, bitch.

I hope you die.

Richard rubbed his chin and motioned out to sea. Now the three of them called in the darkness, Richard moving to the edge of the water, careful not to get his shoes wet. He made a visor with his hands and peered out to sea, his line of sight nowhere near where she was floating, looking at the stars and trying to formulate a plan. She submerged again, only her eyes above the surface in order to watch Richard and the Florentines. She wondered where Ed had found them, if they were friends or only extras from Central Casting. Whoever they were, she doubted they would want to enter the treacherous Pacific. They were land mammals.

Georg-eeee!

No doubt they thought she had drowned herself from shame, remorse, and anxiety; she was so shaken, she had tried to swim to Taiwan.

She knew she couldn't stay in the water forever, though she was comfortable in it, seeing without being seen. She couldn't stay in the water any more than she could stay in Southern California, looking over her shoulder every few moments to check if she was on Ed Smid's candid camera, wired for sound. Wasn't it time to move on altogether? Somewhere in the world the sun was rising on unfamiliar places. She had been too long on the West Coast. She had definitely been too long with Richard Swallow, and while she did not like the idea of being forced, she liked the idea of eternal combat even less. She stretched out, floating; overhead, passenger jets were in the sky. She imagined them traveling to all points on the compass, Vladivostok, Rio, Bangkok, Berlin. All you had to do was buy a ticket and in a few hours you had a new life somewhere else, alone in a city, speaking a language you did not understand — commencing a love affair without the inconvenience of the other party. Undistracted, you could paint what you were capable of painting. No one could tell you what to do or how to do it or to what purpose, and for what price. You could disappear into the canvas as completely as a fish in the sea. She imagined a skein of jets, nose to tail, nose to tail, circling the earth forever. And all you needed was money for a ticket and a valid passport.

Richard pointed at something, then shook his head. He pointed again, calling, and this time she heard the words.

Better watch out for sharks, Georgie.

Lots of big fish this time of year.

We're going to get help.

If you're in there, for God's sake come out.

Why don't you come out now?

We won't hurt you.

One of the Florentines snickered when Richard danced away from the incoming surf. The three of them strolled off, scanning the surface of the ocean, shimmering now in moonlight. When they were gone she floated in, was taken by a wave, dumped, and taken again. She waded the last few yards and sat on the sand, the water swirling around her ankles. She had lost her favorite sandals. She looked again out to sea, watching a fish break the surface, and then another and another. They were small fish being chased by larger fish. Shore birds were skimming the surface of the water. In the rising moonlight they looked ethereal. How beautiful the beach was, soft in moonlight, the water phosphorescent. She leaned back on her elbows and caught her breath, thinking how simple things were when you were alone and unencumbered. It was a shame about the sandals, though.

She looked up suddenly when she heard soft footsteps, ready to run but knowing she had no strength to run. She had no strength for anything, wrung out, tired of the chase, furious at her helplessness, hating Richard Swallow. Looming over her were two beautiful Californians in black wetsuits carrying surfboards. They looked at her a moment without saying anything. Then the boy asked her if she was all right. She said she was but if they didn't mind she'd walk with them a while, up the beach to the parking lot where her car was.

Georgia said, "There was an argument."

The girl frowned and said it looked as if she had lost it.

"No," Georgia said. "I won it."

"That's good," the girl said.

"But it isn't over," Georgia said.

The girl looked at her strangely and said something inaudible. She had a trace of an accent, either German or French.

Georgia said, "I wouldn't mind company for a while."

"Yes," the girl said. "All right."

Richard and the two Florentines were approaching from the direction of Smid's house. Richard carried a powerful flashlight, finding them now in its beam.

"Those three," Georgia said.

The boy squared his shoulders and said something to the girl.

She said, "They didn't, like —"

"No, nothing like that."

The two surfers turned and stared, menacing in their black wetsuits and surfboards. Richard and the other two stayed where they were, not moving now. Richard turned off the flashlight, and suddenly they could not be seen at all.

"Who are they?" the boy asked.

"Industry personalities," Georgia said. When the boy looked at her curiously, she explained. Movie characters.

"What do they want?" the girl said.

"I think they want me," she said.

"I'll go talk to them," the girl said.

"No, you won't," the boy said, and then turned to Georgia with an apologetic smile. "Nicole's impetuous. It's her French blood. Nicole doesn't give a shit about anything."

"They don't look like so much to me," Nicole said. In her skintight wetsuit she looked composed and provocative.

"Forget it," he said.

"Why should I?" Nicole demanded. She added, "David prefers to avoid the conflicts. It's his Mormon blood."

David said, "Maybe they're armed, your Industry personalities."

Georgia said, "They're not. But I don't want to talk to them, so let's go."

That seemed to settle it. Nicole and David nodded in unison, as if it were the most natural thing in the world to come across a fully dressed woman, dripping wet, sitting on the beach at night after an unspecified argument, and wanting protection walking to her car because she was pursued by Industry personalities.

She struggled to her feet, shivering a little, feeling light-headed. The surfers waited patiently as she fell into step behind them, feeling like a prisoner escorted by two jailers. After a moment Nicole and David resumed their conversation. They were talking about surfboards, sounding like engineers discussing the

specifications of experimental aircraft. When Georgia looked behind her, the beach was empty. Far back on the lip of the bluff
she could see the rosy glow of Ed Smid's beach house.

When they were a few hundred yards from the parking lot,
Georgia asked Nicole and David what they did for a living, or
if they were students. Not students, David said. They were not
suited to university life. They did odd jobs, a little of this and a
little of that, just enough work to allow them to surf. That was
what they cared about. They had decided not to buy into capitalism, and the truth was, living in Los Angeles was cheap if you
didn't care about things, possessions, ownership. With a little of
this and a little of that you could surf all day long and into the
evening any time you wanted. Some of the gear was expensive
but you made do. It was not necessary to have the most expensive equipment, and in fact expense got in the way of enjoyment.
This was true generally. Miles Davis used a simple trumpet.
Even Ali wore ordinary gloves, whereas Liberace required a silver candelabrum. Materialism was a cosmetic for the spiritually
ugly.

"Could you teach me to surf?" Georgia asked.

"Sure," David said. "It's not hard."

"It's of ordinary difficulty," Nicole said, except when the conditions were superb, the waves high as houses and the wind roaring. The difficulty then met the circumstances and out of that
came bliss.

When Georgia said that surfing sounded like art, they replied
at once that that was what it was, a kind of art, performance art
in its own way and very exciting. The waves, the feel of the
board on the incoming tide, the sun and salt making their own
rhythm. And of course the speed. It was sexy. Perhaps it was
sexy in a different way from art.

Nicole said, "If you love something it has to be sexy. Otherwise it wouldn't be love; it would be something else."

"It would be ambition," Georgia said.

Nicole nodded emphatically. *Ambition,* she said, giving the
word a French accent.

"It's simple vanity," Georgia said. "If you love the thing itself, ambition cannot come into it."

Nicole said, "So you've thought about it, too."

"It's one of the things I wonder about," Georgia said. "But I know a man who thinks ambition is pure sex. He thinks it's the sexiest thing there is and without it there's no satisfaction in anything."

"A man to be avoided," Nicole said.

"He didn't used to be," Georgia said glumly.

Nicole shook her head firmly.

"People change," Georgia said.

"Never in that way," Nicole answered.

David said gently, "What do you do, Georgia?"

"I'm a painter," she said, but her voice lacked conviction.

"That's great," David said.

"Be quiet, chéri," Nicole murmured.

They talked all the way to the parking lot. Then Georgia offered to buy them a hot dog and a beer, joking that they had saved her life and were owed a reward. They accepted happily but in the event had salad and fruit juice and by nine were yawning and ready to go home to bed. Georgia explained about Richard but they did not seem interested until she mentioned that he had a key to her apartment. Nicole said that if she was worried about the *salop* Richard, she could spend the night with them. They had a couch that converted into a bed. The apartment was small, two rooms only, and there was no telephone or television. They lived quietly. They kept regular hours, except when one of them was forced to work at this or that. Nicole looked at the ashtray and the empty beer bottles and warned that smoking was interdicted, along with drugs or alcohol in any form.

"But you are welcome to stay with us," Nicole said.

"Yes," David agreed.

"We will not allow you to be terrorized," Nicole said.

4

EORGIA thought about it a moment — she had always been independent, and Los Angeles was filled with strange and menacing characters — but at last accepted, happy to give Richard the slip. However dangerous Nicole and David might be, they could not be as dangerous as Richard Swallow. And in fact they seemed openly sympathetic and without guile. The apartment was small and disordered, furnished simply and located in a rundown neighborhood not far from the ocean. It was a world away from Coldwater Canyon. Georgia thought of Nicole and David as California Bohemians and liked being with them, sleeping in the living room while they occupied the bedroom. Nights for them sounded strenuous but in no way — she supposed the word was *false.*

At night their door was always open a crack, and when she thought she heard one of them whisper her name, she ignored it, pretending to be asleep. She thought she heard muffled laughter and ignored that, too, though it was harder to ignore the sounds of repeated lovemaking. There was no ignoring the looks they gave her the next morning, frank to the point of challenge; so perhaps they were not as guileless as they seemed.

They were a nation of two and Georgia was a guest of the nation.

And it was a nation like no other. Nicole and David had no friends and did not know or want to know their neighbors. They never read a book or went to a movie or art gallery. Occasionally they visited the zoo. Some nights they played two-handed solitaire with cards so worn the edges were bound with Scotch tape. Creepy, Georgia thought; but they were seductive, too, in their utter indifference to the world outside. Georgia thought there was much to admire in their self-sufficiency; she began to meditate on her own life. Richard Swallow was gone and for that she had no regrets, yet she missed the lust they had shared. She did not miss his crocodiles or his piranha fish, but she missed his touch, and she missed his audacity. It was if he had taken her to the margins of an undiscovered country and abandoned her there, beguiled and unsatisfied, unwilling to retreat but too confused to advance. Confusion had not been in her repertoire. Confusion caused trouble beyond imagining. And she had never had trouble with her nerve.

What a bastard he was.

One morning after her long bath she assessed the empty apartment. Their clothes were tossed carelessly here and there. The refrigerator was empty and she wondered if somehow they did not require nourishment, having each other; perhaps they were vampires. Ravenous for a cigarette, she went for a stroll in the neighborhood, bought a newspaper, and drank a beer at a bodega. The waiter made a clumsy pass, which she smilingly rejected. She finished the paper in five minutes and decided she might as well have been reading Greek or Chinese. The news was incomprehensible because it had nothing to do with her. And she wondered if in some craven way she was still in thrall to Swallow. She drank another beer and left, emerging into bright sunshine. The street was somnolent, as dusty and deserted as any Mexican hill town. On impulse she walked into a shop called Hair Apparent and ordered a shampoo and a cut, nothing drastic, trim it up around the edges.

To hell with Richard Swallow.

I'll be incognito in Los Angeles.

She had never been so nervous having her hair cut, but when she looked in the mirror she liked what she saw and ordered more taken off.

You know, she said, sort of swept back —

Like a boy's, the hairdresser said.

I guess it would be like a boy's, she said.

Very sexy, the hairdresser said when she was finished.

One hopes, Georgia said.

That night when David and Nicole returned from the ocean they looked at her with astonishment. David looked at her and then at Nicole. Nicole looked at her and then at David. Georgia looked at them both, first Nicole and then David. They were calculating the combinations.

The next morning David went off on an errand and Nicole made an offer. She and Georgia were in the bathroom evaluating cosmetics. Nicole received regular consignments from Paris, tiny pots of face cream and hand cream, tubes of ointments, shampoos, cream for breasts and cream for thighs. She thought that Georgia did not take proper care of her skin and, as all the world knew, a woman's skin, once corrupted, could never be restored. Beautiful skin required continual maintenance, and the face was salient. What was a face after all but a personality's handwriting? Idiot men did not have the problem. Coarse and vulgar skin was a masculine hallmark, at least so far as the face was concerned.

They were staring into the mirror together, Nicole pointing out Georgia's minor blemishes, including what could be said to be the *naissance* of crow's feet. Crow's feet in their first trimester, as it were. She opened one of the tiny pots and began to gently daub a fingernail's worth of cream into the feathery wrinkles. She stood behind Georgia, looking over her right shoulder into the mirror as she worked the cream into the skin around Georgia's eyes and mouth. Georgia thought, Am I getting old? She had never taken proper care of herself, and the results of her inattention were now apparent. Nicole continued to work the cream into her cheeks and neck, and now her shoulders. Their faces were almost touching.

And there is something else, Nicole said.

Georgia turned to look at her.

You are living unnaturally, Nicole said. You are living as a celibate, but that is not your nature, it's obvious. It's unhealthy. She handed Georgia the tube of breast cream.

Perhaps, Georgia said.

Your equilibrium is upset.

Looking at herself in the mirror, Georgia had to agree that Nicole's cream was superb.

You should share our bed with us, Nicole said.

To improve equilibrium, Georgia said.

Nicole turned to face her. There were rules, of course — no aggression, jealousy, or egoism. Georgia must not make more of it than it was, an interlude, a *folie,* a simple *ménage à trois* that was quite normal and healthy. In France it was routine. Of course France was liberal generally, owing to its reverence for privacy and individual rights. In France the family was sacrosanct. The French made unfortunate films about the *ménage à trois,* the films always ending badly for everyone whereas life didn't, necessarily. Films were one thing and life another. Unlike life, films had to have a point. They required symmetry, one thing leading to another with a resolution at the end. Filmmakers were obliged to satisfy a bourgeois public and its bloodlust for the lachrymal and the preposterous. For free spirits, life was helter-skelter. Life was like the sun. You did not lead it; you followed it.

Use the circular motion, Nicole said.

Like this? Georgia said.

In any case, Nicole said, the choice was her's, Georgia's, and must be made in accordance with her own sentiments. Certainly David would enjoy it and she would enjoy him, too, once she got to know him. David was an unusual male American, neither difficult nor *nul.* He was ardent and cooperative, not at all hostile, and extremely strong.

And we already get along, Nicole said. That's obvious.

Yes, Georgia said. She was charmed by Nicole's recital, delivered in a near-whisper in the accents of the lecture hall in a rhythm as regular as a metronome. The temperature seemed to swing as she spoke. Nicole shifted gears, too, one minute a tomboy and the next an odalisque. She never took her eyes from Georgia's body, and then reached to touch her hair.

Ravishing, Nicole said.

An impulse buy, Georgia said.

Do you always follow your impulses?

Always, Georgia said.

Your skin is healthy now, Nicole said.

Feels good, Georgia said.

David likes your hair, Nicole said.

I thought he would. And you also.

Are you still attached to the *salop?* Do you think about him?

No, Georgia said. Never again.

He would not recognize you now, Nicole said.

I am attached to you and David, Georgia said.

D'accord, Nicole said.

So Georgia moved into their bed and the nights were helter-skelter, as Nicole had promised. They were very experienced, which Georgia thought would be to her disadvantage but wasn't. Advantage or disadvantage didn't come into it, such was the velvet anarchy of their *ménage à trois*. The hours were regular. David and Nicole surfed during the day and Georgia sketched and read, always eager for their return. They flew into the room each evening in a state of high excitement, smelling and tasting of sea and salt, praising the aphrodisiac rhythms of the Pacific and their own exquisite equilibrium. David was the more voluble of the two, often causing Nicole to roll her eyes in dismay. She thought him operatic. She preferred northern inscrutability; density, she called it. Excitement existed apart from the words used to describe it, and she preferred the sensations without the verbal clutter. Also, there was the question of propriety. Certain things were reserved for oneself. She quoted with approval the remark of a French general following a humiliating defeat at the hands of the Germans during one of the wars at which territory was lost and not recovered. "Think of it always; speak of it never." Nicole believed that was generally true in matters of sex, and much else besides.

With my attitude, she said, I should have been born a man.

People have told me that. Men have.

But I like the way I am well enough. It suits me.

David and Nicole seemed to exist outside their own time, and whether they had retreated to an earlier time or advanced to a future one was impossible to say. For them, each day was very like the one before; that was the point. They never read a newspaper and did not own even a radio, and this seemed perfectly natural to them. They were interested in surfing and sex. Georgia could not say they were deeply in love, though perhaps they were; love seemed not to be the point. They had their own simple standards, natural foods and an abhorrence of tobacco and alcohol being the most conspicuous. When Georgia asked Nicole if she ever thought about France, she said she did, occasionally. She remembered school drudgery and the routines of daily life in the provincial town where she had grown up and her family still lived, though David was her true family now. She had led a restricted life in France until the day David arrived on his motorcycle and swept her away to Paris and then Los Angeles. She thought French people had shrunken hearts, benumbed as they were by materialism. She would certainly return there someday. She and David would go together to the valley of the Lot when they had the money; and that would not be any time soon. Gathering the money would require a tremendous effort, a much greater effort than they were prepared to make. Surfing and sex would suffer, and it wouldn't be worth the sacrifice. And there was no rush. The Lot would always be there. And her French family would be there, too.

We are not like other people, Nicole said.

We like having you here, she added.

Stay as long as you like.

And if you are uncomfortable without your paints, you can bring them here. Just don't paint at night.

And then, in what for Nicole was a furious burst of emotion, she said, We are only for each other. And you, too. Now we are for you, too.

They tried to teach Georgia to surf but it never worked. She could not find the proper balance and was not at ease. She was clumsy on the board. The size of the waves frightened her and she had no taste for speed. Nicole said she lacked concentration. So one day Georgia returned to her apartment and collected her paints and canvases, leaving a note for Mrs. Clyde: She was visiting friends and would send the rent check by mail. On no account should Richard Swallow be told anything. If anyone asked, they should be told she had taken a long-overdue vacation, destination unknown, date of return unknown. Hold the mail, please.

Georgia returned at six, surprised that Nicole and David were still out. She installed her easel by the open window and set about cleaning her brushes, all the while contemplating the blank canvas. She thought of a blank canvas as a held breath, a void waiting to be filled. The afternoon was torpid, no breeze anywhere, so she took off her shirt. She leaned forward, sweating, listening to Duke Ellington on her tiny transistor radio and wondering if music violated the rules of the *ménage*. Probably they would prefer the Beach Boys or California yé-yé. She sat very still and listened hard to "Sophisticated Lady," waiting for something sublime to move her fingers and cause the canvas to exhale, breathing again. Georgia closed her eyes, sweating, listening to the piano, waiting for her miracle.

A door slammed hard and when she heard them on the stairs she knew at once that something was wrong. They always hurried, taking the steps two at a time, banging into the walls, talking nonstop. This time their footsteps were crisp and there was no chatter. Nicole entered first, stripped off her wetsuit, and lowered herself slowly into the easy chair. David stood in the doorway, glaring.

Nicole threw out a blizzard of French.

"Lie," David said.

Nicole continued, speaking even faster.

"Another lie," David said.

Nicole was speaking and gesturing at the ceiling, as if it were the balcony containing her claque.

"Lies," David said again.

Georgia was looking from Nicole to David and back again. Almost without realizing it, she had begun to draw, first one and then the other, brief strokes, Nicole nude in the easy chair, David bare-chested in the doorway, both wound tight with feelings of injustice. Georgia was trying to draw them in the act of listening, the tension unbearable because neither one wanted to listen. Each wanted to speak, to have the grievance heard. The artist was trying to put them in the still interval between one word and another, as if she had caught them on very fast film, the room silent but reverberating with fury.

"She fell off her *board,* Nicole. What was I supposed to do?"

Nicole tossed her head and muttered something inaudible.

"She could have drowned," David said. "*Drowned.* Teenager drowns off Santa Monica."

"Ah!" Nicole said contemptuously.

"While surfer looks on," David said.

"*Au secours! Au secours!*" Nicole said in falsetto. She fluttered her arms and batted her eyes. "I am drown-eeng. Help me! I am drown-eeng and I have lost my brassiere in the falling."

"She had a bump on her head the size of an egg, Nicole."

"The only bumps she had were on her chest," Nicole said.

"You're insane," David said.

"*Naïf,*" Nicole said.

"Paranoid," David shot back.

"I can see what's in front of my eyes," Nicole said.

"I can't discuss this any longer," David said.

"You betrayed me," Nicole said.

"*She would have drowned,*" David said, clipping each word as if he were speaking to the hard of hearing.

"We are supposed to be only for each other."

David was practicing isometric exercises on the doorjamb, his shoulder muscles bulging with the effort.

"When you live in a small country as I have done you learn to live for each other only, to be for each other because no one else is for you. If you are not for each other, you have nothing." She was staring straight ahead, her feet flat on the floor, her hands white on the arms of the easy chair. "And now you want to share it with a little friend."

David did not reply. He was pushing against the doorjamb with his shoulder, looking like a man trying to launch a heavy boat.

"That is what we have, each other," Nicole said. "We are for each other and for no one else."

"What about Georgia?" David said.

"We are for Georgia, too. While she is here."

"Nicole," David began. The tension in his body seemed to drain away and he stood up now, looking down at her from the doorway. He was sweating heavily, his body slick as if oiled. Georgia was sketching furiously and listening hard, for the temper of the interval was determined by the emotion of the words — and not only what was spoken but what was unspoken.

"You know nothing of women, David. You are a *naïf*."

"I know you," he said.

"No, not me. Me least of all. Nor the teenager. Who was no more drowning than I am, and who had her little blue eyes on you all afternoon and decided that she could have you for herself —"

"Nicole, drop it." But there was something sheepish in his voice now, his words soft at the edges.

Nicole looked at the ceiling, smiling slyly. She had never looked lovelier or more composed. Georgia imagined an audience of rapt French citizens, alert to every nuance, urging her on. Of course Nicole would have their sympathy as a demanding lover, victim of a careless American oaf. Nicole spoke again in French, her voice a kind of purr, its timbre intimate, an aria meant for David's ears alone. Georgia's hand flew across the

canvas as she scrutinized them both, listening for the intervals.
She felt she was invisible to them as they swayed in a wind of
desire, borne along by Nicole's relentless feline cadence. David
nervously shuffled his feet, his arms at his sides like a prizefighter
in his own corner awaiting the ringside decision. Dusk was coming on, the room slowly darkening, the evening heat stifling.
Georgia was working as rapidly as she dared, concentrating now
on Nicole, whose words continued to soar; and from the balcony,
Georgia imagined, she heard a murmur of approval. And perhaps
David heard it too, for now he spoke.

"No more."

"But I am not finished," Nicole said.

"You've forgotten what we say."

She looked at him, an inquiry.

"Think of it always; speak of it never," he said.

She replied in French.

"You ask too much," he said.

"The price is fixed," Nicole said. "We both know what it is."
And then, so softly that Georgia barely heard the words, "We
must be indivisible."

David grunted and opened his mouth to say something, but
no words came.

"We cannot share," Nicole said.

And that seemed to be the decision, for David smiled broadly,
clapping soundlessly.

"It's necessary," Nicole said.

"We share with Georgia," David said.

"Georgia is different."

"So there is only us and Georgia," David said.

"And no one else," Nicole declared.

They both turned to look at Georgia, as if it were her turn to
contribute. The artist was so focused on her canvas that she did
not notice them immediately; in a sense they were absent. She
was taking advantage of the silence, filling in the blanks of her
picture. She had never drawn from life, sketching people who
were not posing and had no idea they were being drawn. She

had never sketched anyone in a moment of high tension. In the sudden silence she looked up; and there they were. She had no idea what they wanted from her.

"What are you doing?" Nicole asked.

"Drawing," Georgia said. She moved her brush to catch the brightness of Nicole's eyes, now in deep shadow.

"I can see that, *chérie,*" Nicole said. "I am not blind. But have you heard anything that we have said?"

"Every word," Georgia said. "Even the French. But I don't understand French."

"Lucky you," David said.

"Perhaps we should not have involved you," Nicole said.

"I don't think you have," Georgia said.

"Oh, yes," David said. "You're involved, all right."

"Show us the picture," Nicole said.

Georgia took the canvas from the easel and placed it on the floor, leaning it against her knees. David turned on the light and in the sudden glare their bare bodies were ghostly white.

Nicole said, "Is this what you see when you see us?"

"It's what I see today," Georgia said. "Tomorrow I might see something else."

"It's interesting," Nicole said doubtfully.

"It could be anybody," David said.

"Is it finished?" Nicole asked.

"Not quite," Georgia said.

"It looks finished," David said.

"There is a certain resemblance," Nicole said.

"If you had a title for it, what would it be?" David asked.

"I don't know," Georgia said. "I hadn't thought about a title."

"All pictures have titles," David said.

Georgia smiled. "A title directs the viewer. Maybe the viewer of this picture is better left undirected."

Nicole was on her feet, then squatting in front of the canvas, peering at it closely. She gripped Georgia's knee, steadying herself. There was sand in her hair. Georgia smelled salt and sweat and the residue of scent, Nicole's face only inches from the canvas. David switched off the light and the room returned to near darkness, something debonair by Ellington in the distance.

Georgia said, "Or I could call it *Drowning*."

"Bad idea," David said from the doorway.

"*Indivisible* would be better," Nicole said.

"You should be in the picture, too," David said.

"I drew the picture," Georgia said.

"David's right," Nicole said.

"Maybe later," Georgia said.

"Why not now?" Nicole said. "We want to watch while you draw."

"Not allowed," Georgia said.

"But," Nicole began.

"There's no space," Georgia said. "There's only room for two in this picture. There's nothing worse than an overpopulated canvas."

David joined Nicole and they both crouched, looking at the unfinished picture. Their argument was over, though who had won and who had lost was impossible to say; perhaps it was not that kind of argument. The anxiety the picture represented was dissipated utterly, gone the moment Georgia had lifted it from its easel and placed it against her knees where David and Nicole could see it; the anxiety belonged now to the viewer. But *Indivisible* was the correct title, if a title were needed.

"You don't have to actually see me," Georgia said. "I'm there whether you like it or not."

"Still," Nicole said. "It would be more agreeable —"

"And we want to watch," David said.

"Present everywhere, visible nowhere," Georgia said.

That seemed to satisfy them. David embraced Nicole. They began to chuckle, aroused, fondling each other. The picture was forgotten. Anxiety was forgotten. After a moment they hurried into the bedroom, leaving the door ajar, an invitation to Georgia. But the artist did not move, entirely absorbed in the canvas she did not want to share.

* * *

The Nation of Three was more spacious than the Nation of Two, and Georgia was a willing sightseer. In the beginning she was suspicious, her natural paranoia asserting itself: What were these two about, anyway, in their enthusiasm and guilelessness and iron code of conduct? They were utterly incurious, yet valued loyalty above all qualities, with the exception of good nutrition and French cosmetics, which made possible the strenuous nights. She was happier than she had been with Richard Swallow, but probably that was because with Nicole and David there was no megalomania; there was only sex all night long, and if occasionally she felt herself a figure in someone else's triple portrait — well, the portrait had color and much movement. She knew that the *ménage* was only temporary, but that was no reason not to enjoy it. She liked the narrow dimensions of the apartment. She liked thinking alone in the daylight and loving at night, the three of them delighted together in the double bed, the window thrown open to the ocean breeze. Some nights she strained to hear the waves breaking, a great roaring in her ears. How odd it was to touch another's breast, she who had drawn hundreds of female nudes. She had never thought of herself as a lesbian and had never been attracted to women, lesbian or not. Yet the love-making three ways came naturally. After the first night she was not self-conscious. Their bodies took wonderful forms and they were secure together. David called it "willying," a word she had never heard but that sounded apt. She kept her work to herself but she could not help noticing that her colors had become more vivid, and abstraction was no longer an enemy.

Georgia tried to think her way forward, setting up her easel next to the wide side window not ten feet from the house next door. When she looked out the window she saw a dark room, an old woman in a chair watching television. The only light in the room was the fluorescence of the video, weird blues and reds. The old woman was motionless, watching talk shows followed by game shows and the midday news, ending with the afternoon soap operas. She sat in profile, her hands in her lap and her head held high. She never switched channels, never laughed, and did not move until five o'clock, her dinner hour. When she left the room, she did not switch off the set.

Georgia began to paint her, having no idea what she was after; the scene was inert except for the flickering in the dark corner of the room. How was it possible to watch television all day long and have no reaction whatever? Georgia thought this a picture of routine domestic life, a canvas of outer stillness and inner anxiety. Perhaps the old woman was not watching at all but daydreaming. And what she saw on the television screen was not a commercial program but her own memories. This woman was working her way forward through her own life, her childhood and adolescence, a marriage, children, the death of her parents, the death of a husband, perhaps of her children; and thousands upon thousands of episodes in between. The screen was a mirror of her own teeming memory, a projection of a life, small moments and large. She was her own director and photographer, projectionist and narrator; and that was why she did not move until it was time for dinner. She would eat to feed her memory, the evidence of her life. In any case it was not necessary to move, nor laugh or cry out loud. It was not necessary to comment on the action. The screen drew her memories from her, and Georgia's blank canvas could capture both.

She was beginning to see art in a new way, working from the outside in. You did not end with abstraction; you began with it. She felt she had found an inner world inside her own heart, terrain that had been denied her, or that she was afraid of. She set about exploring it, inch by inch. She went to work with a density of concentration that was ecstasy. She was working in daylight and believed she was using it up, consuming it as you would consume oxygen in a sealed room. The old woman became a self-portrait.

She painted in succession a dozen saints and a dozen self-portraits, alternating saints and selves. Many of them were androgynous, and this seemed to be unconscious. She discovered it later on. She was not one of those whose experience informed her art; for her, it was the other way around. It was profoundly the other way around and she had not known this before moving in with Nicole and David. Unsettled, she felt she did not have much time and had to work at great speed. Not that she had a choice. The saints and the selves were dictating the pace. And when she finished, she knew she had completed a revolution. She was governing at last.

After three months, time was up; it was necessary to leave David and Nicole's velvet anarchy. This was a day in March on the cusp of the seasons, not that seasonal change was evident in Southern California. But winter was leaving and she knew it was time for her to leave, too. An interlude was only that; and she had used up the daylight. Georgia told them that she had to get on with her work in a different environment, an explanation that seemed plausible enough to her, though Nicole was not convinced. Georgia said she needed to seize a new subject. She had taken everything she could from this light and now had to find fresh ground to break. She was starting to loaf and now required her own place. David called it "space." He was crestfallen. What can we do? he asked, and she replied that there was nothing he or Nicole could do. They had already saved her life; what else was there? They had led her around the corner of her work, and what more could anyone ask?

"This is about work then?" Nicole said.

"Yes, of course," Georgia said.

"Work," Nicole said slowly.

"Does that seem ridiculous?"

"It seems strange, yes."

"You know what it means to me," Georgia said.

"I thought you had met someone," Nicole said.

"No," Georgia said. "Certainly not."

"It would be logical," Nicole said.

"That was what we thought," David said.

No, she said again, it was strictly a matter of her own work and where it was headed, and when Nicole smiled wryly, Georgia protested that it was not ambition. It was love. She asked David to imagine a waveless Pacific. In such a circumstance he and Nicole would surely move elsewhere, searching for the perfect curl. There would be regrets but no backward glances, because Americans were always moving on, to one coast or another, even the interior. It was a question of equilibrium —

"I am French," Nicole said. "What you say is not logical."

And then Georgia understood. Work meant nothing to them. Work was an unwelcome break in the day, as tedious as making the beds or changing your underwear. Painting pictures or selling used cars or doing a little of this and a little of that, all one. Georgia had made work into a kind of religion, call it Methodism. The way they looked at it, she was throwing them away like a piece of used Kleenex. And there was truth to that. Her reward was a new realm. She did not know what their reward was. They were exceptionally friendly, sexy, and good-hearted and everyone had fallen a little in love with one another, and why not?

She admitted, truthfully, that she would never forget them and regarded it as a miracle that they had met at all, and had got on so well, in bed and out.

Didn't we have fun, though?

What fun we had!

Remember the night —

Fall-ink in luff again, Nicole sang in her seldom-used Dietrich accent.

"You didn't think I had found someone else," Georgia said.

Nicole and David looked at each other and shrugged.

"You couldn't," Georgia said.

"Why not?" David asked.

"It wouldn't happen, that's all. That would be a betrayal."

"That's not so unusual," Nicole said.

"But," she began, and said nothing more. She had made her move, and got what she wanted. She had taken what she needed, and looked now for a graceful exit. David and Nicole suddenly seemed much older, though they were only in their twenties. In their stubborn reserve they resembled certain isolated northern nations, perhaps one of the Scandinavian countries, always con-

scious of their borders. They did not often admit outsiders, because of the constant threat of betrayal.

They promised to stay in touch, agreeing that they had had a
formidable *ménage à trois* of the sort that could happen only in
France or in Southern California. Their parting was surprisingly
casual and dry-eyed, almost passive, though when David summoned a fresh round of objections, Nicole told him to stop talking, please, Georgia knew what she was doing. It was not right
to prevent someone from doing what she wanted to do when she
wanted to do it. A *ménage* is not a prison. All spirits were free. If
there was a beginning, there had to be an end. There was disappointment, of course. That was normal, though not usual in
their lives.

Perhaps we are more like other people now, Nicole said.

They were on the sidewalk, David and Nicole in their wetsuits climbing into their van for another day on the waves at
Santa Monica. Georgia thought they were beautiful together;
they looked like brother and sister, perhaps twins. She leaned in
the car window to say something intimate. She kissed them both.
David smiled, but Nicole turned away.

We know so much about each other now, Georgia said.

They nodded.

I blush to think, Georgia said.

Willying, she added. I think I've got the willies now. Don't
leave right away; stay a minute.

They looked at her strangely; then Nicole said something to
David and they were gone, leaving Georgia alone on the sidewalk, fumbling in her pocket for a cigarette. She watched them
disappear into traffic, and then returned to the apartment. She
was changing the bedsheets when suddenly she began to cry, her
head aching, tears coming freely. Their smell was everywhere in
the room. Stupid, she said to herself over and over again.

When the blues were over she wandered into the living room,
where the canvases were. She made a thirteenth self-portrait
on the spot, a vaguely pornographic drawing of a smiling nude
Georgia with two lovers in the background, the lovers in wet-

suits, embracing. Beyond them was the ocean, a huge green wave at the horizon. And then she tore it up, knowing that Nicole and David would be offended by it. They would not care for it, this image. They believed only what was moving in front of their eyes or under their fingers or inside their dreams. Truly, they did not care about possessions of any kind. They were not interested in the twenty-five canvases in the living room except to object to the smell of the paint. Can't you do something about the *paint*, Georgia? It sticks in our nostrils. We can't smell the sea or each other or you. It's disgusting. It's worse than tobacco.

It took her the day to pack her belongings, her paints and her canvases. For a long time she stared at *Indivisible*. She had forgotten about it, a relic of the early days. She wanted to leave it for them but was afraid the gesture would be misunderstood, and Nicole would see it as a false friend. Georgia wandered to the window and stood looking at the old woman staring, as always, at her television set. She tapped on the window but the woman never moved, and then it occurred to her that the old lady was deaf. And she too had served a purpose.

When Georgia returned to her apartment, Mrs. Clyde was waiting with a flurry of questions. Georgia, where have you been? What have you been doing?

You look wonderful! Have you been naughty?

You're so thin! And you have your smile back.

That friend of yours is no good. That Richard. He's been around asking for you.

I didn't tell him anything.

He never fixed the flower bed, Georgia. He didn't give us rose bushes, either. He's a strange one. We felt he ripped us off. He made promises that he never intended to keep. The whole neighborhood was upset.

But your cat is where you buried her.

We did not interfere with the cat.

Would you like a nice glass of wine, Georgia?

* * *

She took her time loading the van for the long trip east. The clothes and canvases and art supplies filled the van, even the passenger seat up front. She was enjoying herself, her last day in Southern California. She took a last look around the apartment, at the bare walls and the sun streaming in the windows. She was calculating the energy left behind. She drained her glass, put it on the windowsill, and departed, leaving the door ajar. It was three in the afternoon and she hoped to beat the rush hour traffic.

The van's engine failed twice but finally caught. When she turned to take a last look at the house, she saw Richard Swallow's face not six inches away.

"What a lucky break," he said. "Another five minutes and I'd've missed you."

"Go away," she said.

"Where are you going?"

"I'll call the police."

He danced back, smiling, his hands moving in circles, palms out. "Calm down," he said. "I wanted to see that you're all right, after that scare you gave us."

"Good-bye," she said, struggling with the shift, trying to get the car in gear.

"Where, then? Chicago? Heading for the Windy City?"

"Get away from me," she said.

He stepped closer, wrinkling his nose. Suddenly he began to laugh. "Jesus Christ. You're *pissed*. You're drunk as a lord. I can *smell* it."

She put the car in gear, looking for something to throw at him. The Clydes were sitting on the front porch of the house, looking on with expressions of disapproval. The UCLA boys were playing catch in the street, and now they too stopped to watch the show. Richard Swallow's voice was loud with his usual sarcasm as he continued to talk, pointing and shaking his head. She searched the floor with her free hand and found what she wanted. She grabbed the wine bottle by the neck and half leaned out the window and threw it at him. It hit him broadside in the stomach and he went down as if shot.

The Clydes cried out. The UCLA boys began to laugh and clap.

Richard moaned, clutching his stomach.

She honked the horn twice, easing away from the curb. Richard shouted something but she didn't hear what it was and didn't care. She gave them all a jaunty wave and began to retrace her steps to Chicago. It was lonely in the van without Liebermann, and the freeways were jammed. She drove forever. Each afternoon the sun was over her shoulder. She seemed to be driving into a dark future. But she was warmed by the image that remained in her mind, and is there still: Richard Swallow astonished, his face crimson, silently collapsing.

Drunk, she thought. Drunk as a lord; that was fair. But not so drunk that she was unable to heave a bottle of Chardonnay and hit the target; and if she had not been drunk, she might not have done it.

In Chicago Georgia drove straight to a gallery on the North Side, demanding that the owner look at what she had brought him — look at once, no delays. She had met him several times when she was a student at the Art Institute, and he pretended to remember. She arranged the saints and selves, *Indivisible,* and the old woman against a long white wall in the order they'd been painted, and stood to one side while he looked at them. She realized then how tired she was, and how disoriented at being back in Chicago, and how much the approval of this gallery owner meant to her. He was taking his time, too, looking at all the pictures.

"My goodness," he said at last. "These are exceptional. Where were they painted? The water doesn't look like our Lake Michigan."

"California," she said.

"Ve-ry curious."

"Isn't it?" she said. "Does it make a difference?"

"Not really," he said. Then, "What do you want? Do you want a show?"

"As soon as possible," she said.

"Not right away," he said after a moment's pause. "It'll take some time. I want to put the word out. No one knows who you are. *I* don't know who you are, and I'm going to have to find out. This will be an event if the word gets out properly. We must prepare the ground carefully. You will allow me to do what's necessary?"

"Of course," she said. "I need the money."

"Everyone does."

"I need it because I'm going to France."

"Oh, dear," he said, giving a little exasperated sigh. "I suppose it can't be helped. I hope you have the temperament for it. All those ghosts looking over your shoulder. I was apprehensive when you walked in here with that look. Are you always so fierce? I thought you were — on something."

"Not always," she said.

Preparing the ground took time, more time than she wanted to give, but the results were, as the gallery owner had predicted, splendid. And there was a further surprise. The day after the opening she bought the *Tribune* to look for the review, finding it briefer than she had hoped but appreciative, with all the expected references and the usual caveat: "Some may find her retrograde." Then she worked slowly back through the paper until she came to the obituary page with Dean Forrest, top left, with a picture taken when he was a young man. She was shocked. She had not seen him in years and knew nothing of his life. The cause of death was cancer. He was a banker and civic leader, a member of boards and charitable organizations and clubs; all these were listed. He was married, with two children, a boy and a girl. Funeral services were private. Burial was private. Friends could make donations to the Art Institute of Chicago. And when she saw that, she broke down and cried like a child.

Georgia did not leave for France right away but stayed on in Chicago for four more years, thinking she could find the vein of rock that had eluded her; but it was gone for good. Yet there were other veins that did just as well, and friends to pursue them with. She was painting slowly but selling everything; and she liked the money and the attention more than she thought she would. Yet her spirits did not improve and she slipped into a despondency that she feared was permanent. All she had was her work, and the fact that she was selling it did not make it what she wanted it to be. She knew she was only at the margins of merit; she thought of it as being in the foothills of a vast range of mountains, and she did not know if she had the strength to climb. That summer, her hair began to fall out; and in the autumn she took her savings and left for Paris, where she did not speak the language and knew no one but depended on Nicole's promise that France was liberal generally and hospitable to strangers. That is, they were indifferent.

She never saw Nicole and David again and came to regard them as a feverish interlude, an interlude to refer back to on cold and lonely nights. An interlude to share with your grandchildren, if you had any and if they were a particular kind of child. She never saw Richard Swallow again either, though she thought of him often. He invaded her dreams. Sometimes she saw him as one of a crowd in a populous Salon painting, *Les Romains de la Déca-dence,* for example. She thought of their last evening on the beach at Santa Monica and wondered what in God's name he had had in mind, beyond getting his own way, what he was owed. Their affair was misshapen; no wonder it broke down. And it was only chance that the dangerous evening on the beach led her to Nicole and David, in whose company she had turned a corner. How she adored them, but they did not invade her dreams as Richard did. She took Richard Swallow home as you take home a picture, believing that it is one thing and discovering that it is something else, and coming to despise it, and yourself, too, for your shallow judgment. The picture understands this and makes no allowances. You are left with your bad bargain and the certain knowledge that the picture is not at fault, though you yearn to have words with the artist who painted it.

ABROAD

1

THE COMMOTION began around midnight, a crowd in rue Blaise. Before long Georgia noticed blue lights undulating on the ceiling of her room and the walls of the elementary school across the street. She was working at her easel, so concentrated that she could not be bothered to investigate. Whatever this demonstration was, it had nothing to do with her. She was working from the edges of her idea into the center, taking her time, sketch after sketch. She thought she was very close. Georgia worked away through the night, living entirely in her own idea, yet aware of the disturbance and the undulating blue light.

Toward morning the street noise settled until there was only undefined and troubling tidal movement, felt rather than heard. When her concentration lapsed for good, Georgia poured a glass of Calvados and set about cleaning her brushes and tidying up. She performed these chores mechanically while examining the sketches, the heart of which continued to elude her. She removed her glasses and leaned in close, studying the brush strokes, the paint itself. But they told her nothing, no more than a poet's grammar disclosed the poem's soul. It takes more than paint and punctuation. She covered the sketches with a swath of burlap, thinking of the burlap as a winding sheet and the easel as a corpse, cold and lifeless and in an advanced state of decay.

And then she remembered last evening's telephone call from her sister Marge recounting Geraldo's awesome morning program, "People Who Have Been Raised from the Dead!" Eight ordinary-appearing men and women who had reached the Upper Room and had been snatched back by medical science or Jesus Christ. Not hard work, though. Hard work didn't figure in the back-to-life experiences, which were, like, miraculous. Even Geraldo was impressed.

It was valuable at these times to recall the philosopher's observation that there was very little difference between one human being and another, but what difference there was was *very important*.

She washed her hands at the sink, using the coarse powder, then cleaned her nails. She stood and stretched, moving her head from side to side, her neck creaking. Slowly she raised her chin and stared at the ceiling and then at the mirror above the bureau. Gorgeous Georgia would be performing no miracles tonight. The mirror told her she needed a haircut. She had rings under her eyes. Her complexion — wasn't the word *sallow?* She shook two vitamin tablets from the open bottle on the bureau, took them down with Calvados, and immediately felt better.

Only when the picture was covered did Georgia become aware of the rustle in the street. It had been there all this time but only now did she sense its weight. She stepped to the window and looked down past the statue of the general on horseback directly below her, astonished to find rue Blaise teeming with people. There were police officers here and there on the sidewalk and in squad cars, and television crews with their cameras and brilliant lights. She listened carefully but heard only the human rustle, and then somewhere the sound of an orchestra and a man singing, a scratchy recording. She thought his voice was off key. It was an ordinary cabaret song, the man's voice thick and furtive and filled with — perhaps sorrow, more likely revenge. The crowd swayed and in places cigarette lighters flared.

Bathed in white light, rue Blaise looked like an unruly stage set.

A vigil, she thought. Perhaps a politician, or some beloved figure of the Resistance. Resistance heroes were dying all the time, an accusing army of elderly men and women, so many that it was mind-bending how the Nazis had managed to administer the nation for four and a half years. The Nazis had administered France as easily as they administered Schleswig-Holstein. But the crowd in rue Blaise was mostly middle-aged and young, and the young had little patience with the Resistance, so long ago and so far away and so fraught with anxiety; and for the middle-aged, it was not distant enough. And there was no politician in France whose death could fill a Left Bank street on a Saturday night, when there were so many cheerful cafés nearby on the Boulevard St.-Germain. A philosopher conceivably, but there were no beloved philosophers either. Sartre was the last. So he — or possibly she! — was an entertainer. Entertainers were the soul of a nation, *very important* for the population's sense of itself, its shared values and emotions, its common destiny. And rue Blaise was exactly the sort of out-of-the-way street that a celebrated entertainer would find congenial. His privacy would be respected. The entertainer would enhance his street rather than the other way around.

At the conclusion of the song there was a murmur but no applause. Someone began to clap but no one else joined in. Georgia saw that many in the crowd were weeping, their faces ghastly in the brilliant lights of the television crews. The crews were gathered around a doorway up the street. The crowd pressed forward to get close, to touch the door. Young people were writing furiously on the stone wall, a sentence or a signature or an awkward drawing. A few stood with bowed heads and others were irreverent, calling attention to themselves. Police watched them but did not interfere. The building was dark so that it was impossible to know if anyone was inside. Hard to imagine a grieving family trying to cope, the house surrounded by importunate strangers, and harder still to imagine a corpse in the parlor. Georgia leaned far out the window, wondering who it was that inspired such devotion from a population that was so notably worldly and self-absorbed.

Georgia looked at her watch; four in the morning.

She perched on the windowsill, hugging her knees, Calvados in hand, watching with mounting excitement. Gypsy flower sellers were now on the fringes of the crowd selling single red roses wrapped in cellophane. Georgia saw a boy and girl embrace in the doorway opposite, the girl's arms tight around the boy's neck, squeezing, her legs scissored around his waist. Georgia looked away, thinking herself a voyeur though the lovers were in plain sight; and others like herself were peering down from bedroom windows, men and women and their sleepy children. She wanted to join the crowd in the street but hesitated. She seldom left her apartment after dark, almost never except when she needed groceries. She was frightened, even though everyone said that the streets were safe. That was because they were teeming with people always, eyes everywhere you looked. She wanted to avoid loneliness, her own and others'. To wander alone late at night in a great city celebrated for its beauty and animation was a definition of loneliness, night shadows in populated streets giving emphasis to a condition that needed no emphasis. The Louvre plaza at night seemed as desolate and wasted as a desert; then without warning a nomad would appear from behind a porch pillar, and a tipsy couple fresh from dinner somewhere on the Right Bank. Alone at night you invited trouble. You asked for it. There were always strange people aprowl, not menacing exactly but not welcoming either. They were melancholy in the darkness. You knew they had a story to tell and that it was one you didn't need to hear. And they feared you, too, except those who wanted company in order to begin a conversation or a friendship.

And of course she had her work.

But there was something seductive about this impromptu four-in-the-morning gathering, so she turned away from the window and pulled on her raincoat. This crowd looked tame enough, and the police were everywhere.

*   *   *

She ran downstairs and slipped through the doorway into the
street and was caught immediately in the current. She moved
close to a party of older people. Voices rose around her but she
made no sense of them, not understanding argot. Her French
was rudimentary, adequate for the market or the pharmacy or
a café, deficient everywhere else. She stopped a well-dressed
woman and asked who it was that had died and the woman
looked at her in surprise, nodding sadly, and gave a name, but
the name meant nothing. An entertainer? Georgia asked. Yes, of
course, the woman replied in English. An entertainer. A great
singer and comedian. A superior librettist. One of the greatest
writers and singers in France and like so many he was an immigrant, a political refugee, a dissident. He fought convention. His
origins were mysterious. He was a Russian or perhaps Polish.
He was one of those who had crossed borders after the war. He
spoke — a dozen languages!

But we loved him, the woman said.

He was ours, after all.

Once, on television, he threatened the master of ceremonies.

And set fire to his checkbook.

To show his contempt.

In that, he spoke for many of us.

And you have never heard of him? the woman asked. She
repeated the name.

Georgia shook her head. The woman turned to her companions, raising her eyebrows. She said, For a short time he had his
own program on television, a Friday night hour, "L'heure de
Réalité." It was a variety show, popular but unpredictable. There
was one scandal after another, so it was canceled by the authorities. Too much *réalité* in the *heure.* Authorities are the same everywhere, on every continent, even yours, madame.

They were moving slowly in a knot, pressed on all sides. The
entertainer's house was a block away, hard lit by television lights.
The wind came up and it began to rain, a light sprinkle.

He was so French, the woman said.

And sexy, she added, digging into her purse to show Georgia

a photograph, holding it up to the bright reflection of the television lights.

A face of character, she said.

And of suffering. So many borders crossed.

It was the cover of one of the glossy French magazines. The entertainer was swarthy, half-shaven, and middle-aged; he wore an earring, and a gold chain around his neck. His face was dissipated, the expression truculent. A burning cigarette lolled in the corner of his mouth, his eyes half shut against the smoke. The face was not familiar but she knew it. She knew it by another name, and recognized it as you would recognize a cartoon by Grosz or a portrait by Bacon. She knew the face as well as she knew her own, not a face easy to forget — spectacularly homely, a naughty boy with untamed thoughts, a boy of sudden impulse, always uncombed, too ugly to be conventionally vain. He would be impolite, the immigrant boy with money to burn. And he would be a great talker, hypocrisy's enemy. His immodesty would be contagious. He would be attractive to women because of his unquiet face and wiry body and surly manner, and because he never flattered women nor hesitated to say what he thought. He would be reckless no less than — the adventurer Cortez slaughtering the Aztecs. Or Casanova. Or Stalin.

"An interesting face," Georgia said.

"Are you all right, madame?" The woman put her hand on Georgia's arm. "You're so pale. You look as if you had seen a ghost."

"No, just an interesting face."

"Sexy, would you not agree?"

"Sexy, yes, I suppose so," Georgia said.

"A bad boy," the woman said.

"I can see that," Georgia said.

"The stories," the woman said.

"I can imagine them," Georgia said.

"All Paris was at his feet."

"Paris is easily seduced."

"Not so easily," the woman said. "This one was unique. He

had one of the best-known faces in France. His nose is as famous as Charles de Gaulle's. He put it everywhere, too. You are from New York?"

"Chicago," Georgia said.

"What a shame about New York," the woman said.

"Yes," Georgia said, uncertain what she meant.

"The crime, the filth. It is the logical consequence of the organization of the city. What a fortunate thing that you can come to rue Blaise at this time. You see how orderly we are?" The woman laughed. "It's rare, I admit."

"I've never seen him perform," Georgia said.

"He didn't travel. He preferred France, where he will be remembered forever, he and his wives and his darling daughter. There were many girlfriends, too. And perhaps there were men. Entertainers live by another set of rules; that's well known. I think they make their own rules."

"They try to," Georgia said. And not only entertainers.

"Well," the woman said. "One forgives them."

"Not always," Georgia said.

"The daughter did. And there was much to forgive. But of course the daughter is an entertainer, too. It goes with the family, a matter of genetics. And there is a natural sympathy among those who practice the same métier, as if they are all members of the same club. The daughter is a star in her own right. When he died today she was with him. She was holding his hand, and they sang a final duet together. That's according to the radio. They interrupted programs to bring the news. Would they do that in America? I suppose not, unless the man were a politician or capitalist. The word spread and those of us who loved him came immediately to rue Blaise to pay our respects and show our appreciation. It's the least we can do for one who gave us such music. You can see how many of us are here, and of all ages. We are his true public. We loved him. He was ours. An entertainer belongs to his public." The woman put a hand on her arm. "Listen. Someone's playing his song on a tape deck. That's him singing."

It was the same song Georgia had heard before as she sat on the windowsill, and listening to it now she was certain that the rasp in his voice was revenge. It was not hard to identify. The thought depressed her, and the woman's ignorance depressed her. She had been foolish to leave her quiet apartment and her work to come into the street. She felt claustrophobic, shouldered by the crowd. Smells of cheap scent and wine were all around her, along with the incomprehensible conversation. The rain was falling a little harder now and she hunched her shoulders against it. She worried about getting back to her apartment because the crowd seemed to be growing. She heard the cough of a motorcycle. She wondered what it was really about the Russian waif. Whatever it was, he had touched a nerve. Inside their own rules, such men were irresistible. But they were rules that everyone else was expected to follow, and when you declined — sorry, darling, this isn't my idea of a life — they called you hopeless or worse because you took the fun out of it.

Do you know the trouble with you, Georgie?

You have no imagination.

Georgie, you're old before your time.

Your mind's in the suburbs.

Lighten up, Georgie.

Live a little.

Naturally the photograph had upset her. Why wouldn't it? She thought she had seen a ghost.

They had been standing still but now the current began to move. They were passing the little park beside the school, the one containing the statue of the general on horseback, her subject, the heart of which eluded her. The general towered above her. Perhaps an anarchic heart beat behind the iron tunic and that was what she could not grasp or refused to acknowledge. The crowd slowed, growing silent as it approached the entertainer's house, and now Georgia noticed that the Frenchwoman was carrying a red rose in cellophane. Flowers of all kinds were strewn in front of the man's house. Then the white light flared and in the darkened doorway at her elbow she saw the teenagers she had watched from her window. She was almost close enough to touch them. The boy's back was against the big double doors, the girl's legs around his waist, her arms around his neck, her skirt hiked up to reveal the perfect moons of her bottom. Georgia felt their heat. The boy's eyes were squeezed shut, the girl's head moving from side to side, her long hair swishing like an animal's mane. They were whispering to each other in a soft breathy language. The boy's head began to nod rapidly and his eyes popped open, though he saw nothing. His hands were somehow tucked into his crotch, his knuckles distended. Then in the moment of the light's flaring Georgia saw that they were not his knuckles, nor were his eyes sightless. She abruptly moved away as the television lights went out and rue Blaise was cast into darkness, with no sound she could identify except for the whisper of the lovers and the entertainer's song on the tape deck.

"Are you there?" the woman asked.

"I'm here," Georgia said. Her voice shook.

"I must go with my friends," the woman said after a moment. "It's been pleasant talking with you. I hope you have a fine time in Paris. Be sure to watch television tomorrow. We'll all be on it."

Not everyone, Georgia thought but did not say.

"I must present my rose now," the woman said.

"Wait," Georgia said.

"It's just ahead there. The house where he died this afternoon."

"*What*," Georgia began.

"They said it was liver failure. Or heart trouble. One of those two. It's possible that it was something else. Doctors never tell everything. Doctors never tell the whole story. Doctors are *bastards*." The woman paused. "And we live in dangerous times. He did not take care of himself. Perhaps he thought he was in the hands of God."

"*What*," Georgia said again.

"So he has been taken from us. A part of Paris is gone, madame. We are a small country. We are like a family. And when one of us dies, we all feel it. We come to pay our respects, as family members do. And when the death is unexpected, we are shocked as well as saddened. It is our *heure de réalité*, madame. I wish you a pleasant journey."

"Wait," Georgia said. "*What was his name?*"

But the woman had rejoined her companions and moved on, and was now lost in the crowd. Georgia called out once and stood on her toes, but the woman had vanished. She did not want to be alone in the street, in the darkness no longer tame but unruly. She wondered if the teenagers had finished loving each other and decided they probably had, for the moment; but there would be other moments, public and private. She was close to the entertainer's house now, the doorway protected by police as if it were the scene of a crime. Georgia lost her balance but she was propelled by the surge of people around her. How strange it was, knowing so much about a man but not knowing his name. When she heard it the first time it meant nothing to her, and then she forgot it amid the details, the wives and the lover and the darling daughter and the illnesses and the rest. No doubt he was a local cult figure, locally notorious, cut from the same shroud as Lenny Bruce or Jim Morrison. Not to mention Richard Swallow, who was an entertainer in his own way, and notorious in Los Angeles. She had not expected the face of Richard Swallow in rue Blaise.

Georgia heard the motorcycle again and began to struggle, to untie the knot and slip to the edges of the mass, but she was held fast in the darkness. She dipped her head, believing that if she concentrated on the pavement she would regain her composure. But she swung from side to side like a dory at anchor, the entertainer's coarse voice pursuing her, reverberating in the narrow street. Tipsy people sang along, everyone off key. The song was monstrous. For a moment Georgia thought she would faint, pressed on all sides and tethered to the anchor, weightless and lightheaded, her breath coming in sharp puffs. She raised her head, searching for the general's statue, but she could not locate it. Her apartment was behind her somewhere. It was raining harder now. If she could find the statue, she knew she would find her way home, but it was the entertainer who held her now. She heard him whisper *Georgie* and begin to hum a new song, something raunchy and familiar, something from America. She believed that something marvelous would happen. Richard had the magician's power of astonishment. His thick baritone was as consoling as a rough caress.

The song faded away, then stopped, and she looked up to find the crowd silent in the rain. She lifted her face to the sky, raindrops on her skin. The crowd began to stir, surly in its anxiety and anticipation, its grief and desire. There was a scuffle behind her. Then someone said something rough and suddenly she was off her feet and moving backward, away from the crowd of people and the gendarmes overseeing them. A woman cried out. As Georgia flew backward she seemed to rise, weightless and erratic as a feather. She was borne above the crowd like a martyred religious, her flimsy body manhandled. She saw her desperate general on horseback and above her head she thought she saw the first pale stripes of morning. And then she fainted, because above the commotion she heard the gleeful laughter of Richard Swallow.

The laughter, fainter now, pursued her. She was seated in a chair in a brightly lit room filled with people drinking Champagne from crystal flutes that glittered in the light. They glittered as brightly as the marquee of a theater, little lights winking on and off. And when they finished a glass they threw it into a marble fireplace and took another from a white-coated waiter. Richard's low laugh mingled with the sound of breaking glass and high-pitched conversation. From time to time one of the guests — for that was who they seemed to be, guests at a party — would turn and smile in her direction, raising a flute in a toast.

Take a bow, Georgia.

Take a bow before it's all over.

They crowded around, leaning over her. Some of the faces were familiar but she could not put names to them. The names were there but she could not give them voice. They formed a sort of human wall around her chair, pressing closer now. She could smell the Champagne on their breath and feel the heat of their bodies. The men were slender as reeds, the women heavily made up and garlanded with jewels, jewels around their throats and wrists, jewels on their dresses. She had the idea that if she allowed them, they would suck the oxygen from the room and she would suffocate. In a panic she looked at her fingers and saw they were crawling with jewels, the jewels swarming, moving, and biting as insects do. Blood was on her fingers.

Someone bent down to purr to her in a voice soft as cotton.

Georgia Whyte, you cannot know what it is to be mourned by a city, to have your work so revered that the public weeps, comes with flowers to the front door of your house, feels your death as it feels the death of a beloved member of the family, remembers your most casual and thoughtless remarks as emblems of a whole nation, is drawn to you as iron to a magnet, sees you in their dreams, adores you, would raise you from the dead if they could —

No, she said, turning her head from side to side.

The wall of people parted then, swinging left and right like figures in a costume musical, and she saw her pictures displayed, suspended from the ceiling, turning like corpses on a gibbet. It was an exhibition of her saints and selves, the Brownes in conversation, Winnetka Boy, the old woman in Los Angeles, Nicole and David, all her finished work. Then to her horror she saw pictures and sketches she had thrown away, drawings from her teenage years and before, every single thought she had had in her lifetime — sketches in the margins of pages from schoolbooks, stick figures drawn in Crayola on rough yellow copy paper. And on the frame of each one, a dime-sized red dot. All the pictures had been sold and were now hanging in this brightly lit room, admired by their owners.

She had nothing left.

You belong to them now, the voice purred.

They own you.

You're *theirs*.

And in return you get — adoration!

They'll put flowers on your doorstep.

And see you in their dreams.

Try to raise you from the dead.

So there's no turning back, Georgie. Lucky you.

You've chosen a performing art. Entertain them!

Because if you sell one, you've got to sell them all.

I am not an entertainer, she said through clenched teeth.

The cat's voice went away. The owners drifted out of the room, dropping their Champagne flutes into the fireplace. The lights dimmed, and went out one by one. The room was in dusk. Georgia struggled to rise but the chair held her fast. Her vision was unnaturally clear, and now she saw her pictures turning, hanging by their slender cords. She thought they were in a kind of agony.

She was half in the dusky room and half on the sidewalk in rue Blaise, neither place exactly but suspended between the two. They were far apart with no connection between them at all, and now the nightmare vanished utterly. She was weary, hot and cold at the same time, without any firm purchase on her own identity, who she was or where she was and what she was doing, half sitting, half lying on the pavement in front of her apartment building, dense morning light coming on in purple stripes. Her eyes came slowly into focus, and when she raised her head she saw that she had a torn fingernail. She was surrounded by strangers who looked at her with embarrassment, averting their eyes when she raised her head. A woman bent down and said something in rapid French. Apparently they thought she was drunk. Georgia looked at her torn fingernail, dismayed because she had stopped biting them, had grown them beautifully, and now one was lost; dumb bad luck.

The woman took her arm, and at last she understood that an ambulance was on its way because she had fainted, though fainting was not her habit. She had never fainted before. Slowly, piece by piece, she remembered the laughter, loud, deep, and derisory. She struggled to rise.

Ambulance, someone said.

Non, Georgia said.

No, it wasn't necessary.

I'm home, she said. I live here, thirty-three rue Blaise.

I have my own doctor.

She imagined the high thick walls and wide corridors of a French hospital, a dozen patients to a room, attended by nuns in blue speaking a language she did not understand. If she was committed to a French hospital, she would never survive its nineteenth-century practices, being bled by leeches while confined in a canvas straitjacket, because naturally they would think her mad, a hysterical American woman far from home. Georgia struggled to her feet and leaned against the building. She was better now that she was upright. Her eyesight was blurred and she had a terrible headache, but that was no reason to go to a hospital.

How long? she asked.

Not long, the woman said. A few minutes.

You should be examined, the woman added.

I have a doctor, Georgia lied.

The woman drifted off in the rain. Georgia heard the bleat of the ambulance and remembered then that there had been a commotion in the street. An entertainer had died and people came to pay their respects, an unruly street mass for the dead. She had been shown a photograph and the entertainer reminded her of Richard Swallow. She remembered music in the street and a boy and girl making love in a doorway. She had been overwhelmed by the crowd. She panicked and fainted. She did not remember getting to the sidewalk where she was now, being stared at like an animal in a zoo. She put her hand on the door, feeling better. Her only souvenir of the incident was the torn fingernail, beginning to sting. The Frenchwoman was again at her elbow, looking at her closely. Georgia gave her a bright smile.

I'll go now, she said.

I live here, fifth floor.

The woman said something she did not understand.

It was the crowd, you see, Georgia said.

So many, many mourners.

So much commotion.

And I don't understand the language.

The woman said, Madame should be more careful.

Georgia smiled her thanks and stepped inside as the ambulance turned into rue Blaise. She had trouble with the heavy door but it was cool and quiet inside the building. The concierge was nowhere to be seen. Georgia's hair was wet and she shivered in the chill. She had a vague feeling that someone was behind her as she moved slowly up the stairs; but when she turned she could see no one in the shadows, and it didn't matter because she was safe inside now. She touched her finger to her lips, feeling the torn nail, sharp as a razor blade. She mounted the staircase a step at a time, balancing herself against the wall. Her fingernail continued to sting as she made her way painfully up the narrow winding stairs to the fifth floor.

She faltered at the fourth floor, falling to one knee, her hands flat against the dark wood. God, she was tired. She was exhausted and cold, and her head hurt. She noticed blood on her raincoat. God, what a mess. She had been very stupid but probably that was because she was not herself. And had not been for a good many weeks, more than she cared to remember. She lived out of time, as people who were alone usually did. Sometimes she had difficulty remembering the exact date, always consulting a calendar when she wrote checks; otherwise, it did not matter. Another week or another month gone, but the meadow was limitless and she could not graze it all in a thousand years. She thought she was a better painter when she was not herself than when she was, so perhaps not being yourself was a precondition of the *very important* difference between souls. And where better than in incomprehensible Europe, where you could leave your apartment at four in the morning to participate in a demonstration that did not concern you and find a street full of temptation and the devil himself whispering at your elbow. You were transported into the past like a parcel, Return to Sender. Unwholesome memories arrived, fully detailed and in Technicolor and you had to sit through them until the reels were empty, and all because of a cheap magazine photograph of an unknown entertainer and a garrulous Frenchwoman to explain it all. The bad boy and his *heure de réalité,* canceled by the authorities.

Are you all right, Madame? You look as if you had seen a ghost.

Sexy, would you not agree?

Madame should be more careful.

The Frenchwoman was shrewd; she knew fear when she saw it. And she observed it then, in Georgia's eyes and her mouth and the way she had shivered and taken a step backward as if she thought the picture would become animated. Ghosts collected around her like flies around a carcass, and the ghosts bred more ghosts until she thought she was living inside a medieval legend.

Georgia touched her head against the wall and hugged her knees, thinking she would rest awhile.

She stirred as she heard the floor creak, felt soft hands under her arms. She opened her mouth to protest but could not find the words. She was so tired, she had no strength to speak. She allowed herself to be helped up the stairs to the door of her apartment. The corridor was still dark. She fumbled in her pocket for the key but when she found it she was unable to fit it into the lock. A match flared, and the key was taken from her. She heard a sharp click and then was inside. The window was open and the apartment frigid. Papers were scattered on the floor. Rain flew in the window and she could see the faint undulations of the blue light, no doubt her ambulance. The small room with its bureau, bed, and easel was achingly familiar. She put her hand to her forehead and realized she was burning with fever. That she was slightly delirious she already knew. She felt a rush of gratitude, but when she turned to thank her benefactor there was no one in the room or in the hallway. Had she imagined that, too? She closed and locked the door, leaning against it, looking at the easel and the palette on the bureau. She stepped to the bureau and poured a full glass of Calvados, taking it all the way down. The liquor burned her throat until it settled uneasily in her stomach. She drank too much, always had.

Half in the bag, Richard called it.

You drink too much, Georgie.

You'll get fat. You'll lose your looks.

You've got a drinker's face.

She closed the window and took off her wet raincoat and pulled on a heavy sweater, curling a scarf around her neck. She lit a cigarette and poured another glass of Calvados, reaching to move the burlap to one side so that she could see her sketches. She sat on the windowsill in the dawn light and looked into the street, where there were only a few dozen mourners milling about. The ambulance was gone, and there were no police in sight. She saw the woman who had shown her the photograph of the entertainer, and the teenagers who had been making love in the doorway. The wall of the entertainer's house was covered with graffiti, incoherent splashes of paint. What an effect he had had, holding a nation in thrall. Surely that had been his ambition — and the only question was, Had it satisfied him? She turned from the window in order to look again at her own work. She was farther along than she thought, though there was still a way to go. She sat staring at her sketches, leaning against the window until her eyes closed and she was asleep.

2

T HE DAY AFTER the entertainer's death the curtain came
down and she was as sick as she had ever been in her life,
with convulsions and a fever that seemed to reach to the
center of her bones. It was one of the Central European flu
strains, Bulgarian, Romanian, Hungarian, she never knew which.
Bugs swept west like a medieval plague infecting the civilized
world. There was no cure. She lay in her narrow bed and watched
the clock, time itself accelerating and disintegrating, winding
down, even reversing course. It seemed to her that she was an
island of illness, inert, unable to defend herself, accepting each
wave as it came. She thought she would die, alone and friendless
in France, her work uncompleted, her life half-lived. She did not
struggle against the waves but bent before them. She offered no
obvious resistance, thinking of herself as an exile, a castaway, a
prisoner of war with no secrets and nothing to hide. Whatever
they wanted she would give them.

She lost track of things, as prisoners do. That day or the next
the snow began and the street outside was abruptly silent. There
were no cars or buses, and no children's voices from the school

across the street. Nothing moved except the fat white flakes drifting in from Normandy. A young doctor arrived and gave her an
injection and various powders and bitter lozenges that dissolved
on her tongue. He shook his head at the disarray of the room
and said she needed someone to clean. It was irresponsible to
live in such chaos. He would speak to the concierge, but mean-
while Madame had to take care of herself. Above all she should
stop smoking. Employ common sense, he said. She had been foolish to go out in the night rain with such rabble in the midst of an
epidemic that had brought all Europe to its knees.

An epidemic? she asked.

La grippe, he said. The Americans call it Romanian flu. But it
is no more Romanian than I am. Do the Americans have a complaint with Romania? Is it because of their Communism?

I'm dying, she said.

You'll survive, he said. You're rundown, that's obvious. But
you're healthy. The worst is past. You will have fever for a few
more days.

How bad is it? she asked.

He shrugged as if he didn't understand the question.

He said, You have flu like everyone else.

That's comforting, she said.

He stared at her a long moment, then pointed to the medicine.

Take these as prescribed, he said.

She nodded.

And don't drink, he added.

The doctor went away and she slept. When she woke she
discovered a thermos of rich fish soup, hot and delicious. She
dissolved the powders in a glass of mineral water, ate the soup,
and smoked a cigarette. She tried to read. She was reading about
the sculptor Rodin, his great fame and his many women, his
scandalous work. He was often denounced by his inferiors. At
the end of his life he had drawers full of plaster-of-Paris feet:
large feet, small feet, broad, thin, short, long feet, feet for any
occasion. Feet fit for Balzac. Feet fit for a Calais businessman or

a Chicago debutante. Friends and colleagues came to his atelier to admire the feet, astonished at the muscular lines. They looked alive, as if at any moment they would climb out of the drawer and walk out of the atelier and into rue de la Université. Sometimes Rodin gave them away as presents, in the manner of Picasso donating a doodle on a cocktail napkin. She read a page but could not concentrate and drifted off again.

The next morning there was another thermos and a bowl of fruit, the bitter lozenges next to the fruit. The room had been tidied. Georgia struggled to stay awake so that she could thank the concierge, who had brought the fruit and summoned the doctor. The woman had always been so cold and indifferent. Waiting for the concierge, she tried again to read about Rodin, his rudeness and egoism, his many quarrels with the French establishment, his appetite for young women. But again she was unable to focus and found herself driven back into her own memory. Concentration was still difficult. Thinking was like wandering in and out of badly lit rooms with no destination or design; often, the rooms were unfamiliar. For three nights she was in and out of consciousness. She could not let go of things. She was trying to account for her life before the entertainer's death and the adventure in the night rain with the mourners. It was difficult for her to separate what she was remembering and what she was dreaming. Her dreams and her memories fused and became one, and in that there was a kind of coherence. Think of them as a drawer full of tiny feet moving this way and that, here a dream and there a memory, tapping as a jazzman does at a piano and then becoming still altogether when, at the conclusion of the piece, the audience applauds.

The building on rue Blaise had a history.

A celebrated Impressionist died in it a hundred years before, apparently a suicide. This was the grisly story the concierge told, her eyes widening to judge whether Georgia was charmed or spooked. She was neither, since she didn't believe the story.

Your own flat, Madame. He died *right here.*

A noose around his neck, hanging from the water pipe.

No note, Madame. The Impressionists loved mysteries; this was well known.

There were initials carved above the window, E.M., and a date effaced by the years. You would never notice the initials unless you were seated at the window and looking closely. The gouges were deep, as if carved in a moment of high emotion, but there were many marks and notches, the normal wear and tear of a turbulent century. Sitting at the window, you could think of yourself as frightfully ordinary, not unique at all, only the latest of many tenants young enough to climb five flights of stairs and old enough to live alone. Experienced enough for high emotion, which led Georgia to the obvious question: Was E.M. the tenant or the lover? Tenant: The word in French is *locataire.* When she was sick she stared at the initials until they were branded on her brain.

From the window she could see a restaurant and an antique shop, a boutique selling underwear, and a *tabac* and a little park with her general's statue and the school next to the park. And on the corner, the Café Mercure. The street has its own slow rhythm, the busboy sweeping the restaurant stoop before dinner, the tourists window-shopping the antiques, the reclusive concierge walking her dog, the postman hurrying by on afternoon rounds. Many of them found their way to the Mercure at some point in the day, for a cold beer or corrected coffee. The sun made its transit, and except on the cloudiest days, Georgia could tell the hour within five minutes.

Her day: Rising slowly, she bathed quickly, drank a cup of Nescafé, poured a glass of Calvados, and went at once to her easel to wait, watching the street while she waited. Around her everything was within reach and in sight: the unmade bed along the wall, the wooden bureau next to the bed, a corduroy couch along the wall opposite, the bookcase next to the couch, the easel convenient at the window. She waited for dusk and then worked,

without interruption, except on Wednesdays, when at seven P.M.
her sister Marge called to see how she was doing, to see if she
was all right, to ask when she was coming home.

She says, I am home.

She began work when the light died and stopped when she
saw the first faint traces of dawn, a dirty sunrise, gray no matter
the weather. Of course her eyesight was blurred after the long
night at her easel. It was the morning light she was trying to
capture on the canvas, an atmosphere to match the general's dis-
consolate mood. At night she worked by the glow of the street-
lights, the reflection so sallow and gaunt that at times she could
barely see her subject or the paint on the canvas. Shadows flick-
ered on the ceiling overhead and on the walls, and it often
seemed to her that her little room was alive with spirits, perhaps
the Impressionist and his rowdy friends come to visit and share
a glass of Calvados. Perhaps E.M. or the object of E.M.'s desire.
Artists love to interfere with each other; it is what they do for a
living. So at night she painted by touch only, the long brush on
the canvas, the feel of the reins or the horse's mane or the saber
in its scabbard swinging and scraping against the saddle, and the
general's haunted gaze as he moved forward on his reconnaissance in the rising eastern light.

She broke for dinner an hour or so after midnight. She lit a
candle and heated something on the hotplate, opened a bottle of
wine, and turned on the radio, listening to news in a language
she could not understand. The only words she grasped were
proper nouns; the sentences themselves were atonal arias, dis-
sonance without content or form. Occasionally she heard what
she supposed was an obituary or market analysis or a small war
somewhere or the weather report. After dinner she turned off the
radio and turned on the television set and relaxed with a pornographic movie, usually French or Scandinavian, costume drama
or seaside mischief. She turned off the sound and watched the
women love each other, inexpertly she thought; she had many
memories, watching the pornographic films, and often she got
an idea from the angle of an arm or torso. The men were coarse

and loutish, the women lithe and merry. Georgia thought, No wonder they prefer each other. And she preferred drawing them, though whether it was the image on the television screen or the image in her memory that she transplanted to the canvas depended on the time of night and her own balance.

She drank two glasses of red wine and watched the movie, soft core, soft focus, soft-headed; but now and then there were wonderful arcs and angles. In the middle of the night her eyesight was cockeyed, her head thick, her thoughts ponderous as she replayed the mundane events of the day and awaited the day to come, all the while studying her portrait of the general on horseback. More than once she dozed off, or simply forgot where she was and awakened to a blank screen, her sketch pad in her lap. The spirits were all around her then, crowding so close that it was difficult to breathe — but what can you expect in a cold unlit room with a sputtering television set and Calvados followed by red wine followed by Calvados? It was difficult to return to work, but she believed she was most productive in the hours before dawn, her senses chaotic but her mind stretched and alert. Georgia was exhausted, yet was drawn to the canvas for whatever remained of the night. She wanted to use wisely what time she had. The memory of the old woman in Los Angeles was often with her.

She wrote to her sister — one of those letters which alarm the recipient, as they are surely meant to do, consciously or not — "I am never happy to see the dawn. I watch for it patiently, with appreciation, because I am painting it. But I am not eager to see it because it means my working day is ended. I make a desultory stroke here and there, and mix the paint again. The room fills with gray light and I know now that I must give it up and return to my nest like any nocturnal bird. I must cover the canvas, put away my tools, swallow aspirin, and prepare for bed. As morning light fills the room, I see that my general is taking form, though not the form I expected. I am not disappointed because the painting is acquiring a life of its own. An outsider cannot understand this, that a work of art is no different from a life. With each brush stroke, the choices narrow. Things are done that can't be undone; if you undo them, you have a different work, perhaps better, perhaps worse, but anyhow different. And the canvas remembers. You begin with a man, tallish, on horseback. He has a certain cast to his face, the sum of victories and defeats, some courage, some vainglory, some honor, some cowardice; and the art is knowing which is which. Of course as an artist you make mistakes that can be corrected — recovered, as a human being recovers from injury or emotional distress. But the scars remain. At the end of it the general is no longer himself, or the sculptor's, or mine. In a practical sense he is you — the witness — since he will be seen with your eyes, meaning your vision, imperfect and biased as it is bound to be. However, he *belongs* to me."

And finally, in a hand that wandered the page, in places barely legible: "Water rushes through the pipe in the hall. Somewhere in the building a door slams. I can hear voices, traffic in the street, an ambulance siren far away. I pull off my sweater and step out of my jeans, hanging them on the doorknob. I could be anywhere, except for the morning noises that are particular to my building and my street in Paris. Anticipating insomnia, I commence my bedtime rituals, beginning with my hair. I wear it short again, for convenience, but still I brush it fifty times, staring into the mirror. Then I take a final look out the window, say my prayers (the same ones our father taught us when we were children), and try to sleep. I do or I don't sleep. If I don't, I take a glass of Calvados — and, in a few moments, another. I love its bouquet, the flavor so light on my tongue, then the catch in my throat as the liquor works its way down, thickening, spreading itself throughout my body. My fingers fill up with it, my will wanders, and I am able to begin my American dialogues, imaginary conversations with absent friends. Before long I am in deep sleep, resting easily, surely smiling."

Georgia's postscript, not written but spoken to her absent friends: "This is not a life that most people would choose, yet I can imagine many that are much worse and people who are unhappier by far than I. Despite appearances I am not lonely. I am fatigued, but that is a natural condition. My work is demanding: grazing is not as effortless as it looks. I have resources enough for the way I live, which is after all my own choice. No one forced me. I have elected to live as a fugitive among strangers, remote from the life of my own nation, unconnected to the life of this one. I have my work and my reflections, my prayers, my American dialogues and my French time; and I believe that even God is lonely, and perhaps God most of all. I am trying to live without disorder so that I can discover my next step, when it will be and in what direction. It could be that I will remain where I am; there is no law against it and I am content here after my own fashion. In a manner of speaking, I am waiting for instructions. I am waiting for a convincing voice, either my own or another's. Just yesterday I read that in many mosques around the world the Imam has the use of a strong-voiced interpreter. The Imam speaks quietly from the maqsura, and the interpreter shouts his words to the congregation gathered in the courtyard. Sometimes this is only a version of the Imam's words. The devout call the interpreter the Exaggerator. Sins exaggerated, consequences exaggerated, forgiveness exaggerated. There is wit to this. I am in rue Blaise listening for the Imam's true voice, but I cannot hear him above the shouting of the Exaggerators. A common enough complaint; you hear it all the time. It is a plague of the modern world."

At last she met the man who lived down the hall.

She was curious about him because his hours were similar to her own. He was earlier to bed and earlier to rise but not by much. He came in around four in the morning and rose in the early afternoon, always careful to be quiet. She heard his radio turned very low, as no doubt he heard her moving about. Perhaps he heard the squeak of the cork of the Calvados bottle, or the shuffle of her sandals on the wooden floor. But he had no more true knowledge of her than she had of him, though the squeak of the cork would tell him something. As his deep cough told her something.

They never met, in the hall or anywhere else. Then one night she heard a light tap at her door, a tentative tap-tap that could easily be ignored. It was eight o'clock and he was dressed in a tuxedo. His hair was brushed straight back and combed to within an inch of its life. He was freshly shaved and smelling of cologne and his shoes were polished, the uniform of a man about town. The tuxedo was very worn, the cuffs frayed and the trousers shiny. However, the shirt and black tie were new, so it was easy to overlook the suit. He presented a neutral European appearance, the sort of man described as interesting-looking. His age was indeterminate, somewhere between forty and sixty, she thought.

He asked in English if he could borrow some coffee; he'd run out and had no time to go to the shop in rue de Seine. And he always liked a cup of coffee when he finished work; it relaxed him and helped him sleep. He apologized for disturbing her but he had seen the light under the door, and. She left him standing in the doorway while she fetched a jar of Nescafé.

He thanked her and said he would replace it the next day.

"Are you feeling better?" he said.

"Yes, much," she said and when he nodded sympathetically, the penny dropped. "So it was you."

"Me?"

"Who helped me up the stairs and got me into bed and called the doctor and brought the fish soup and otherwise saved my life."

"You were not yourself," he said.

"No kidding," she said. "But I thank you. I thank you very much."

"We were all worried," he said.

"You were?"

"The doctor thought it might be pneumonia. That night I saw you in rue Blaise, and I knew you were unwell."

"You were very kind."

"It was my pleasure to be of help. You're an American?"

"Yes," she said.

"And a painter," he added, nodding at the easel.

"An American painter," she agreed.

"Who paints at night," he said.

"Always," she said. "And in the dark."

He nodded as if this were unsurprising, a natural routine. Everyone knew that artists had erratic work habits. No need to explain them. They went with the temperament.

"And you work very late sometimes," he said.

"Usually. Why not?"

"And I, too," he said. "I enjoy it. It suits me. It's not so bad, working through the night, except you miss the morning. On the whole it's a good bargain. Mornings are overrated, don't you agree? I've seen you occasionally at your window, when the children are leaving school. When there's all that racket. We call it *l'heure de maman,* mother's hour. That's when I'm returning from my walk. I often take a long walk in the afternoon, to the Luxembourg Gardens if the weather is good. It clears my head. You should come with me sometime. A walk before dark. A walk before work."

"Sometime," she said.

"I'm going to work now," he said after a little pause. "I need the coffee because I have no time now and everything is closed when I finish up at three. I'm a musician at the jazz club around the corner. Maybe you've seen it? The little place, down the flight of stairs under the hotel. There's no sign in front; they want you to think it's a private club. They like to think they're exclusive, but anyone can go there. I'm the pianist. I play between the sets."

"Sets," she said.

"What?" He leaned forward, through the doorway.

"Between sets," she said. "That's the idiom."

He nodded, reaching into his pocket and handing her a card.

"Please," he said. "Come hear me sometime. Some night when you're not working or are tired of working. Some night when you're bored and want to listen to music. Come any time, but around midnight is best, things are most loose then. I admire your Fats Waller and many others." He said the card would entitle her to a free drink. A drink on the house. All this time he was looking at the easel, but because the room was dark he could not see it clearly. There was a traffic jam in rue Blaise, an ambulance's blue light reflected on the ceiling, and the sounds of horns all around.

"I wondered what you did," she said. "Because of your late hours, almost as late as mine. And when I saw the tuxedo — "

"You thought I was a maître d'."

"No," she said. "Not really."

"That's what they take me for, when they see me in the street on the way to work."

"Maybe they think you're going to a party."

"It could be," he said. "It's possible. It's barely possible," he said, shooting his cuffs and smiling. "I knew you were a painter because I saw you working once. From the street I saw the easel. You were staring out the window at the general's statue. You had the brush in your hand."

"My subject du jour," she said.

He said, "That one was a bad general. Perhaps he is a good subject. Soldiers are fools."

She said, "Like your Bonaparte?"

"Him worst of all," he said.

"They're not all fools," she said.

He laughed sourly. "Have you ever known one?"

"No," she admitted.

He raised his eyebrows and looked away, either abashed or amused, it was hard to tell which. He thanked her for the coffee.

He said, "It's good to meet you at last. I hope we will meet again soon. Perhaps we can share a meal."

Georgia smiled and moved to close the door, realizing then that she was still holding her brush and the glass of Calvados. He was looking at her fingernails. In the half light of the hallway her neighbor in his shabby tuxedo was suddenly reassuring, a companionable presence. They were the only two tenants on the fifth floor, not counting ghosts. He checked his wristwatch and began to move down the hall to the stairs. On impulse she asked if he wanted a drink.

"Before you play your gig," she said.

"I don't mind," he said.

"Are you sure? Perhaps another day — "

"I have time," he said.

He took a glass of red wine, holding it delicately by the stem, leaning carefully against the doorjamb, checking first to see that it was free of dust. The tuxedo was in terrible shape but he was being solicitous of it. The room was so littered, in such disarray, that the doorway was the most convenient place to drink.

She said, "I don't have much company."

"It's logical," he said. "You're working."

They stood in silence a moment. It was dark in the corridor except for a soft shaft of light that came from Georgia's window.

When he asked her what she was doing in Paris, she did not know what to say.

"Is it a sabbatical leave?"

"I suppose it is," she said. "Something like that."

"So many Americans come to France."

"It's because the French leave you alone."

"Most Americans think we're rude."

She smiled. "That's why it's better not to speak the language."

He smiled back. "Then you can't know anything of the country."

She said, "Precisely."

He nodded at that but did not reply.

She said, "Is it true about this building? That an Impressionist lived and died here a hundred years ago, a suicide?"

"The concierge thinks so," he said. "But the concierge also thought you were a German. She was positive about it. *Une boche,* she said."

"An unreliable concierge," Georgia said.

"It would seem so."

"I liked the story, though."

"Many find it morbid. That's why she tells it."

When she asked him if he had lived in the building a long

time, he said he had. The building was convenient to the jazz club. The concierge, though an unreliable historian, was a competent superintendent. The rent was reasonable. The plumbing was trustworthy. The heat worked in winter and in summer the rooms were cool because the walls were fifty centimeters thick and there was always a breeze on the fifth floor. The tenants kept to themselves, mostly. He shrugged, taking a cheroot from his inside pocket, rolling it between his fingers. In the darkness his appearance was sinister, but his voice was soft.

He said, "I'm sorry what I remarked about the soldiers, the generals. I didn't mean to upset you."

"I wasn't upset. It's a common enough opinion."

"Their foolishness?"

She nodded.

He said, "I pass the statue every day. It's plastered with pigeon shit."

She replied, "I can't see the pigeon shit from my window, the altitude. But there you go, ruining things. My fine general covered with pigeon shit. Your English is excellent."

"It's not so much," he said. "It's not as good as it was. I don't use it often. Sometimes I use it at the club when Americans buy me drinks so that I will play 'Your Feets Too Big' between the sets. And they're always disappointed when I tell them I don't sing. Singing's not in my repertoire. And it's the vocal that succeeds. Otherwise it's not much of a song. It's only a left-handed song and my left hand is not so good."

Somewhere on the fourth floor a door opened, discharging music and laughter. He had lit the cheroot and now the odor of tobacco mixed with his cologne. Georgia had never liked cologne on men, but his was mild enough and it seemed to suit him. He sighed suddenly, causing her to smile. His sigh reminded her of Richard Swallow when he was exasperated or impatient. She had been by herself for so long that she had forgotten how to conduct a conversation. Between her and the stranger there was a thick, not unpleasant distance and she realized then that she knew no musicians but had always thought of them as pleasant characters, amusing and irresponsible. Downstairs the door closed and the building was silent again.

He tapped his foot on the floor and said, "Italian girls and their boyfriends."

"Downstairs?"

"They work for one of the Italian designers."

"And the boyfriends?"

"The boyfriends are idle. Indolent as lice."

"Lice are industrious," she said.

"Are they? Idle as slugs, then."

She said, "My name is Georgia."

"Georgia," he said. "That's an American state."

"A very American state. But I wasn't named for it. I was named for my uncle George. My family calls me Georgie. I can't stand it."

He laughed. "That's the other song they like me to play, 'Sweet Georgia Brown.'"

"I don't like it either."

"It's better than the other one, though. At least you don't have to sing it."

"'Georgia on My Mind' is another one."

"My family picked my name out of the air. It isn't even French. It's a stupid name. I've hated it all my life. *Alfred.* It would've been so simple if they'd named me Jean, Jean-Claude, Jean-Marc, Jean-Louis. Any of the Jeans or Pierres or Henris. Sometimes it's troublesome. But you can't choose your name any more than you can choose your parents or your nationality or the tune they ask you to play." He looked at his watch and sighed again, draining his glass. He pushed off and stood in the darkness of the hallway, his hands in his jacket pockets. He said, "I must go to work now."

She said, "Good luck with the Americans."

"I have to be there at nine. They insist on it. I warm up the band, then the band plays its set, and I go on between the sets, and so forth and so on through the evening."

"It seems we both have our routines."

"Yes," he said. "It's disgusting."

"Why disgusting?"

"It's perverse," he said.

"It isn't perverse," she said. "It's only a routine. That's what life is, a routine. That's how we get along, day to day. Get up at one hour, go to bed at another hour. You take your walks, I watch the street. You play the piano, I paint. You see the pigeon shit, I see the general. You end your day with coffee, I end mind with Calvados. Begin it with Calvados, too."

He shook his head sadly.

She said, "Don't make more of it than it is."

"All perversity begins with routine," he said.

"According to who?" she asked.

"Sade," he said. "And Sade's right, for once."

She began to laugh.

"We should beware of it."

"I'll try," she said.

"It's not funny," he said. "It's bad business because once begun it's hard to end."

"That's right," she said. "Look what happened to Sade."

"That's what I mean," he said. "The pig."

"Alfred," she said, "I don't think he meant routine. He meant ritual."

"It's the same thing," he said. "It's absolutely the same thing. There's no difference between them at all."

"You're sure about this," she said.

"Completely."

"All right," she said.

"I'm glad you agree."

"To Be Continued," she said.

"Thank you for the coffee," Alfred said. "And for the wine," he added, handing her the glass. He had long pianist's fingers and seemed conscious of them. "I must go now and play 'Your Feets Too Big' for the Americans. Think about what I said. Try not to work so hard. The general will be there tomorrow and the day after tomorrow. And you must try to break your routine; it's healthier and more productive. Come tonight and have a drink on the house. There won't be too many people. The club will be quiet tonight."

"I'll try," she said. "Thanks for everything. Thanks for helping out when I was sick."

He put the jar of coffee in his jacket pocket and, with a dapper wave of his cheroot, was gone, his footsteps echoing on the stairs.

But she didn't go to the jazz club that night. She was unwilling to step outside her narrow boundary. She had no desire to do so, content as she was in the altitude of her fifth-floor world. She ceased to think of herself in any circumstance other than the here and now, except occasionally at dawn, when she thought about then. She lived as a recluse in Paris as she might have lived in any capital city, Ottawa or Lima or Cairo, except that Paris had become familiar and she liked it. It was familiar as the Sphinx was familiar from hundreds of photographs from childhood on, and then no longer a photograph but the real thing in front of your eyes, whole and alive though no less mysterious. And anyone would agree, yes, it's everything the photograph promised. But somehow it was the photograph that was the original. Years after the Spanish Civil War, Picasso encountered a German general who remarked that he had seen, and admired, "your Guernica." Guernica was yours, Picasso replied. But was it really?

So Paris was her Sphinx, its gaze as hollow and its haunches as worn. She meant no more to it than a grain of sand in the western desert meant to the great cat. She spoke the language carelessly and was indifferent to the city's politics, culture, and rates of exchange. She had never seen the Invalides at night nor strolled the Champs-Elysées nor lit a candle at Notre Dame. From time to time she visited the Musée d'Orsay, dressing up for the adventure. It was a way of touring Arles and Giverny, Barcelona and Berlin and Florence. She strolled through the Musée d'Orsay as a naturalist would wander in a forest; and when her eyes became tired, she left, taking the long route home, walking slowly along the river until she came to rue de Seine. Molière's house was there and, around the corner, an apartment that Richard Wagner had occupied during his disastrous voluntary exile from Riga. She learned these quaint facts courtesy of Alfred, who believed that a *locataire* had a special responsibility to know the neighborhood.

But Paris did not care. Paris made no demands, asked nothing, and gave nothing unless you made a specific request. She liked the idea of an indifferent universe outside her window, the random animation of the street and the general's statue always provocative in the little park next to the school. *L'heure de maman* began her day, children spilling from the school into the arms of their mothers. She enjoyed watching the tourists with their maps and green guide books and carrybags window-shopping the antique stores. And at night they vanished and rue Blaise could have been any anonymous bourgeois street away from the boulevards. Its night shadows were deep and suggestive. The rooftops swung away to the west, a crabbed and ragged mountain range where the Eiffel Tower glittered like an iron Matterhorn. She saw it from her window. She thought of herself as living in a quiet corner of an obscure museum of urban history. There were no guards, but the rules were strict and you were on your honor. You could look but you couldn't touch, and if you complained no one cared.

Alfred's sudden appearance altered her routine. Each evening at eight he stopped by in his tuxedo for a glass of wine. The doorway was a kind of frontier. They stood in it and talked, mostly about commonplace things like the weather and life in the quarter and the progress of his work and hers. He was assembling a new repertoire for his younger customers because this year they were far more numerous. It seemed to happen overnight. Of course the management was pleased; a younger crowd tended to be spendthrift; and music helped them along. Alfred said that every time he saw a death notice he thought, One less Fats Waller fan. Young people thought of Fats Waller as an antique and listened quietly to the first few bars out of respect, and then the hum of conversation began and grew louder until at the end he could hardly hear his own left hand. There were still requests for "Your Feets Too Big," but fewer each night and they were always from older Americans and occasionally Japanese, who were surprisingly knowledgeable and always polite and generous with tips, though they sometimes confused Fats with other, less talented, personalities. When they asked for "Frat Froot Froozie with a Froy Froy" it was hard to know what to do, and not to laugh when you did it.

Georgia's easel was always in darkness, so he could not see her progress with the general. But he remarked that it looked like more paint, each time he saw the gummy palette and the squeezed tubes that littered the floor. He had the idea that more paint on the canvas meant a more substantial picture, like more notes in a musical piece. Brubeck gave you more to chew on than Hoagy Carmichael. Bach gave you more than Albinoni, and Mahler gave you most of all. She said that was true enough, up to a point. It did seem that the general got more difficult each day.

As generals usually do, he said.

It was a companionable time for her when Alfred arrived, her own working day already well begun, his about to begin. She started to make an effort, tidying the room and combing her hair. It seemed the civilized thing to do. He was always well turned out in his tuxedo and polished shoes. In the darkness of the hallway she could forget about the shabbiness of the tuxedo, and when he lit his cheroot she imagined him on the deck of a yacht somewhere, the sound of a cocktail shaker in the saloon and music aft. When she told him that once, he snorted and said she was drinking too much Calvados, an observation that she could not disagree with but was not disposed to discuss, either. Still, she thought his dignified presence lent a decorous air to their eight o'clock rendezvous and as the weeks passed they came to depend on each other as neighbors do. He was happy to shop for her and she for him, on those infrequent occasions when she ventured into the street. Alfred seemed to have no friends in

Paris and no social life beyond his work at the club. He told Georgia that he was born in Saint Denis of a French father and a Russian mother, both gone. He thought he had a bit of the Gypsy in him, from his father's side. There was a sister living in Canada somewhere.

His mother died the day Leonid Brezhnev did, in 1982.

Alfred said, She was like a person from another civilization. Sumeria, Carthage, a civilization about which little is known.

He said, The news came that afternoon and I had time to hurry to the hospital to tell my mother. I knew it would ease her last hours. And indeed she smiled and gripped my hand and snarled something I did not understand completely, since it was in Russian. It was a proverb — is there any culture with more proverbs than Russian? — to the effect that when one oak dies the forest does not change. It would never change.

She was a White and lived in the past. She hated the Reds.

You could say she could not see the trees for the forest.

She was thrilled that Brezhnev was dead. She had enough strength to ask me how he died and when I said I didn't know, she said of course you don't, they never tell. It would have been poison or gunshot. Or, if natural, a heart attack or hardening of the arteries, a consequence of cannibalism, feeding off the flesh and blood of the people.

At that, Alfred began to laugh, shaking his head, tapping the ash from his cheroot into the big bronze ashtray. He said, She was from old Russia, Saint Petersburg. She claimed to be an aristocrat, Princess Something-or-other, and maybe she was. She was very beautiful, even as an old lady. She had beautiful manners. She loved to speak obscenely, but that had nothing to do with class; it was a Russian thing. She knew her time was finished forever but she continued to cherish the old days, as she called them. At Christmas she read from the Bible in Russian. My father loved her but was dubious about the blue blood. If she's a Russian princess, then I'm a Gypsy king, he said.

The last night she said to me, Tell me, darling. Do you think he suffered?

His body was aching and wracked with pain, I said, lying, because I had no idea what he died of.

I hope so, she said. Good. *Da.* I hope he died like Dzhugash-vili, choking on his own vomit, his stomach swollen with shit.

She claimed to know how Stalin died.

She claimed to know who killed him.

So that's my story, Alfred said.

Or *her* story. My story's another story altogether.

He was silent a few moments and then he said, "I'll bet you don't remember how Brezhnev died."

"No," she said.

"And you don't remember anything about him?"

She thought a moment. "Nixon liked him."

Alfred expressed surprise, smiling gamely.

He said, "My mother loved Nixon because Nixon hated the Reds almost as much as she did."

Georgia said, "He did at one time. Then one thing led to another and the times changed and he didn't hate them any-more."

"Nixon changed with the times?"

"That's what he did best."

"Thank God my mother never knew," Alfred said.

"So who killed Stalin?"

"My mother said it was the White Underground, aristocrats who had been hiding out since 1917. Her relatives, she said. Cousins, nieces, and nephews. One grand duke, a prince, several princesses. They ganged up on him in the Kremlin, cut off his nose. Eviscerated him. Castrated him. Gouged out his eyes. And if you objected that the corpse in the open casket was whole and intact, she would tell you that the corpse was a double, and that Stalin lies in an unmarked grave somewhere near Odessa."

"A bloody end," Georgia said.

"Not bloody enough for my mother."

Georgia learned much more about Alfred than Alfred learned about her until one night he asked if she had ever been married. The question was tactfully put. Alfred had been married once

and hadn't liked it and wondered how she had taken to the routine, the *ein-zwei* of domestic life. Wasn't it tedious?

No, she said. Not tedious.

How was it then? he asked.

Well, she said. Let's see.

At one point my hair fell out.

I took up ice dancing.

I joined a Marxist study group.

I began to paint in the dark.

And then the fun began.

All those things were true, though perhaps not in the order
given. But that was what she said and at the end of the dreary
inventory she gave a little laugh. She'd surprised herself and Alfred, too. He had not expected the *ein-zwei* he heard, probably
imagining tales of suburban cookouts and car pools and a television set in the family room and romantic hijinks, until something happened, which it obviously had because why else would
Georgia be in rue Blaise alone. Of course that was what he was
asking. What he wanted to know was, Why are you here? What
are you doing in France? What occurred that caused you to
journey across the ocean to live alone without friends or family
or any objective except to work on a portrait — if that was the
word — of a man on horseback, a statue seen from a fifth-floor
window? But Alfred was much too tactful and probably he suspected that she had no taste for the confessional. And theirs was
not that kind of friendship.

"And I wasn't married," she said. "All but."

He did not say anything, drawing on the cheroot and exhaling
a great cloud of smoke. "My wife and I never had children."

"You're lucky," she said. "The child would've grown up to
hate Fats Waller and then where would you be?" She smiled, but
he shook his head sadly and murmured that his wife did not want
children and nothing he could say would change her mind. Looking at him, Georgia felt bad that she had made a joke.

She said, "For a while I thought about children, and then I

didn't because I didn't see how I could accommodate one. And there were other problems."

He nodded and said, "And your — the man you were with?"

She said, "It was hard to know with Richard. Richard didn't always say what he meant. Most of the time, in fact. Richard used words the way gamblers use money. I think he liked the idea of a child more than the child. It's a common enough thing with men. And some women."

"Not with me," Alfred said.

"There are exceptions to the rule."

He said, "We lived in a very small apartment. It was in the suburbs, too small for three. That was her excuse. I tried to talk her out of it but she didn't want a solution. She wanted the excuse."

"Where does she live now?"

"Here," he said glumly. "She lives somewhere in Paris. I think she's married again. She hated my work, the nights away from home, the sexy atmosphere of the cabarets. I think she thought I'd run away with one of the dancers. She thought I was infatuated with the dancers. I worked in Pigalle and then in Montparnasse before coming to the club. That was six years ago and it's been a good place for me. The money is adequate and the hours are predictable."

"And were you?"

"Infatuated with the dancers? There was one I cared for but it never came to anything. It was meaningless."

There was a little silence and as if to fill it he made a gesture with his hand, a slow sliding motion such as a pilot might make to describe a descending aircraft. Alfred said, "I have no idea what brought you here."

"Air France," she said.

"You are a personable American. You are really a very beautiful woman. You seem — decent. Yet you leave this room only to go to the market, and occasionally to the Musée d'Orsay. You work all night long and sleep during the day. You are ruining

your health with Calvados. I don't understand what you are doing *here,* this place, with no association with the outside world
except me, the musician who lives down the hall, and if I had not
come to borrow coffee one night we might still be strangers. I
wish you were happier. You have a right to be. But one must
make an effort in order to complete a life." He paused and then
added, obscurely, "What's past is past."

Georgia's attention had wandered, as it always did when
someone lectured her. She did not respond well to lectures. She
concentrated on the doorknob and thought about Monsieur E.M.
and waited for Alfred to finish. And when he did, she raised her
eyebrows and let them fall, remaining silent.

He nodded as if he understood and then said lightly, "And
your hair fell out?"

"Not all of it," she said. "A lot, though. I wore a wig for a
while. And then it grew back, and I was able to give up the wig.
And just when I was getting used to it."

"Nerves," he said. "It's well known."

"I lost my nerve for a while," she admitted.

"I know what you mean," he said.

"No, you don't," she said quickly.

"I don't mean the specifics."

"*But I got it back,*" she said.

He made a conciliatory gesture. "When you took up ice dancing?"

"I knew a man once who skated to stay in shape. He was
such a shit. I was feeling pretty shitty myself, so I thought that
if it worked for him it might work for me, but it didn't so I turned
to Marx."

"I could never be a Marxist," he said.

"It's difficult, all that bogus science."

"Impossible," he said. "And my mother would have cursed
me. She would have laid a Russian curse on my head. Maybe it
would be a curse that would sentence me to play 'Your Feets
Too Big' for American tourists until it's Last Call."

He looked at his watch as he always did when it was a quarter to nine. He straightened his tie, patted his pockets, and lifted his shoulders, Bogart-style, gesturing with the cheroot. He shot his cuffs and winked, smiling rakishly; but the demonstration was tired. His shabby tux only added to the effect. Alfred gave a short bow and wished her a pleasant evening. Then he seemed to come to a decision of some kind, for he wheeled and spoke roughly, not to her but to the darkness of the hallway.

"Come to the club tonight, we'll have a late drink."

"Some other time."

"I'll play your favorites, after the Americans go. It's quiet then at the club."

"Not tonight."

"I wish you would change your mind."

"I'm working."

"We could have a late meal. My treat."

"I'm working."

He looked at her sideways and said, "Georgia? When does the fun begin?"

"You ask too many questions."

"I suppose I do," he said. "But where's the harm?"

"The harm is that I don't like answering them."

"All right," he said.

"You should know better."

"It's not good to keep so much to yourself," he said.

"I decide that."

"It's not normal," he said.

"I decide that, too."

"It's not normal," he repeated.

She threw back the last of her Calvados, furious now. Who did he think he was? What right had he to investigate her life? Alfred was another one who did not recognize boundaries. "The man I was with is — defunct." What a strange word to use, she thought. It had popped into her head, along with the source, the Cummings poem about Buffalo Bill. Defunct meant dead, which Richard was not, so far as she knew. But the word also meant having ceased to exist, which was very close to the mark.

Alfred looked at her with his mournful eyes.

"You should have known that," she said.

"Yes, of course."

"Or guessed it," she said.

"I'm sorry, I did not mean to upset you," he protested. Alfred had moved into the corridor and stood facing her, lifting his hands in a gesture of entreaty.

"Then you should keep your mouth shut," she said, and closed the door.

3

L'HEURE DE MAMAN — mother's hour — began around four in the afternoon on the sidewalk in front of the school across the street. The mothers were there to collect their children, and they were not alone. In fine weather the beggars from the little park on the corner came to solicit. I am hungry. I have no place to sleep. Madame, can you spare a franc? They were rarely successful, receiving only bored looks and minute shakes of the head, except for the red-haired woman who occasionally reached into her purse for a coin. Georgia wondered why. Was it the appeal of the man? Perhaps it was superstition. Perhaps the woman had cashed a lottery ticket, or she had heard a sad story that day and when the man approached she felt she should do something for someone so obviously down and out. The beggars were always polite so that she would not feel in any way menaced; and she was the only one who gave a sou.

Georgia worried about the inner lives of the women waiting patiently for their children. *L'heure de maman* seemed a lonely time for them, a kind of motionless parenthesis in the day. They were not convivial. They rarely spoke to one another, and Georgia naturally wondered if this was a normal thing or only a characteristic of these particular women. Worrying about them put her in a mood to think of her own work, her reconstruction of the man on horseback who towered above the women from his pedestal in the park. She wonders if it is fate, to be overseen by one who did not disclose his purposes, one whose face was hidden; and perhaps that is all it was, oversight. Not direction or supervision. Not judgment. Not anything sinister or even scrutable, but ubiquitous nonetheless, like the beggars soliciting francs, taking what was given and never far from view, always in the vicinity, watching.

The school is a blank-faced building of red brick and white limestone, four stories high. Rue Blaise is narrow and the sidewalk is very narrow, so that when the women arrive at mother's hour pedestrians must detour into the street in order to pass by. They don't like it, but the mothers see the sidewalk as their own territory, an extension of the school, which has the lifeless ambiance of a prison of the previous century, glum and dark and without effervescence. No child could feel comfortable in it, but perhaps that's the point. It would be logical, for elementary school is a serious and disciplined affair. In fact, the mothers have the resigned look of relatives of prison inmates waiting for visiting hour. The blank-faced building looks as if it should have bars on the windows and blue-suited armed guards, but of course it doesn't. It's just a school in the Sixth Arrondissement.

The red-haired woman, as Georgia watches her now, is staring vacantly up the street. The young mother in the blue sweater and jogging shoes consults her wristwatch with a look of impatience, glancing at the double doors, waiting for them to open and the children to spill forth. Several of the women are reading paperback books, as engrossed as if they were in the reading room of a library. Then they look up and dog-ear the page. They can hear the shrill voices of the children behind the doors. The women back away. There is little animation on the sidewalk, much less than at a theater during intermission. And there are a few fathers as well, solitary and conspicuous on the perimeter, ill at ease and almost furtive in the atmosphere of purposeful

women. Such a routine scene, a moment of the utmost common-
placeness, yet to Georgia, alone, an artist without a family, it
seems freighted with mystery and consequence. That is why she
takes care to observe closely, her eyes moving from the school
to the statue and back again. She does not neglect the beggars
collected around the pedestal. She tells herself that she is trying
to discover the connection among them, the effect of one upon
the others.

A few minutes after four the doors swing open and the children spill down the steps and onto the sidewalk, and then into
the street in a continuous lazy ooze. They move as if in slow
motion. Traffic halts. The children carry packs weighing ten
kilos, schoolbooks and notebooks and slide rules and compasses
for the evening's homework. The packs weigh them down — a
burden, as someone said, that stays with them their entire lives.
The youngest children move sluggishly to their mothers, a few
of the mothers sexy in tight sweaters and jeans and oversized ear-
rings, looking young enough to be older sisters. Perhaps a few
of them are, though when they reach down to caress a shoulder
or an arm and then kiss twice, both cheeks, it is with motherly
concern. The children are mostly subdued; it has been a long day
and they are hungry. And homework remains. Presently everyone begins to disperse, the fathers the first to go, leaving quickly,
leading their children by the hand, bending to hear the day's
news, juvenile entanglements, examinations passed or failed, who
has been disciplined and why, and of course the homework. The
impatient mother in the blue sweater and clumsy jogging shoes
move off slowly with her two children, who look like twins, boys
who evidently favor their father; and Georgia is reminded at
once of Marge's sons, her nephews, who are about the same age
but seem much less poised, more urgent, demanding, and nervous. What she means is less grown up, but "grown up" is not a
concept she associates with young children. Their mother looks
years younger than Marge, though Georgia estimates their ages
to be about the same. There is an avid lightness to her slow step,
what she takes to be a kind of pride in her children, so poised,

so like their father. Marge's sons favor her, and now Georgia wonders if along with her looks they took her energy as well.

She remembers that she has not written in weeks.

When Marge calls on the telephone, she speaks only of her own unhappy life. She is visiting a psychiatrist, who has uncovered very many strange and interesting conflicts in her childhood. Did you know that I saw you as a rival, Georgia? And that I hated it when our mother gave you my clothes, dresses, and sweaters? I've kept my anger inside but now I'm supposed to let it out —

And Georgia, bored to distraction, fills her glass with Calvados.

The beggars are passing around a wine bottle, and the general is now entirely in shadows, more or less benign, and unnoticed. In a few minutes there are only half a dozen mothers on the sidewalk, waiting for children who have been detained. Then the children appear and in seconds everyone is gone, the sidewalk vacant and the building quiet, traffic moving normally in rue Blaise. From one of the upper windows a young teacher stares into the middle distance, her eyes cloudy and unfocused, her palms flat against the windowpane. She yawns, and her eyes begin to close. She places her forehead against the cool glass, her eyes closing. What a long day it's been. I thought it would never end, but now I can go home. Something pleasant occurs to her and she begins to smile and then looks up, fumbling with something in her hand. The window shade falls like the curtain at the end of the play, and Georgia knows that it is time for her to return to her work, the business that keeps her on rue Blaise across from the school.

She begins cautiously and without imagination. The truth is, she continues to worry about her sister Marge. What a calamity it would be to commence psychiatry in early middle age, a time when your faculties should ideally be focused outward to the world. She was too old to be grubbing around in childhood's sandbox, sifting resentments, uncovering enemies and belatedly settling scores. And in Evanston no less. Evanston, the Vienna of suburban anxiety —

Georgia is feeling her way, trying to locate the center of her general, his balance and direction, his utter carelessness. Her angle of vision is lofty, almost Olympian, and that seems to be at odds with her Expressionist technique. From this angle of vision his features are obscure. But it is not his face she seeks; it is his physical balance, his density. He is a heavy man on horseback, bent at the waist, his head forward, elbows in. His saber is in its scabbard, establishing that the enemy is not at hand. His slender fingers grip the reins. Shadows are gathered around him as the sun dies. He is on the march alone, but alert to every nuance. From this height, above and ahead of him, it is impossible to know his precise objective, and indeed there may be none beyond an ambitious forward motion. Perhaps he is on reconnaissance, moving ahead of his troops; reconnaissance would be logical. But he is deeply concentrated, entertaining an unwelcome thought; there was a moment not long ago when he lost his nerve. And this was such a surprise; he had never lost it before. If it was gone for good, then he was ruined. That accounts for his bent waist and his downcast eyes. So Georgia goes at him from above, her fingers moving slowly, concerned now with the shadows and the shape of the unwelcome thought. Shadows reveal personality and the mystery of existence. With each long stroke her fingers sting, hurting, because the nails are bitten to the quick. Filthy habits are hard to break, and she has taken up biting again; she bites them in her sleep and when she is alone staring out the window, bites them absentmindedly, remembering that Freud had several explanations, of which the salient seemed to be "repressed infantile longings." But she had no infantile longings, repressed or otherwise, that she knew of. Of course, if they were repressed, she wouldn't know about them. Probably there was a therapy for it, heavy mittens perhaps, a digital chastity belt.

And so her work is laborious. But time is not the essence.

And then, two light taps at the door.

She held her breath, knowing it was Alfred, hoping he would go away. She did not want to leave her general, now that she had invaded his mind. But her own concentration was broken.

"Georgia?"

She opened the door and Alfred bowed forward in his tuxedo, handing her a dozen long-stemmed yellow roses wrapped in cellophane, bearing the mark of the expensive florist in rue de Seine.

"My peace offering," he said.

She looked at him and did not reply and did not accept his flowers, either. But naturally she smiled, and from a distant region in her mind she heard a dance band.

He said, "I saw you at the window watching the children."

She said, "I do that every day."

"And I thought you would like these," he said.

"It's thoughtful of you," she said. "You didn't have to."

"Put them in water," he said. "They'll spoil."

She took the flowers, the cellophane crackling in her hand. They were very pretty. Of course she had no vase, nor any glass deep enough to hold a dozen roses unless she amputated the stems. When she turned back to him, he handed her a ceramic vase; it was from his own apartment. She filled it with water and put the flowers on the bureau. They were out of place but welcome, a splash of color in her drab room.

She said, "Will you have a glass of wine?"

He said, "I would be pleased to."

"I've missed our evenings together."

"And I," he said.

She laughed then. "Do we deserve each other?"

"Perhaps we do," he said.

She opened a bottle of red wine and poured two glasses. "Our health," she said and they clinked glasses.

She covered the general with a swath of burlap and opened the window wide. It was still light outside, the days longer now in early summer. The evening was soft. She thought she could smell the river. As always, Alfred had lit a cheroot and was leaning against the doorjamb, sipping his wine. There was a companionable silence between them and Georgia was suddenly happy that he had come with his yellow roses. She had missed him and realized that she had been too harsh the last time. Alfred had meant no harm, was only inquisitive the way people are. He was alone as she was, and enjoyed their evenings together as much as she did; and it was Alfred after all who had picked her up on the stairs, taken her to her room, summoned the doctor, and brought the fish soup the week she was so sick she thought she was going to die. And he had asked nothing in return.

"It's been weeks," she said.

"Many weeks," he agreed.

She thought he looked thinner and not so dapper. He was certainly reticent, but that was no doubt his reaction to her words the last time. She said, "And what's been going on with you?"

"Not so much," he said.

"Have you a new repertoire?"

"My wife is suing me," he said abruptly.

"What for?"

"Her husband left her and she has no money."

"Shouldn't she sue him?"

"Him, too. She's suing us both."

She said, "Sounds bad."

Alfred took a sip of wine and did not reply.

She said, "Will she win?"

"She might," he said. "She has an excellent lawyer."

"And do you? Have an excellent lawyer?"

"I have no lawyer at all," he said.

"I don't think that's so smart," she said.

"I hate lawyers," he said. "They're villains. *Maître* this, *Maître* that. They're arrogant. And expensive."

"I suppose they are."

"And I don't want to have anything to do with her."

"Of course not. But —"

"It's a closed chapter."

"— if you have no representation, they'll have you for lunch."

"I beg your pardon?"

"You'll lose in the courts," she said.

He sighed heavily and looked at his shoes and when he saw they were scuffed he rubbed their toes against his ankles, first one and then the other. He looked like a man who expected the bailiffs any moment.

He said, "I'm thinking of going away."

"Going away? Going away where?"

"Dordogne," he said. "I have friends in Auvergne also. I could stay with them for a while and then go on to Dordogne. You can live cheaply there and no one cares who you are. It's very beautiful in Auvergne and wild in Dordogne. I could stay with friends or rent a little place. And if it was dangerous for me there I could go on to Italy or Spain. My papers are in order. It would be easy to drop from sight. What do you think of that?"

"It's never easy to drop from sight. But it can be done."

"Have you ever?"

"Not entirely," she said.

"I've done it before," he said defensively.

She said, "You've got to get one thing straight, though. You're not going away. You're running away. There's nothing wrong with that. Sometimes you have to do it. Sometimes it's the only thing left for you to do, when the cards are stacked. But that's what it is, Alfred."

"Call it what you want," he said.

"A lawyer could help you. The more villainous he is, the better. He's *your* villain, and the case against your wife would be strong. It's not as if there were children to be taken care of."

"There are certain support payments," he said.

"That you didn't make?"

"I did, for a while. I was careful about that, each month. And then I stopped. She was living with him; why shouldn't he support her?"

Georgia said nothing to that, and tried now to picture Alfred's ex-wife living in one of the government housing projects to the north and east of the city. They were glum and featureless places with architecture reminiscent of Poland. She assumed that the ex-wife's new husband had left her and she wanted out and Alfred was her ticket. Georgia knew nothing of French domestic law and whom it favored and suspected that Alfred knew as little as she did. But she could not imagine any breaks for women in La Belle France.

"Maybe a settlement," she said.

"It would ruin me."

"Not necessarily," she said. "If the settlement were fair — "

"Everything was fine for me here," he said. "This is where I have made my life. I have no desire to leave Paris. I enjoy working at the club. My apartment is livable and I have put money aside for retirement. I have never been extravagant. It is true that I have been thinking of living in the country. I mentioned it to you once. But I wanted to make my plans in my own time. One does not like to be forced. This suit seems to me unjust. I did not expect it and there is nothing I can do about it. I am a lamb to the slaughter. I must disappear. I must not become involved with French justice."

"Is it bad?"

"No worse than anywhere else. No better, either."

She looked at him closely, seeing something in his face that she had not seen before. She said, "It wouldn't be the first time, would it?"

"No," he said. "There was another time, a few years ago. It was only a small police matter, the usual confusion and incompetence. I was taken to the Conciergerie and questioned, but nothing happened."

"Was there a charge?"

Alfred thought a long moment, gently tapping his cheroot against the doorjamb. Then he sighed and said perhaps he had not been quite truthful, a moment ago.

"Perhaps my papers are not quite in order," he said.

"I thought you were a French citizen."

"There are different kinds of papers," he said obscurely.

"I see," she said, though she did not see at all. The concept of "papers" was foreign to her.

"It was a stupidity," he said. "I was not myself. I was daydreaming and went into a Métro station without considering the possibilities. And they were making identity checks. The Métro was Réaumur-Sébastopol and I knew better than to go there. It's worse even than Barbès-Rochechouart or Stalingrad. It's always best to enter or exit at the quiet, out-of-the-way stations like Saint Georges or Vavin or the fashionable ones like rue du Bac or Parc Monceau. Réaumur-Sébastopol is filled with Musselmens and other illegals, underworld characters, draft dodgers and homosexual people. Often they are selling drugs. Sometimes they are selling each other. It's disgusting. So the police make identity checks and I was caught up in one and taken to the Conciergerie for interrogation. They held me for hours."

"It sounds dreadful."

"You can't imagine," he said.

"You weren't harmed?"

"Fortunately," he said.

"And your papers — "

"I am an immigrant," he said finally. "My mother, as I told you, was Russian. My father? He always maintained he was French, given citizenship owing to heroism in the last war. But the details of the heroism, and the citizenship, were vague. My father had many stories, but I don't know which ones are true. My father had numerous stories about who he was and where he came from. The stories varied according to the listener. Sometimes they were harangues. What is it anyway but an accident of geography, who you are and where you come from? You would not think that God would care, although all the evidence is to the contrary. But I should not mention God. God has nothing to do with it. It is, as you say, a police matter."

Georgia asked, "Your father was an illegal?" She was trying to get things straight in her own mind.

Alfred moved his shoulders this way and that and took a long draw on the cheroot. He said, "Not in his own opinion. I think he was like an actor. A Catholic one day, a Jew the next. Tomorrow a Greek, yesterday an Egyptian. Once I heard him swear that he was a Hungarian born in Transylvania. Hungarians are everywhere in Europe, and if he was a Hungarian born in Transylvania his nationality could be either Romanian or Hungarian, depending on his date of birth. I heard him say once that he was of mixed German and Hungarian ancestry, but that his great-grandmother was Turkish. Born in Macedonia. And if he was, as he once claimed, a Gypsy, then that would be another matter altogether. An interesting man, my father, a great storyteller. He left me much. But he did not leave me a passport."

Alfred took a small sip of wine, then moved his hand as if to say, So what?

"My father had a great feel for the land, whichever land he was from that day. When he talked of the land, it was almost as if he were describing flesh, its contours, the way it smiled or frowned, its illnesses and delights, its neuroses, and the blood beneath the flesh, and the bones swimming in blood. You know the face of the land as intimately as you know the face of your brother."

She said nothing to that.

"Of course he hated France."

"He did?"

"He did not think it *gemütlich*."

"He didn't?"

"He preferred the East. He thought French people too serious."

She said, "What did he do? Did he work?"

"He said he drove a taxi."

"And did he really?"

"I don't know. That's what he said. But it's doubtful, because he hated capitalism."

"But he had money," she said.

"Oh, yes," Alfred said. "My father always had plenty of money. To my father, capitalism was one thing, money another thing. You needed money to fight the capitalists. My mother often challenged him on this point but he said she was not qualified to speak because she was a Russian and Russians knew nothing of money because the ruble was worthless. It's an unreliable currency, unconvertible."

Georgia was barely able to keep a straight face during all of this, and now poured more wine into her glass; Alfred covered his with his hand.

"So," he said, smiling again. "What are you thinking? I suppose my father is not very much like your father."

"No," she said. "Not very much."

"And Europe not much like your America. Have you been to California? I've thought about California often but I never considered going there."

"Someday you'll get there."

"Never," he said. "It's too late. I wouldn't know what to do there now. And in any case it would not be possible without a passport."

"You could apply — "

Alfred shook his head, raising his eyebrows in dismay. He said, "But don't you think California should be a place where you didn't need a passport? Just show up at the door and they let you in? Isn't it that kind of place?"

"Yes," she said. "But the problem isn't getting in. It's getting out."

"That's the trouble here, too," he said.

He turned away, sighing again, looking at his wine. He had hardly touched it. They stood in silence. He looked so disheartened, and she could think of nothing encouraging to say to him. The way he described his situation, it was a dead end; and nothing in her experience was any help. He seemed to be in a no man's land, in some profound sense — unauthorized. Georgia could imagine nothing worse than being caught in the French legal system or any legal system. Alfred was certainly not equipped for it, he whose papers were "not quite in order." He who avoided certain stops on the Métro. She wondered if his papers were forged or stolen. Probably they had been purchased and could not withstand scrutiny. And if he were deported, where would he go? Where would they deport him to? Who would have him? Who would have need of an aging jazz musician, in a threadbare tuxedo, whose left hand was not quite perfect?

"You must think all this very foolish," he said. "But what can I do?"

"You have to fight them," she said.

"Oh, no," he said, beginning to laugh. He threw his head back and laughed at the ceiling. "No, it's impossible. Whatever you do, you must never do that. You have to be serious with them. You have to make them explain everything. But never fight them unless you are interested in a *beau geste* or making a political point of some kind. And that is why I will never step into court with them."

She did not reply to that.

"You're very kind," he said. "I have not told anyone of my troubles, because you never know where that will lead. You never know what people want or what they're willing to sell. It's only a question of disappearing for a while. The authorities have many things to worry about, and dossiers do get lost."

"I want to help," she said, "but I don't know what I can do in this situation. Alfred, do you need money?"

He drew back, offended.

"I'm very sorry," she said. "Do you have friends here? Perhaps friends could help."

"I have a few friends, but they are not in a position to help me. They would not want to become involved."

"It was a silly question," she said.

"I'm sorry," he said.

She said, "Don't be ridiculous."

"It's a bore. I shouldn't have involved you in it. I've been stupid. But perhaps — she'll forget about it. She was never an attentive woman. You have a word for it in English. She's a squanderbrain."

"Scatterbrain," Georgia said.

"She could never stick to anything. Here today, gone tomorrow. She was never good with details, to take a thing and go with it to the end. Do you see what I mean?"

"I suppose I do."

"So she might just forget about it," he said.

"I wouldn't count on that, Alfred."

"You wouldn't?"

"No," she said.

"Well, you don't know her."

"That's true."

"You never saw her trying to work a crossword puzzle and if she didn't have it well started in five minutes, she'd throw it away. She threw them all away, the apartment was littered with them. She was terrible with crosswords because she was such a scatterbrain."

"Was she good with the checkbook?"

"Excellent," Alfred said. "She was good with numbers. Very attentive. And she was a materialist."

"Well, then, Alfred." Georgia paused, struggling, "if she was a materialist and cared for the checkbook — "

"I see what you mean," he said slowly. And then he added, "She has nothing to do all day long except start crossword puzzles and think about the lawsuit. That's all she does, and she's welcome to it. She's a very disagreeable person, Georgia. Even her name. Dido."

Dido? Georgia was looking at the floor because she was having such difficulty suppressing her laughter. Alfred was such a — loser. He would never fight for anything because he believed he could never win, that the deck was always stacked and the odds favored the house and he was unlucky in any case, and what could be gained would never be as valuable as what would surely be lost. Alfred had no idea how the world worked and how you had to struggle to achieve anything in it, and how you had no guide except your own good intentions and whatever God you believed in, if you were a believer. Alfred did not understand that nothing was written. And then she wondered whether he understood all too well, saw the formidable force arrayed against him and decided to keep at all costs what mattered to him most, whatever that was, his Fats, his tuxedo, his memory, his privacy, and his unauthorized way of life. He did not choose to fight because to fight would be to expose himself, and he had too much to lose. Perhaps he was a man who would always live between the sets, playing what people paid to hear, and listening to his own tune. Georgia looked at the yellow roses in the plain ceramic vase, and then at Alfred smiling his grave, distracted smile. And something caught in her throat. He was so very gallant.

"Alfred," she said. "Don't lose your nerve."

He sighed heavily, slumping suddenly, and the wine spilled. A few drops fell on his white shirt. He looked at the spots as if they represented the final wounds of a long, bruising, losing campaign.

He said, "*Merde.*"

Georgia touched his arm and said lightly, "The end of a perfect day."

"But it isn't the end," he said. "I have to play tonight."

She said softly, "I know. It was a joke. I think if you button your coat, the spots won't show. Try it."

He looked at her doubtfully and buttoned the coat.

"See? It'll be fine. No one can see anything. Can you play Fats Waller with your coat buttoned?"

"I never have," he said.

"It'll be a new thing for you then, something unusual when you're playing between the sets."

He looked at her sadly and said again, "I'm sorry."

"You have nothing to be sorry for."

"I'm burdening you. You have troubles of your own. I only wanted to bring you the flowers, as a peace offering, and instead I'm telling you the story of my life. There's nothing that can be done about it anyway."

She said, "Stay awhile. Have some more wine." When she moved to pour wine into his glass he covered it again with the palm of his hand, shaking his head emphatically and saying that he had to go to the club. It was almost time for the set to begin and he liked to be there early, to inspect the crowd, the mix of tourists, Japanese and American, in order to prepare the repertoire.

"I'd like to," he said. "But it's impossible."

"Then later, when you're finished."

"But you'll be working, and you won't want to be disturbed."

"I won't mind."

"If you're sure."

"Of course," she said.

"It'll be late. But I'll come."

"I'd like that," she said. "I'll be waiting."

"I'll bring something from the club."

"No need," she said. "And Alfred? Thank you for the flowers. They're lovely."

And then he smiled, put the wine glass just so on the bureau, straightened his tie, shot his cuffs, bowed, wagged the cheroot, and was gone. When she closed the door she could still hear his footsteps on the stairs, and when she went to the window she saw him emerge into rue Blaise. He unbuttoned his coat from habit. The night was so warm. From above he did not look shabby; he looked like the worldly maître d' of one of the better restaurants in Boulevard St.-Germain. One of the street musicians was playing Schubert on the steps of the school, and when Alfred went by he dropped a coin into the musician's hat and was rewarded by a dip of the violin. Alfred strode on, the skirts of his coat flaring. It was almost dark.

She watched him advance up the street, thinking what a nice man he was, and how droll, perhaps not always intentionally. She had thought when he first started to speak that he looked defeated, one of the condemned waiting patiently on the gallows for the hangman to fit the noose, all appeals exhausted. But he wasn't defeated; he was only on the run. He was trying to find a secure niche from which to combat the forces arrayed against him. They were powerful forces, much more powerful than he was, and there was no question of his prevailing over them. Men like Alfred did not prevail, unless you considered evasion a victory. She thought of him now at his club, settling in, checking the wine spots on his shirt as he prepared the evening's program, playing the blues while worrying about the forces arrayed against him. The stakes were high; and surely it was conceivable that if he slipped away to Auvergne or Dordogne his tormentor would forget about him, throwing away her lawsuit as she threw away crossword puzzles, and he might fall between the cracks. This was easy to do in North America, where the authorities were not vigilant and it was a casual matter to move from place to place. The more obscure you were, the easier it was. In Europe, the situation was reversed. But Georgia liked the idea of a gallant neighbor whose papers were not quite in order, and decided to do something for Alfred.

She stood at the window in the darkness for some time. The violinist was still playing Schubert, a greatly deliberative and furry adagio that put her in mind of poor Liebermann, the narcissist that would lie for hours in front of a mirror, waking occasionally to check her appearance. She was a barn cat, formal and dapper as a tuxedo; she had a flash of white at her throat. Remembering Liebermann, Georgia felt her eyes fill. Liebermann's final days were undignified. At age seventeen she went dumb and then she went blind. It was obvious she was blind, because, checking herself in the mirror, she would have her back to the glass. Apparently she was running on instinct. This was terrible to watch, her eyes clouding to the color of steel. Her appetite failed. She moved head down in a kind of crawl, using her whiskers as antennae. But still she banged into table legs and the wall next to the door. She scratched feebly to be let out and then, once out, she lost her way. She slept in the petunias like an exhausted Sphinx, tail twitching in the sunlight. Georgia took to carrying her from place to place, the water dish to the davenport and back. At night she slept in Georgia's bed. She no longer went outside and was reluctant to use the litter box. Richard Swallow suggested that she be put down, an act of mercy that Georgia described as murder and would have nothing to do with. Liebermann retained her sweet grave nature to the end, and seemed apologetic for the trouble she caused the household. Ever proud, she began to withdraw. She was no longer interested in her mirrored self-portrait and wished only to get by from day to day, each hour a gift. Needless to say, in his self-possession and droll fatalism, his reticence and modesty and courtesy and pride, Alfred reminded Georgia of Liebermann. Of course she was a cool cat, but affectionate in her own way.

She listened to the thick Schubert adagio. When she looked up she could see the unmistakable crabbed rooftops of Paris and on the horizon the summit of the Eiffel Tower beyond the curve of the river, lights glittering on the water. Her turn-of-the-century predecessor would have seen the same spectacle from the window; and when he looked into the street, as she did now, he would have seen nothing distinctive except the general on horseback. He could have been anywhere, even the North Side of Chicago. Shadows slanted this way and that. She could not locate the musician in the gathering darkness. He was playing by ear, and she wondered now what had brought him to rue Blaise, where there were so few nighttime passersby, and no tourists to give him a franc. And then she concluded that he was playing Schubert for himself alone, in the spirit of one who says a silent prayer. In such a circumstance an audience is always a distraction, the audience believing that the work is theirs and the artist knowing that it isn't. Perhaps that was the difference between an artist and an entertainer. She wondered how many in rue Blaise were listening to Schubert in the humid darkness, grateful for the concert, preparing applause.

The invisible musician brought her back to the task at hand. She closed her eyes, trying to summon her concentration for the work ahead. It was necessary for her to become impersonal, to banish any concerns beyond the canvas, thinking of it as the perimeter of the known world. She lost track of everything but her eyes and hands and the canvas, bringing herself to it by stages, thinking about Liebermann motionless on the davenport, Alfred at his club, and the musician alone in the darkness as she was, unencumbered by audience. Focusing on the canvas, she found it hard to remember the false starts and mistakes, and the occasional bursts of pure joy. You were indistinguishable from the thing you had made, always less than you believed it could be, and a miracle that it existed at all. No wonder Liebermann had sat with her back to the mirror.

The violinist allowed his final note to hang. He stepped from the shadows and took a quick look around. Then he packed his instrument and sauntered off in the direction of Boulevard St.-Germain. She watched a man drift into the park, relieve himself, and move on. He walked with a sailor's rolling gait, and she realized he was drunk. She turned away from the window and removed the burlap from her canvas. Everything was as she remembered it. She took brush in hand and stood looking at her picture, thinking that if she looked hard enough it would spring to life and speak to her, perhaps drunkenly like the sailor, perhaps sadly like Alfred, or perhaps — most likely — in a tongue she did not understand and would have to decipher, crack like any code.

Touching the canvas was like touching a human being. The canvas seemed to move from side to side as she applied the paint, composing her general but remembering Alfred's face, long and thin, his dark hair slicked back in a widow's peak, eyebrows that swung up like hinges, dark Slavic eyes that seemed greatly aged. He was beginning to speak and without taking her eyes off him she poured a tot of Calvados to take the edge off the chill. Alfred was present in his tux and scuffed shoes, smiling his shy smile, beginning to speak. And then he dissolved, leaving her with her general, and her general's weight, and the canvas.

She finished when her eyesight began to fail and her concentration to liquefy. It was three in the morning. She covered the canvas, cleaned her brushes, brushed her hair, put on a fresh shirt, and poured a glass of Calvados. Without being conscious of it, she had turned on one light; now she turned it off, noticing at once how quiet rue Blaise was, the night air dry and balmy, smelling of smoke and the river. She sat in the dark at the open window, looking into the street, waiting for Alfred. She closed her eyes, her mind wandering, winding down. She had worked hard and was warmed by the effort, and the time had flown, as it does generally when you devote your whole heart to the task at hand.

Her skin was hot and the Calvados cool and sharp as she sipped it. She felt it working into her, softening her resolve; she was wondering whether Alfred would like the picture, and whether she was being foolish. At three in the morning she thought of herself as a scientist in a laboratory, practicing a kind of alchemy, transforming the base metals into gold. And when you brought the goods out of the lab it was always a disappointment, because the energy that created them was left behind. No one but you could ever fully possess it, but this was a thought you kept to yourself.

Commercial realities. Once in California a woman bought a self-portrait, paying too much for it, but thrilled because of what it represented to her, a political statement of feminist determination and grit. This was one of two Georgia had painted after Smid had bought the famous six, and grit did not figure in its message. She knew that the woman had brought too much of herself to the canvas and was going home with a false friend, one she would learn to hate or become a rival to; and then she would feel betrayed and later she would take the picture down and put it in the basement, unless of course it had become valuable in the meantime, in which case she would look on it as an investment that had paid off. She would tell herself that she was a connoisseur after all, and possibly could make a living with her shrewd eye. What she had seen in the picture was an idealized image of herself, when actually it was Georgia at a moment of defeat. She would not understand this until she had lived with the picture, and then she would know that she was the pacifist who had bought stock in a napalm company.

You could do nothing about any of this. When you put a picture up for sale, it was available to anyone who wanted it.

The buyer was not obliged to take an examination to see if she was worthy of it or understood what she was buying. Love did not come into it. Ambition did. The picture was hers and she had a right to see what she wanted to see, to furnish it with her own dreams or nightmares as she would furnish a bedroom. But this was always a disappointment because of the energy left behind and because a part of your own soul was in the paint. To misunderstand the picture was to misunderstand humanity, and while that was the normal course of things generally, you did not have to like it. You did not have to value it. When Georgia told the woman that she was buying napalm, she was offended, naturally.

Fuck you, she said.

Fuck you, asshole, she added.

So I was not wrong, Georgia thought.

Carole Fox explained it all. Georgia was bothering about matters that were better left to professionals. She had to understand that her job was not finished when the picture was. In a profound sense, her job was just beginning. The picture was but an expression of a personality and the buyer of a picture bought the personality of the artist as well. This was obvious, as the careers of Warhol and Picasso attested. The personality had to be as carefully drawn as the canvas. What if Warhol had been a Republican, a frequent guest of Nixon and Rebozo at Key Biscayne? What if Milhous had hung Jackie and the Campbell soup can in the Cabinet Room and offered the artist the Presidential Medal of Freedom? Andy'd be a joke. They'd call him an illustrator and rank him somewhere between Norman Rockwell and James Montgomery Flagg. This was the unwritten contract: the customer looked at the picture and saw a personality, and more often than not it was the personality that counted; the more exposure you had, the better off you were. And the customer was always right. You gave the customer what she wanted, the moment you figured out what it was. And then you fitted her for the picture the way Coco Chanel fitted a silk suit. It was very important to fashion a specific personality, even an elusive one — but if you chose to be elusive, you had better be alluringly elusive, the sort of sly, kicky personality that would fit easily into the pages of a glossy magazine. Or you'd better be a master, Georgia. You'd better be Jan Vermeer. You'd better be a whole lot better than you are now, honey.

You have to cooperate, she said.

Relax and enjoy it.

Market forces are moving your way.

Exercise leadership, Carole Fox said. You are on the threshold of *fantastic success.* So we'll want to do a retrospective real soon, before they forget who you are and what you do. Before they forget your signature, the way you move and what you look like and stand for, up close and personal. And what you're doing, on the canvas and in your own life. They want to know *you,* honey. They want to know your personality and you owe it to yourself to give it to them, any version you like so long as it's alluring, 'cause they're indispensable. They're the *consumers,* Georgia.

They were, too. Everything in sight.

She poured another glass of Calvados and thought how much she envied Alfred, his composure and his focus, his paranoia, which gave a shape to things. He was a professional and worked within that perimeter, observing life in his own way, trying to compensate for his poor left hand. She imagined him playing his finale, rising from the piano, closing its lid, and unbuttoning his coat now that the customers were gone. He said good night to the maître d', refusing the offer of a nightcap. The band had already dispersed; there was only Alfred, the maître d', and the bartender and the busboy cleaning up. The maître d' tried to insist, but Alfred refused.

Thank you, no. Some other time.

I have a late date. My neighbor in rue Blaise.

A painter, a night owl.

An American night owl.

Then he would check to see that his papers were still in the inside pocket of his jacket, say good night again, step outside, and pause a moment to look up and down the street. He would take two deep breaths because the air inside the club was foul. And then he would move off, keeping to the shadows, walking softly, smelling the wood smoke and the river. He would remain alert. Alfred would be cautious, because for him the streets were unpredictable. Each street was a border crossing. He would be careful and if he encountered the police he would step up to them and ask directions frankly — perhaps to the Café de Flore or the taxi rank at the rue du Bac. He wanted a glass of Champagne to cut the chill. He would be companionable, exceedingly polite — and if they asked him for his papers he would hand them over casually, still talking in a low, polite voice, and standing confidently in his tuxedo, buttoned again to conceal the wine stains. How heartening that the authorities were on patrol, mindful of the safety of ordinary citizens.

You couldn't be too careful late at night.

Actually, monsieurs.

I have an assignation.

A woman who is often — occupied.

But mercifully free tonight until (consulting his wristwatch) only an hour from now!

And then he would stride off again, feeling the sweat on his backbone, breathing easier. In his mind he would hear a tune and presently he would begin to hum, something from Fats Waller or Franz Schubert, a bluesy tune to keep him company as he hurried down Boulevard St.-Germain, past the Deux Magots and the Flore, the church on the corner, turning left now at rue Bonaparte, the street so silent and empty, only a few blocks now, and all this time he would be thinking of Dordogne or Auvergne, a place to fall between the cracks, eluding the heavy arm of the past while he considered the future. Or perhaps not. Perhaps he would be thinking not of the French future but of the American present.

It was pleasant sitting in the open window, smoking a cigarette, sipping Calvados, waiting for Alfred. And when he finally arrived he apologized for being so late, only minutes after he left the club he encountered two policemen, both very young, boys almost, but rough and suspicious. It was advisable to speak politely to them. In the event, they did not ask for papers; they noticed the tuxedo. When he told them he was a musician, they wanted to know what music he played. Then they told him bawdy jokes. Still, it had been a nervous few minutes.

Alfred took a glass of Calvados and said that the crowd at the club had been tame and unresponsive, though a drunken middle-aged American had tapped his foot to the music and put down a good tip. And you? he said. How have you passed your evening? She said her work had gone very well but that she missed him, and was happy he had come even though it was late. He said, Why are you sitting in the dark? She replied, I like the glow of Paris at night and you can see it better in the dark, the lights on the street and so forth. She said, I watched you come up the street and wondered if you would go on, or come in and go to your own room, leaving me here alone. I imagined that your evening had been frustrating. I predicted the encounter with the police — as you said, a nervous few minutes.

"You should have told them you had an assignation," she said.

Alfred smiled and kissed her.

"No," he said. "I came straight here."

"You didn't have a nightcap at the club with the boss?"

"He would never offer me a drink," Alfred said.

"And if he had?"

"He wouldn't."

"Should I turn on the radio? Would you like to listen to music?"

"No," Alfred said.

"Maybe I could find some Schubert. Would you like that?"

"No Schubert," he said.

"I thought you liked Schubert. I saw you give money to the musician — "

"Not at three in the morning," he said. "Not when I'm in a good mood."

They sat in silence a few moments, and then Alfred confided that there had been a strange table of three men. Perhaps tourists, perhaps not. Likely not; they were dressed in dark suits and carried leather briefcases. They looked familiar; one of them reminded him of his father, being short and swarthy, surely of Slavic ancestry. The men talked very little but drank steadily, regular as metronomes. They were unnerving. They seemed to be interested in me, Alfred said. They were staring at me the whole time.

"Of course they were," Georgia said.

"Why should they?"

"You were the talent. You were the entertainment, playing the piano between the sets. That was why they were there. People normally watch the talent they pay to see."

"Are you sure?"

"Certainly," she said. "They're listening to Fats Waller but they're looking at you. One buys them the other."

"I'm worrying for no reason?"

"No reason at all," she said.

Alfred kissed her again. He began to tell her some of the bawdy stories, struggling to translate them into American idiom. Often the stories depended on puns, so he had to explain them. She thought the stories were stupid but goodhearted and his explanations hilarious. There were two or three cuckold stories, antiques that could have come from *Cousin Pons* or *Lost Illusions*. The cuckolds were always credulous, ridiculous figures. There was one story about the wand of God that seemed untranslatable, and another one about an Englishman and a unicorn. All the stories had humorous endings, slanting toward mild paranoia, the source of all humor, modern and ancient. Many of them had to do with encounters among European nationalities, French and English and Germans and Russians. Attitudes of women, attitudes of men, and the sexual glue that held them together. Georgia tried to remember American jokes with a paranoid slant but could not. She had heard somewhere that most American jokes came from Wall Street, a place she had never been; and when she told that to Alfred he laughed and said it was logical, most bawdy French jokes came from the Garden of Eden, a place they had never been either. He went on and on, the stories funny and baffling at the same time. She had the feeling he was making them up on the spot.

They undressed and slipped into bed. He took her hands in his. The sheets were crisp and stiff and Alfred's skin cold to the touch. The window was still open to the mild Paris night. Somewhere in St.-Germain-des-Prés they heard the bleat of an ambulance, and then a car idling in rue Blaise. The river barges were beginning to move and the city to waken generally. The city and the river worked to a cycle different from theirs. The dawn was not far off now. Georgia could see Alfred's slender face and smell the Calvados on his breath. She closed her eyes and when she opened them he was looking at her with an expression so grave and tender that her breath caught. She looked ahead and saw no misfortune. His eyes shone in the gray light. He was subtle and without urgency, and in that spirit she cast all doubts aside.

They were happily bound together until dawn. Just before he slept he laughed quietly and said something in a language she did not understand, so she asked him to repeat it in English, every word.

He said, So beautiful, my American night owl. Worried about a future that doesn't deserve worry. So beautiful and so badly cared for.

And then he laughed.

Why do you bite your nails when I could bite them for you?

Laughing again: You don't have to worry about my nerve.

4

THE EARLY SPRING was very cold and wet but May was
warm as midsummer and dry. There was drought in western Europe generally. The days lengthened, the schoolchildren were dismissed for their summer vacation, and tourists
appeared. Street musicians arrived in the general's park to play
for the tourists, mostly Japanese and Italian with an American
here and there. There were never very many tourists but the
venue was agreeable. There were accordionists and organ grind-
ers along with the young violinist who played Schubert. The
most accomplished musicians were two middle-aged Frenchmen
who arrived in a wrinkled Citroën van with an upright piano and
a soprano saxophone. They played the Sidney Bechet songbook,
swinging wildly through "Petit Fleur" and "Bye-Bye Blackbird"
and "Baby Won't You Please Come Home." The saxophonist
must have had a lip of iron because he could play nonstop for
an hour, gathering an appreciative crowd, neighborhood people
along with the tourists. Occasionally Georgia would see Alfred
in the vicinity listening to the pianist; he would look up to her
window, wave, and blow her a kiss. One afternoon the unreli-

able concierge saw the pantomime, her eyes widening before she frowned; a story to be retailed up and down the street.

Some stayed for the whole hour, paying for the privilege, dropping coins and an occasional bill into the saxophonist's black beret, which rested on the sidewalk next to the piano. When the Frenchmen moved on, they had a beretful of money along with the applause and cries of "Bravo!" and "Yeah!" Georgia heard later that they played various locations around the city, the plaza of the Musée d'Orsay, the rue de Rivoli across from the Louvre, and Boulevard St.-Germain near the church. They were excellent musicians and could have made a living but preferred the ambiance of the street, apparently a political statement of some kind.

When she heard them in the park she would stop work and lean out the window and listen, the jazz so blue and familiar because Bechet was a great favorite of her father's. Tears jumped to her eyes and her feet moved in rhythm with the music, her mind flooding with memories from childhood and adolescence. Her father listened to Sidney Bechet on Sunday afternoons while he read the *Tribune*. "Petit Fleur" seemed to Georgia as stately and formal as sacred music. Of course it was Bechet's signature piece, and the Frenchmen played it beautifully, each taking a long solo before ending ensemble. Her father claimed that the essence of the blues was its emotional contradiction. The blues broke your heart and lifted your spirits simultaneously and when Georgia replied yes, that was a characteristic of great music generally, Bach for example, Brahms and Beethoven and Mahler and Mendelssohn and Tchaikovsky and Telemann and Verdi and Mozart and Puccini not to mention Portuguese fados and Venetian barcaroles, he said she was probably right but why do you have to be such a god-damned wiseacre, Georgie, ruining a perfectly good remark with needless international clutter? Her father preferred the explanation of the experience to the experience itself, an attitude that kept his disposition sunny and his faith unshakable. She rested her head against the windowsill and thought about her cooperative father, newly retired and happily improving his golf game, shooting to break ninety. He had a menu signed by Sidney Bechet, a collector's item because Bechet was famously surly and rarely signed anything unless it was a check in his favor. But Dan Whyte was a great appreciator, and probably Bechet had seen that and decided to give Whitey a thrill.

In the good weather the musicians came once or twice a week. She looked forward to them as you look forward to the postman bringing letters from home. It was like having a private orchestra or your own Imam, and after a month of free concerts she slipped an envelope with a hundred francs into Alfred's hand and asked him to give it to the jazzmen, please. The next day she saw him do it, indicating with his head where the money came from. Alfred put the envelope in the beret and moved off without a glance but poised and deliberate, knowing he was being watched. The saxophonist looked up and saw Georgia and swung at once into "Petit Fleur," the pianist picking up immediately. She thought of an old married couple completing each other's sentences. She leaned far out the window and gave them a closed-fist salute, tipping the Calvados bottle to her ear, an impulsive confession that caused them to laugh and break rhythm. The pianist looked up, so startled that his hands flew off the keyboard, his left foot stuttering, then resuming its heavy beat. The saxophonist pointed his horn at her window and began again, the first few notes of "Petit Fleur," duhhhhh-*duh*.

She was very tight.

Alfred was angry.

The weather was so warm and swollen, like one of the late spring days when she was in school and unable to study or attend class and partied all afternoon instead, drinking and carrying on and listening to music and dancing and carrying on generally. She suddenly felt twenty years old and disobedient, feverish in the spring. And she was impassioned because in the early evening the setting sun was fierce in the ancient narrow street. It came right at you, the yellow light so brilliant it hurt your eyes and then reflected off the dancing sax, transforming it into a bright golden wand. Wand of fire, she thought; and she remembered Alfred's joke the first night they went to bed together, the one she didn't get.

They had such good times together. Alfred worried about her and became angry when she drank in the afternoon. You're ruining your health, Georgia. And when she tried to explain that she thought she would explode, and drank to relieve the pressure, he shook his head in disbelief. Explode? With love, she said without elaboration, leaving him to wonder whether it was love for him or for her work or merely unspecific passion.

She could still hear them below, winding down now. The pianist was carrying things because the saxman's lip had turned to glue, his high notes failing to gain altitude and his low notes thick as mud. Soon they would be gone in the Citroën van, perhaps to the Musée d'Orsay, a glass of something at the café on the corner, a marc or pastis. She wished she played an instrument, the bass or traps. They could use a sideman to relieve the pressure. Didn't everyone? A sideman was helpful generally. She thought, Perhaps now it is time to stray a little. Alfred was always telling her to get outside, and her room was becoming claustrophobic. She was fond of the café down the street; and how fortunate for her, the time was just six.

The Mercure was owned by a young couple who were trying to upgrade the place and had decided that they needed an American accent, so every evening at six they had a happy hour. They called it *l'heure de Mercure*. They thought the happy hour and the American accent would bring in some of the new people who had moved into the neighborhood. But it never happened because the new people were not café people. They were professional people who stayed home with their children and watched television. The regulars drifted away because of the American accent, hanging plants and a wood bar to replace the zinc. The new owners had seen pictures of cocktail lounges in Boston and San Francisco and thought they could duplicate them, and the profits too, in rue Blaise. When they took out the pinball machine, the regulars felt insulted and left en masse for the café up the street, Café le Sport.

Georgia enjoyed coming by and sitting quietly, drinking a Scotch alone at the end of the wood bar. Alfred had convinced her that she had to get out of her room and see the city, not only because she had a household errand but because it was enjoyable for its own sake. He was insistent. She had to look on the city as a naturalist would look on the Great Plains of America; there were many species of city life and they were fascinating. And when you got away from work for a while you were refreshed and could return to it with heightened imagination. Alfred made her promise to get out at least every other day, to investigate his city, so beautiful and tranquil in early summer. So she developed the habit of stopping at the Mercure around six each evening, drinking alone while the owners tallied the accounts. After they removed the pinball machine there were very few patrons, so it puzzled her how they could spend so much time calculating profit and loss. At six o'clock on a weekday there was only Georgia at one end of the bar and the owner of the antique shop next door at the other end, and one of the teachers from the school, who graded papers at the table by the window. The antiques dealer had a collection of toupees and after a while Georgia realized he wore a different toupee for each day of the week. If he wore a pony tail, she knew it was Tuesday. Occasionally a passerby would look in, pause, and then move on. The Mercure was not inviting, unless you wanted to be alone with your own thoughts. She thought of sketching it, perhaps bartering the sketch for Scotch. But she immediately discarded the idea: the Mercure was Edward Hopper's material.

She wanted to tell Alfred about the antiques dealer but didn't because he assumed that on her outings she was strolling along the river looking into bookstalls or visiting the Impressionist galleries at the Musée d'Orsay, at the very least feeding pigeons in the Luxembourg Gardens or snooping around the Invalides. She did not want him to know that she was sitting in a café drinking Scotch and soda two hours after rising. Alfred worried about her health generally, and it was easier deceiving him than telling him to mind his own business. And that would have been untrue in any case. By that time they were minding each other's business. She knew that sooner or later he would discover her in the Mercure, and they would have the reckoning then.

She was the only customer who drank Scotch and over three months' time she drank everything they had, a bottle of J & B and one of Black & White and two of Haig & Haig Pinch. At six in the evening it was light in the café and pleasant to sit and daydream in the stillness, feeling ever so slightly brazen because the sun was bright outside. The Mercure had a wonderful dusty smell and the sense of conversation just ended. She seldom had more than two or three drinks at a time, and never doubles. She drank enough only to wake up and begin thinking about her picture, where it had been and where it was going. She was so ill at ease the first time she went in, she was certain she would never return. But no one bothered her once they understood that she did not wish to talk and that, indeed, she could not speak their language well enough to converse seriously. She was convinced that they thought her dangerous in some unspecified way, a woman not to be patronized or mishandled.

In time the Mercure became as familiar as her own apartment. She always chose the same stool and nodded at the regulars, who replied with a soft *Bon soir, madame* before returning to their own worlds. The barman brought her Scotch without being asked, always very polite, asking her how she was and wasn't the weather — whatever it was, filthy, fine, or in-between. And then he would return to the caisse, where his wife was settling the accounts. The schoolteacher scribbled in the corner and the antiques dealer admired himself in the mirror and Georgia drank, thinking often about Alfred and how long they were likely to last. At least she was hearing no more about Auvergne or Dordogne, or the false papers. Alfred had agreed to hire a lawyer to defend him against his ex-wife. They seemed to be settling in like any long-term affair, though they had known each other only a short time; it was as if each had a spouse elsewhere, and these spouses had their own claims. They slept in her apartment and ate in his and their hours continued topsy-turvy, except when she strolled up rue Blaise for a Scotch at *l'heure de Mercure.*

No mystery why she chose the Mercure. Back of the bar was a poster for a gallery offering drawings of Constantin Brancusi. The drawing shown was of a sculpture of Mercury. No doubt the owners of the café thought this fortunate, for the poster had pride of place behind the bar; but for Georgia it recalled Alfred's story of the sculptor Louis Brian, working in wretched conditions in the frigid Paris winter of 1864, removing his only blanket from his shoulders and wrapping his clay figure of Mercury. If the clay froze, it would break. The temperature plunged and naturally it was Monsieur Brian who froze and died and was given an important Salon medal posthumously and even his many enemies did not object because of the supreme sacrifice the sculptor had made. Brian's act was a gift to all artists, a kind of psalm or memento mori. No one would ever feel obliged to emulate it; the act was sui generis. Repeated, it would lose force. Repeated, it would become a clumsy plagiarism. The story has been told through the generations — Alfred's mother had heard it from her father, who said she had heard it from the great Turgenev himself — as emblematic of the artist's responsibility to his work, absolute fidelity, devotion unto death. Devotion reached beyond the grave no less than artworks. Maître Rodin was greatly moved and thought Mercury a useful piece, well worth saving. Indeed, he thought it Louis Brian's masterpiece. Rodin was said to be in sympathy with Brian's sacrifice, as was only natural for one who declared, in answer to his own numerous critics, that in nature there was no morality. Probably he meant depravity.

Mercury: the god of eloquence and feats of skill, protector of traders and thieves, conductor of departed souls to the Lower World, God's messenger.

And humble Louis Brian? It is doubtful he expected a reward, and in any case there was none. No street or square is named for him. His work is not displayed in the Musée d'Orsay. The sculptor founded no school, and is not even mentioned in the compendious *Petit Robert*. Louis Brian is remembered today only as the artist who gave his blanket to a dummy, and died as a result.

The poster was not easy to see in the gentrified light of the Mercure, so Georgia was free to make of it whatever she wanted. And when she was not daydreaming about her general or about Alfred and their future, she tried to imagine Louis Brian's last night, the sculptor removing the blanket from his shoulders and covering the statue, wrapping it carefully around the clay, perhaps tenderly embracing the package, trying to transfer heat from his own body to the god's image he'd made. The blanket would still be warm, and it would be then that he remembered his happy childhood, the thick comforters on every bed, and the anemic winter sunlight spilling through the window of his room. From the kitchen came the smell of real coffee. He heard his mother's voice: Dress warmly, it will be very cold! Brian put on everything he owned, shirts and a coat and three pairs of ragged socks, and as he sat on his step stool and watched his sculpture grow cold and brittle he forgot about the comforters, the anemic sunlight, and his mother's voice.

The papers had predicted minus 14 C. He leaned forward now, trying to see the form beneath the blanket, reconstructing it, every curve and angle, and then began his revisions. He was fifty-nine and his memory for small things had begun to fail, but now he saw his Mercury whole — eloquent, protective, consoling, fleet. He saw the idea of it, and what he had made from the idea, and wondered what else could be done. He became drowsy and took drink to stay awake. His head became cold and heavy as marble, and his fingers were stiff as claws, the nails bone white. He envisioned himself a marble-headed bird, some god from the Americas. He held the glass on his knee and rocked back and forth, gratified that blood seemed to be returning to his head; but as it did he wondered if the marble would crack. The candle's flame dipped this way and that and he put his hand near it, not too close because he had lost all feeling in his fingers. The quick shadows from the candle made sinister shapes on the wall,

as if an illusionist were at work. He believed that ghosts from
the underworld were gathering round, inspecting his clay figure.

Through the night the temperatures fell, the wind blow-
ing from the northern plains. It would be a wind from Scandi-
navia, originating somewhere near the Arctic. All northern Europe would be locked in and the cold wind would move south,
gathering speed in the Low Countries, rising as it fed on the
land. Around three in the morning snow began to fall. Louis
Brian heard it, hard little flakes banging against his window like
tiny pebbles, pushing and then loosening the latch. The snow
beat against the glass in a kind of furious rhythm, a child banging
a tin drum, the bassoon-wind in the wings. The window flew
open and Brian moved to close it. But his fingers would not
work, he who had always been so deft with his hands. He took
a very deep breath and the cold seared his lungs with a pain not
unlike fire. He thought he would faint, then took another drink
of vin ordinaire, the wine so cold it scratched his throat. Seated
again, he noticed that the blanket had become undone, flapping
stiffly in the wind like a frozen flag. He had not closed the window after all. The sculptor struggled to his feet, found twine,
wrapped his Mercury as tightly as he dared, and tied it in a sail-
or's knot; it had the appearance now of a corpse in a winding
sheet. Brian was exhausted and returned to his step stool. The
glass fell to the floor, shattering, but he did not notice. His eyes
closed but he did not notice the darkness, either. He felt the beating of his own heart and willed its pulse inside the clay form. He
gave Mercury all he could spare and then some. He began to talk
to it with a fervor religious in its intensity, and was thrilled when
it replied with humility. Finally, the sculpture had all that the
sculptor could give.

When she finished this romance she was near tears. The story
was so vivid, her imagination yielding extraordinary details. She
invented conversations with Mercury and recollections from the
sculptor's young manhood: early successes with work and with
women, estrangement from his family, constant struggle, terrible
poverty, grandiose dreams of driving his elephants over great

mountains. And all the time wondering whether his vision could be transferred to clay, and from clay to bronze, and retain anything of the ideal inside his own head. Alfred had heard about Louis Brian from his mother, an unreliable provenance. Princesses made things up all the time, or took gaudy stories at face value, especially when retailing them to sons. Mothers loved a good story and seldom let the facts interfere, most particularly if the story was sentimental and pointed to injustice. Extreme behavior made a stark novel. Naturally Georgia wanted the story to be true because she liked the idea of the artist martyred by art. She wanted to think of the stubborn sculptor alone and freezing, delirious with cold and fear, donating his blanket and then his heartbeat and his voice to God's messenger and succeeding: Mercury brought back from the underworld.

Needless to say, the comforter, the yellow sunlight, and the mother's voice came from her own experience, though she had never been cold or hungry or poor. She had had what you could call an ordinary middle-class childhood, no blue blood in the family and everyone's papers in order. When Alfred asked, she told him that her mother was a housewife. Her father worked for the archdiocese, something to do with finance. He invested money for the church. Her father was an amateur historian of the city of Chicago, his library filled with scholarly books on transportation and politics, architecture and society, the grain trade and the mechanics of credit. He had written a monograph on the city's warehouses, intending to prove that inventory was the foundation of the region's astounding growth in the nineteenth century. He believed that prosperity had taken Chicago far from Christ's teachings, but all was not lost. "It is sown in corruption; it is raised in incorruption." He thought Chicago the first modern metropolis, a city more powerful even than Venice or Hamburg; yet it had not yielded to the sin of pride. It swaggered, but it was filled with self-doubt.

We are fortunate to live here, he said.

Vulgarity is only venial.

Pride goeth before the fall.

Chicago was his obsession, a private thing he could not communicate. He seemed almost ashamed of his passion, as if he were collecting Satan's works. When she asked him about Leopold and Loeb or Capone or Big Bill Thompson or Jane Addams or Marshall Field or Hack Wilson or any of the other local heroes, he would answer in the dusty language of the accountant and refer her to a book. She thought at heart he was a teacher with no talent for instruction. At night he would sit in his big leather chair in his study, reading, a drink in his hand. He would have one drink after another, pouring from the decanter on the sideboard. He seemed to her the essence of contentment, a man wholly at peace. He required only his drinks and his books. She remembered as a child watching his big hands turning the pages, a dreamy look on his face; elsewhere in the house would be the sounds of commercial television, but he never paid any attention. And then he would fall asleep in his chair, his hands over his belly, the drink on the table, the book open in his lap, Sidney Bechet on the record player, the volume turned low. It was so low you could not hear it outside the study. At the end of the evening the stack of records would be turning silently, the air still heavy with the blues and the smell of whiskey. Later, when Georgia was older, returning home late from a class or a date, he would invite her in, offer her a drink, and they would sit and talk, often for hours. It was during one of these whiskey evenings that he asked her if she had met mother's friend.

Alice? she asked. Her bridge partner?

No, he said. The man she sees.

Georgia knew at once that he was not joking; but she didn't believe him either. She sees him on Saturday nights, he said. She's with him tonight. I thought she might have introduced him to you. She's proud of him. I'm surprised she hasn't said anything. It's no great secret with her.

She managed to ask, Have you met him?

No, he said, I haven't met him. I know all about him, though. He's a doctor. She met him when she was doing her volunteer work.

Georgia rose slowly and went to the sideboard and poured Scotch and stood there drinking it, waiting for her father to say more. When he handed her his glass, she filled it.

I can't believe it, she said finally.

It happens, he said.

But what did you *do* to make her — go off.

I don't know, he said. Maybe it's something I didn't do. Maybe it's who I am. I'd guess that would be it.

You must have done something, she said.

He shrugged and mumbled something noncommittal. And then she saw that he was very drunk. He was so composed it was difficult to know when he had been drinking heavily. He never slurred his words or stumbled and the only way she knew now was that his face had gone slack, and if she had seen him in a crowd she might not have recognized him. He was sweating, holding his glass in both hands. His gruff voice had dropped an octave but was still so neutral that he might have been discussing his warehouse inventories. Georgia wanted him to say that he was joking after all, but there was no chance of that. Nor did he seem to want sympathy, or an alliance against his wife, Georgia's mother.

She said, I wish you hadn't told me. Why did you?

It was time, he said.

I don't know what that means, she said.

I want you to understand things, he said.

I don't want to know about it, Georgia said.

Of course not, he said. Of course you don't. It's how people live, that's all. And that's the point.

The whiskey had filled her up, too. She felt it in her head and the tips of her fingers, and she was thankful for it. It seemed to make them equals. She balanced on the arm of his chair and put her hand on his shoulder but he did not respond except to shift his weight. When she looked up she saw all his books, his Chicago books and other heavy books, and in the corner the turntable silently revolving. On his desk were photographs of Georgia and her sister, and a signed photograph of the Cardinal, and him in a golf cart on the first tee at the South Shore Country Club. She knew she would never again enter his study without remembering this conversation; and in that sense a frontier had been crossed with no return. Her father had always been a mystery. She believed that he had a fabulous inner life. His very ordinariness and imperturbability she had seen as a façade concealing — she did not know what it concealed. When he went to confession, what were his sins? Did he count his blessings? She asked him what there was she could do.

Just don't tell Marge, he said.

I wouldn't think of telling Marge, she said. Why would I?

Just don't, he said.

Why? she demanded in a conspiratorial whisper, a tone of voice she had never used before, but would often use again. She thought, My father and I against the world, though still she wondered what he had done to drive her mother away.

Dan Whyte stared at his drink and at his daughter's and then, absurdly, he clinked glasses as if they had concluded a pact. He said, Marge isn't like you. She's a girl; you're grown-up. You've always been grown-up. You don't play by the rules. You don't replace your divots and you don't take the two-stroke penalty when you go out of bounds. Marge doesn't know the game. Marge doesn't *know* the rules. Marge doesn't have the heart that you have. Sweet Jesus, you have a beautiful heart because you see things clearly and know what you have to do to get ahead. You always have. You're serious-minded. And the more things you *see,* the more things you know for certain, the better your heart will be. And you will prevail, no matter the odds. What I have said to you is a truth I wanted you to have because you should know how things are in this house.

She was listening carefully, not trusting what she heard. It seemed to her that she had always obeyed the rules, whatever they were. She did not surrender herself to them but she tried to obey them. It was true that she had always been determined to see things clearly and for herself. And it was also true that to get ahead you had to break things.

I don't know if I can face Mother, she said.

He laughed then, too loudly, his voice filling the room.

Your good health, he said, clinking glasses again. Whiskey bound them together now, and she put her arm around his shoulders, squeezing. She leaned close, feeling the sweat and stubble on his chin. He was a powerful man and she could feel his shoulder muscles moving under her fingers. He had picked up a golf tee from the table and was balancing it in the palm of his hand. When he spoke his voice was thick but the words were clear enough.

Of course you can, he said. I face her every day. And you're just like me. You're a Whyte, Georgie. You're a Whyte, lock, stock, and barrel. You and I, he said. We Whytes, we see things through. We take life seriously. We look life straight in the face. We never give up.

Yes, she said. She believed him absolutely.

You can get me another drink now, Georgie. And have one yourself. Where were you tonight? Where did you go?

Winnetka, she answered from the sideboard. Some country club.

You're moving up in the world, Georgie.

That depends, she said.

There are fine people in Winnetka, he said. Some of the finest people in Chicago are in Winnetka.

Not all of them, she said.

Did something happen? he asked. He took the drink she handed him.

A man told me I had a hard heart, she said, and burst into tears.

So when she went to the Mercure in the late afternoons, still fuzzy from sleep, she thought about Louis Brian in Montparnasse and her father in his study on the West Side of Chicago, and much else besides. It was a place for Scotch drinking and daydreaming because the atmosphere was private. The Mercure was a kind of club except that the patrons were strangers, each to the other. They did not know one another's names or family situations, likes and dislikes. When Georgia lit a cigarette her lighter made a scratch in the silence; and for a moment, that was her identity. The barman had a perpetual cold and his wife a perpetual scowl, and that was theirs. The antiques dealer had his various toupees and the schoolteacher had a nervous tic, though that may have been disappointment at the papers he was grading. When one of the men used the toilet, the flush sounded like an avalanche.

That afternoon, things were quieter than usual. But Georgia had so much going on inside her head, Louis Brian and then her father, that she did not notice. At a little rustle at the table behind her she looked up, into the mirror.

The schoolteacher gathered up his papers, nodded at the bartender, murmured *Bon soir 'sieurdames,* and left the café. They all watched him go, offering sympathetic smiles, a close friend obliged to leave the party early. Georgia wondered about the antiques dealer, who was studying a racing form, concentrating hard, chewing on his pencil. His widow's peak had slipped a little and she knew that very soon when he looked into the mirror he would notice it, and tidy up. The light was very bad at the end of the bar and she wondered how he could see, but his pencil kept working.

When she called for another drink — her third, and she had a feeling it would not be her last, so fraught had been her daydream — she saw Alfred looking through the front window. She looked at him as she would look at any stranger standing indecisively in front of an unfamiliar window. Would he choose the Mercure or Le Sport? The choice would define him. Alfred looked first at the antiques dealer, then at the barman, and finally at Georgia. And he did not recognize her right away. She was not in a place she was supposed to be. He frowned and looked away, and as quickly back again. He gave a little start and she saw his eyebrows lift, staring at her hard to see if she recognized him, perhaps also to judge whether she was tight.

She crooked her finger, beckoning him. She sat up a little

straighter and tried to appear composed and cheerful, difficult as that was in the louche atmosphere of the Mercure. The antiques dealer and the barman saw this pantomime and looked at each other in alarm.

Alfred smiled wanly, then entered, standing in the doorway without moving. She thought of the tenderfoot in the Western movie, the background music suddenly quickening. The regulars were looking at him, and the audience would know without being told that he would order a sarsaparilla and that would be the beginning of the end. Someone would make a crude joke and guffaw and then hit him or shoot him. When Alfred walked up to Georgia, the barman scowled and reached for his towel. No one had ever approached Madame in the Mercure, and it was far from certain that his attention was welcome. The barman folded his arms across his chest, scrutinizing Alfred as if he expected trouble. The antiques dealer followed every move.

"Well," Alfred said.

"Take a seat," she said.

"So this is where you go?"

"Off and on."

Alfred nodded.

"Once or twice a week," she said.

He said, "I was passing by and looked in. I can't think why I did. I never have before, and I pass this place every day. Of course it's difficult to see in, with all the vegetation."

"And here I was," she said.

"I didn't recognize you at first."

"Have something," she said.

"Coffee," Alfred said to the barman. He glanced about at the hanging plants and the round wooden tables with the Cinzano ashtrays. The barman came with Alfred's coffee and a fresh Scotch for Georgia, then retreated to the caisse, where he whispered something to his wife. She looked up, her face dark with disapproval. The barman would have remarked on Alfred's French, which did not have an American accent. They would identify him as a provincial, perhaps from Alsace or the French Alps. Alfred was dressed in a dark suit and tie, as if he had just come from church; and then she remembered that he had had an appointment with his lawyer. He had wanted to make a good appearance, to seem a respectable and sober musician. By no means prosperous, but respectable. He wanted to be seen as a man whose debts would never be large but would always be paid. The antiques dealer was still looking at them, and Georgia wondered whether he spoke English. She poured Perrier into her Scotch and drank. Alfred sipped at his coffee and made a face.

"It's filthy," he said.

"People don't come here for the coffee, Alfred."

"Do they re-use the grounds?"

"I don't come here for the coffee, chéri. I come here because it's quiet."

"Quiet?" he said. "It's a tomb."

"A good place to sit and think," she said.

"And drink Scotch," he said. "And what do you think about?"

She did not answer right away. What, indeed? She pointed at Brancusi's Mercury, then at the barman and the antiques dealer. In the stillness of the room they seemed to her as composed and settled as a painting, perhaps one of Edward Hopper's because she had the sensation of suspended conversation, and things withheld or inaccessible, beyond reach. As an afterthought she pointed at Alfred. She thought of them as the four points of a compass, with Mercury dead center.

"And what have you decided from your thinking? Is there a verdict?"

"Nothing," she said. "It's just a daydream."

"But pleasant," he said.

"Not very," she answered. "I was remembering a conversation I had once with my father. It concerned my mother. And not two weeks later, she left home with her doctor, never to return. After that, we were no longer a family. We were blood relatives, but we were not a family. Marge and I collected her things and brought them to her new place, a beautiful apartment on Lake Shore Drive. She loved the apartment and she loved her doctor and I guess she still does. They're still together. That's what I was thinking about and it wasn't pleasant, though we were all old enough to understand, wish her the best, and so forth and so on. Everyone has a right to happiness, even married people. So my mother started out a hausfrau and ended up a Chicago princess."

Alfred said nothing, but leaned over and kissed her hand.

"Such a surprise," she said. "And such a scandal at the archdiocese. My father was very popular."

"You've never told me about your mother."

"I was thinking that your mother started out a princess and my mother ended as one."

"Russian princesses are a dime a dozen," he said.

"In Chicago, too," she replied.

"Do you," he said. "Do you come here every day to drink and daydream?"

"A few times a week," she said. "Always at this time. They have a happy hour, *l'heure de Mercure*."

"Happy hour?" He laughed. "Georgia, this place is not *happy*. The Luxembourg Gardens are happy. The Musée d'Orsay is happy."

"It depends on where you are in the Musée d'Orsay," she said.

Alfred looked around the room and shook his head.

"It grows on you," she said. "The Mercure is good for daydreams. I daydream about you, too."

"Me?"

"Sometimes," she said. "Not always."

Alfred nodded and did not reply. At the end of the bar the antiques dealer was adjusting his widow's peak, looking into the mirror and preening. He was very vain, turning this way and that, mugging. She had decided that he probably spoke a little English, though they were talking so softly that he could not have heard anything, and could have made no sense of their conversation if he had. It didn't matter anyhow. She was feeling the effects of the whiskey.

Alfred looked at his watch, then through the window at the empty street. Dusk was coming on.

"How did it go?" she asked, remembering that he had seen his lawyer. Her mother had been in her mind's eye all this time, standing in the bay window of the Lake Shore Drive apartment, the lake over her shoulder, white sails against the pale blue water, she and Marge fragile in the bright formal room, and then her mother's curly-haired doctor in the doorway, putting them all at ease with a tender joke, offering tea, apologizing for his lateness, an emergency at the hospital, a very difficult birth but successful, mother and twins doing fine; and then the memory feathered away as Alfred raised his eyes.

"He wasn't in."

"But you had an appointment — "

"There was an urgent matter. He was called away."

"I'm sorry," she said.

"His office is in Montparnasse, very difficult to find. And when I got there his secretary said he was in Mantes-la-Jolie on an important legal matter, and she did not know when he would return, except that it wouldn't be today. I was to call back and make another rendezvous. His office was cluttered with those caricatures of lawyers and judges, and of course defendants. Who did them, Daumier? They're sentimental. They're tripe. I suppose Maître Besse thinks they're ironic, but they're not. They're tripe. And his secretary was curt."

"They're bastards," she said.

"I suppose they are," Alfred said. He fingered the sleeve of his coat, frayed where it met his wrist. She noticed that his fingernails were dirty, and she hoped he had not gone to Maître Besse's office with unclean hands.

"But there are other lawyers," Georgia said. She thought they were talking softly, but there was a bass echo, as if they were in a barn. Alfred was uncomfortable in this atmosphere, so heavy and dour. He had turned his back on the others, and now he lowered his voice again.

"I had a dream last night," he said. "It was fantastic. I dreamed we were in Auvergne together. We were living in a stone farm-house. The farmhouse had a huge fireplace with old-fashioned andirons. There was an Alsatian dog. There was no other house in sight, but in the distance we could see the mountains, their summits and slopes covered with snow. In the evenings we read and listened to Gustav Mahler on a wind-up phonograph. You painted during the day. You were tremendously productive, there were canvases everywhere, portraits mostly, but also landscapes. We lived like normal people, Georgia. We got up at dawn, and went to bed after dinner."

"And what did you do while I was painting?"

"I don't know. That wasn't part of the dream."

She held up her hand for another Scotch, but the barman did not notice. He was staring out the window.

"But that's not all," Alfred said. "Suddenly we were no longer in Auvergne but in California. Auvergne was black and white, and gray and green, and mountainous. California was flat and pastel. It was otherworldly. We had a red car. We lived in a house surrounded by palm trees. And the ocean was nearby. Listen to this: There was a parade of animals, elephants and kangaroos and the like."

She held up her hand again and said, *Monsieur,* her voice loud and tactless. When the barman turned, startled, she pointed at her glass and Alfred's cup.

"And there were children," he said.

"Ours?" she asked.

"I don't know," he said. "They were in the pastel house so I suppose they were ours, except they weren't very friendly. They were surly children."

"California children," she said.

"I suppose they were. They were children of all colors."

"It sounds like quite a dream," she said.

"It was very pleasant. Did you know any children in California?"

"I only knew one."

"And was he surly?"

"No, he wasn't surly. He was almost mute because he was beaten up. In America they called it abused. But what they mean is beaten up."

"How terrible," he said.

"He was beaten up by his father."

The barman brought Georgia's Scotch and Alfred's coffee, and took a bill from the little pile of coins and bills on the bar. There were only two marbles of ice in her glass and she wondered why they could never get it straight, the glass filled with ice, the Scotch poured over the ice; and then you added your own Perrier. It was such a simple thing that seemed to elude them.

"It was a wonderful dream," Alfred said.

She said, "It was the wrong one. I would never again live in California, never. Not with you or anyone."

"Because of the boy?"

"Not only him," she said.

"Perhaps the boy's father," Alfred said.

She did not reply.

"It's just a place like any other," Alfred said.

"To you it is. To me it isn't."

"In your own way, probably you miss America. California."

"I do not miss America," she said slowly. "I do not miss California. Good riddance to California. I want nothing to do with California."

Alfred was silent a moment, moving his cup this way and that on the bar. She felt the familiar buzz in her head, something tugging at the roots of her hair, and took a sip of Scotch and then another and the buzz receded. She didn't understand why they couldn't get it straight about the ice, such an obvious, elementary thing that improved the taste of Scotch. They were scrupulous about subtle things and slovenly about simple things. She looked up the bar, thinking that if she could get the barman's attention she could eke some ice from him; five or six additional cubes would be about right. But the barman and the antiques dealer were deep in conversation, and suddenly she knew that they were talking about Alfred.

"Shut up!" she said loudly.

Alfred started. "What?"

"Not you," she said.

He looked at her evenly.

"Those two," she said, nodding at them. They were still tête-à-tête.

"What about them?" he said.

"Nothing," she said. "Forget it."

"Really," Alfred said after a moment. "Tell me the truth. Why do you come here, this place?"

"I like it here," she said truculently.

"Yes," he said. "But why specifically here, instead of the place up the street, or one of the cafés on the Boulevard Saint-Germain."

"It doesn't have to suit you," she said. "It suits me."

"I was only curious," he said mildly.

"It's a mistake to think that one size fits all. Cafés are not stockings. It's an error to think that because I like something you have to like it, too. It's childish. I come here because it suits me and the cafés in Saint-Germain don't suit me, because they're like stage sets, people making entrances and exits and speaking lines they've heard in their stupid movies. They kiss a lot. And there's too much noise."

"Well," he said. "No chance of that here."

"None whatever," she said.

"Are you coming home now?"

"Whenever I damn well feel like it," she said.

"I see," he said.

"I'm having another drink. Perhaps two drinks."

"What a good idea," he said.

"Doubles," she said.

"Good luck to you," he said.

"And to you," she replied.

Alfred looked at his watch and slipped off the bar stool.

"I'll see you later, Alfred."

"Will you be all right?"

"I always have been."

"Don't stay too late, please."

She nodded, turning to search for the barman.

"How late do you think you'll be?" he asked.

"As long as it takes," she said.

"It's hard for me to understand," he began.

"Later," she said. "Some other time. Now isn't the time."

"That's true," he agreed.

"You should know that. It's obvious. You shouldn't come in here when I'm enjoying myself and ask questions. I don't like questions. I like a drink at the end of the day —"

"It's the beginning of the day," he said.

"Whatever."

"All right," he said.

"— when I can look things straight in the face. And not blink."

"Perhaps I should stay."

"Alfred? Do you see other women?"

"No," he said. "Of course not."

"Don't look so surprised," she said. "It happens."

"It isn't happening with me," he said.

"I had to be sure," she said.

He nodded, smiling sadly.

She said, "Dear Alfred."

"Will you tell me about California sometime? Not now. I don't mean now. I mean some other time, tomorrow or next week or next month or whenever you feel like it."

"All right," she said.

"It was such a pleasant dream," he said.

She had to smile at that.

"I'll go now," he said.

"Yes," she said. "And would you mind telling that blockhead to bring me another drink. Lots of ice. Tell him that, *beaucoup glace.*"

"*Beaucoup glace,*" Alfred repeated.

And she replied, "Don't start in on me, Alfred."

"Lots of ice," he said. "And you'll want a double?"

"A double," she said.

"I'll tell him," Alfred said, and was gone.

Georgia remained at the Mercure for some time, deep inside her memory. The antiques dealer left and someone else arrived but did not stay. She seemed to be thinking several thoughts at once. The thoughts were like people entering a crowded party, mixing and then leaving, making way for others. You had only time to say hello before they were gone. Sometimes they returned, holding her attention for many minutes and then vanishing. When they left she could not remember their names or what they looked like, or what their business was. And in the corner, alone and apparently friendless, was her general in his unfinished state. He was undefined. Every so often she would look hard at him, fixing him in her mind. He became uncomfortably abstract, a fugitive thought that she wanted to pursue. In this light he could be any horseman from any century on any continent. And then she took a sip of Scotch and her attention wandered, slipping this way and that, sometimes to a friend or to an episode in the past, sometimes to the many pictures she had painted. She tried to recall the six self-portraits as they rested against the wall in her apartment in Southgate, appraised by the Clydes. And the dozen saints and the dozen selves in the back of her van traveling from California to Chicago, and back again to the general. Perhaps the general would never be completed. Many things in life were not. Perhaps the general would be like a human being, always changing and never dying until she did. When you finished a picture, it was the same as killing it. When she looked at the general, she always saw something new. Unfinished, he was an inspiration. In a continual state of becoming he would resemble the artist. He would be like life itself. And she could go on to another subject. Many subjects, hundreds of them, were at her disposal.

When she thought of Alfred she thought of the future, but the future was never specific. It was at the horizon and shrouded. Having no dimensions, it was not something she could see clearly. His formlessness attracted her. She smiled to herself, thinking that Alfred had the formlessness of granite, but he had a grip of iron. He would never let go, and never let her let go. He had such a good heart. She tried to imagine Alfred in Auvergne, cultivating his garden while he avoided the authorities, succeeding for a while but only for a while. She tried to imagine Alfred in a golf cart motoring down a fairway at the country club in Winnetka, and this amused her, it was so loopy. It was an idea that was felt rather than seen, Alfred in his tuxedo alighting from the golf cart with his nine iron, touching the ball to improve its lie, straightening his arms as he addressed the ball. A figure from an English sporting print, no less. She laughed out loud and looked at her glass, empty again. The truth was, the general would always be in a state of becoming, while Alfred simply was. He appeared suddenly, but vanished when, implausibly, Georgia heard a voice.

"Madame," the barman said sadly.

She looked up. She was alone in the bar.

"We must close, madame."

"Yes," she said. "Of course."

"I'm sorry about the ice, madame."

"It doesn't matter," she said. She pushed ten francs across the bar, a gratuity.

"*Bon soir, madame.* Thank you."

"*Bon soir, monsieur.*"

"It is always a pleasure to serve you, madame."

"What is your name?"

"Jean-Marc, madame."

"*Bon soir, Jean-Marc.*"

"Madame will be careful?"

"It's only a few steps," she said.

"I could call the gentleman, the one who was here with you earlier, monsieur — "

"Alfred," she said. "Monsieur Alfred, my lovely fiancé. He is a very great musician, Jean-Marc. And a fine golfer. He has a noble spirit. His mother was a princess. From Russia! I love him, you know. I love him completely." She paused, losing her bearings, remembering then that Jean-Marc had offered to call. "However, it won't be necessary," she added, but, struggling to her feet, she had second thoughts. Her head was spinning and her eyesight cockeyed. She gave Jean-Marc a telephone number and waited, hoping that Alfred had not left for his club. But in the event, there was no need for a telephone call. Alfred was striding through the door in his tuxedo, signaling to Jean-Marc, putting an arm around her shoulder, and speaking softly as he helped her to her feet.

A week later she came by the Mercure and it was closed. There were no lights anywhere and the chairs were piled on the tables. The cash register was gone and papers littered the floor. The mirror was dusty. There were no bottles behind the bar, though the Brancusi poster remained, aslant on its hook. She thought it was like looking at a house you had lived in and loved, and finding it derelict, the same house but changed utterly. She was shocked. She could not imagine what had happened in the week since she had sat at the end of the bar with her Scotch, daydreaming of Louis Brian and then her family, and seeing Alfred at the window, Alfred on the outside looking in as she was doing now. She leaned against the glass, bereft; another touchstone had vanished. When you live quietly and work obsessively, the small change of the day — where you market, where you buy your books and your toothpaste, or the route you follow on a walk or where you go to drink a Scotch — assumes an exaggerated importance. Her life was not one of Mahler's grandiose symphonies or the immolations of the Ring Cycle or Guernica or Homer's Odyssey; it was a simple, slow-walking blues, a blues with some rhythm but little percussion. This was an artist's ordinary life, a life of grazing without drama or ceremony. It involved drink, a drink to start the day and a drink to end it, a drink to give her thoughts a human face; and now that too would become a thing of the past. She could not bear Alfred's stricken look, and naturally he had taken responsibility; and now the Mercure had closed. She knew she could find another café, but it would not be the same and she had the feeling that Louis Brian and her father would be welcome nowhere else.

And just when Jean-Marc had learned about the ice, she thought as she turned away.

5

EXCEPT FOR TOURISTS Paris was empty in August. The weather was filthy but Alfred's club was filled every night with free-spending Japanese and Americans. He was rarely home before four, but at the end of the month everyone got a bonus. Georgia continued to work but her heart was not in it; she understood that her general would be permanently on reconnaissance, better for everyone. She began to consider other subjects and a fresh point of view. She thought of herself as temporarily fallow, a field waiting for spring. She was brimming with ideas but could not choose among them, so she began to visit the museums, the Louvre and the Marmiton and the Musée d'Orsay, and the chic galleries in rue de Seine. She began to adjust her own hours to the hours the museums and the galleries were open.

The first week in September the tourists left and the Parisians returned. The rain stopped and the sun came out, the days long, warm, and golden. The city resumed its normal rhythms. When the children returned to the school across the street, Georgia noticed a new cast of characters at *l'heure de maman*. Naturally they looked younger; every year they would be younger. The musicians were gone, and she wondered if they were on vacation or were playing elsewhere in the city. Marge continued to call every Wednesday with harrowing tales of her hours on the couch, each call ending with the identical question: When are you coming home? And the identical answer: I am home. Georgia realized she had been in Paris a year.

The boss gave Alfred a week off and he and Georgia went to Normandy, putting up at a tourist hotel at Arromanches. The weather continued fine, and under the influence of the bright sun and the great wide beach and the remains of Operation Overlord in the harbor, she told him about her California days. They seemed very far away now, and not easy to parse. They seemed not to have the weight they should have. But they had to be got out of the way sooner or later, a question of her peace of mind. Biographical gaps were not fair to Alfred, either, although she had to strain to hold his interest. Then it was time to return to Paris.

"I'm glad I told you about my life among the entertainers," she said. "Doesn't it make a good story?" She leaned across the table, grinning, watching him.

Alfred plucked an oyster from the bed of shaved ice and held it at arm's length, weary Hamlet contemplating the skull of merry Yorick. Smiling thinly, he cut the muscle with his fork, then slid the oyster into his mouth, chewing while he held the shell at eye level.

"I didn't leave much out," she said, giving a little hopeful laugh.

"Try the papillons," Alfred said, tapping the tray with his fork. "The little ones. Sublime."

He spoke in his normal voice but she had to lean far forward to hear him. They were in the crowded buffet car of the Cherbourg-Paris express, surrounded by giddy British tourists off the Portsmouth boat for a lost weekend in Paris. They all carried identical shoulder bags advertising a travel agency. Georgia was unnerved by so much English being spoken so loudly around her.

"Except the Marxism later. I didn't say much about that."

Alfred continued to chew.

"What are they anyway but old war stories," Georgia said. And in this ambiance, a railroad car hurtling across Normandy, it was hard to recollect the atmosphere of the battlefield. It was her life but it was far away now and only dimly seen. In Chicago she had known a Vietnam vet, a poet who wrote earnest pornographic verse about the war. Late at night he retailed his own experiences in the rice fields, insisting that what he said was completely truthful though not entirely accurate owing to the passage of time. The poet's girlfriend was a minimalist playwright who performed her own one-woman show, *Rosa Luxemburg,* and was thrilled when an old Red walked up to her one night, embracing her and weeping great German tears, saying that she was more Rosa than Rosa. They were a companionable group, Georgia, the poet, the playwright, a professor of sociology at Roosevelt, and a gay worker priest, all struggling to create an anticulture. They met in a tavern on the far North Side; she could not remember its name but saw vividly the Schlitz sign behind the bar. Then the playwright got a grant and she and the poet went to live in Alaska. The professor moved to Berkeley and the priest went into retreat. It was the 'eighties, after all, and everyone was moving on. And when you moved on, again and again, you forgot where you had been, what the places looked like, what you had done there and what you thought when you did it. As the vet said, stories went slack owing to the passage of time; and Alfred had his own Marxist memories.

She said, "But just because they're old doesn't mean they're not real. I gave it a try. I read all the holy texts, stopped drinking, took up skating, moved to a mixed neighborhood, drew Expressionist posters for the poet and the playwright, listened to the sociologist, tried to comfort the priest. I tried to convince him that he was the victim of class antagonisms. His church hierarchy was a manifestation of bourgeois oppression. Bad fit, though. I was never a real political, and I wish I were because it might've helped. Politics can be a balm. Politics can take your mind off things. But I guess it was just a phase that started in California and ended in Illinois. It wasn't hard to be a Marxist in Chicago, because you were indignant all the time. It took a lot of energy."

Alfred sighed and repeated himself, "Very sublime."

"When my hair fell out I thought it was a signal. But it was only nerves and bad nutrition."

Alfred fluttered his hand over the bed of ice, touching the oysters in turn. There were several different kinds of oysters arranged in circles around a bright yellow lemon. He looked like a jeweler inspecting gems.

"Nobody cares anyway," Georgia said.

Alfred nodded vaguely as he touched the oysters, squinting at them. Then he grunted loudly, screwing up his face in irritation, glancing over his shoulder, cursing under his breath.

She thought, Am I boring you, *chéri?* Am I driving you around the bend? Would you rather hear about ice dancing, gliding to the music of Strauss or Cole Porter? Anything Goes? An oyster was not usually such stiff competition. Probably you would rather hear the story of the worker priest, searching for God among rough trade, tormented every hour of every day, believing himself damned and beyond redemption, until he gave himself over to the night. At the tavern on the far North Side he was always the first to leave, rising round about midnight, so agitated he could hardly keep his hands still. Georgia, can you lend me twenty dollars? Then he asked her to paint his portrait, agreeing to sit in the late afternoon before he began his evening prowl. When she finished, he was astonished. Is that what you see? he asked. Is that *me?* She had painted what she saw beneath his skin, devotion of a certain kind, not the church kind. She had drawn him as a musician, sitting patiently on a plain ladderback chair, his horn in his lap, waiting his turn to solo. She drew the padre in ascending shades of blue. Tears jumped to his eyes and he had kissed her; and then he asked her to keep the painting for him. Not long after that he went on his retreat and she never heard another word except for a cryptic postcard from a small town in Wisconsin, months later. The message was in Latin but she got someone to translate. Reach for the stars, it said.

She murmured, "Am I boring you?"

"They are," he said. He gestured with his fork. "The British swine. They want more lager, so they're shouting at the barman in their terrible French. They think that if they shout he'll understand and move faster, and he knows that so he slows down. They have unforgivable accents. It grates on my ears, the barman's too. They sound like Albanians. Worse than Albanians."

A child began to howl.

"They even bring their children," Alfred said.

"Is that bad?"

"If it isn't bad, why is the child crying?"

Georgia stared out the window at the lush rolling fields rushing by. She was sitting backward, looking into the sun, shadows leaning toward her. Cows lumbered here and there, grazing in the pastures, guarded by shaggy dogs. The earth seemed to her profoundly settled in the frail light of the afternoon, stone farmhouses and barns framed by stick fences, orchards beginning to blossom. Every few minutes a church spire would announce a village, the houses jumbled together but all of a piece, the spire dead center. The landscape and the civilization it supported put her in mind of a well-laid table, everything just so. This part of the country seemed out of touch with contemporary life despite the thickets of television antennae, and new sedans speeding along the narrow lanes. But there were stone crosses, too, beside the roadbed and in places on the hillsides. All her life she had lived in cities, at ease on pavement and comfortable with noise and disorder. She liked the city's hard edges, its inwardness and anonymity, its struggle and promise. But now she was drawn to the pale light, which cast deceptive shadows between the rolling hills and compact forests; hills became fields and hills and forests again until it was hard to know where one left off and the other began. In the farmyards men in blue trousers and women in black dresses were grimly bent to private tasks, ignoring the children underfoot; and every child looked up at the sound of the express. This country was in twilight while the world was at high noon, and she wondered how it would be day to day, looking at the Catholic shrines on the hillsides, the somber crosses inviting belief. Reach for the stars, the padre had said. And while you were stretching, the children would be waiting for the Cherbourg-Paris express, listening for the whistle. Lulled by the train's rocking motion, she filled her glass with Muscadet and poured a little for Alfred. He had scarcely touched his wine and now made a show of covering his ears against the unforgivable accents. She thought he had a countryman's face, bony and weatherbeaten; yet he was an inside man, a man of the indoors, a musician no less. She turned away, back to the beckoning fields and villages, thinking hard, trying to ignore the English voices. They had not bothered her until he complained about them.

She said, "It's so pretty out there."

He said, "Do you like it?"

She said, "Very much."

"I thought you were a city woman."

"I am. I've never lived in the country. It never occurred to me. Maybe I'll try it sometime."

"It would never work," he said.

"Why not?"

"Your material is city material. Street musicians, the cafés, the Musée d'Orsay. You need something to absorb all that spare energy."

So he had been listening after all.

"Still," he added. "People change."

"Is your Auvergne like this?"

"More rugged," he said. "Less cultivated. Older."

She shifted in her seat and closed her eyes, fighting a wave of nausea. The train was swaying from side to side as it flew through Evreux and the car was thick with cigarette smoke. A blast of laughter caused her to start. She said, "I thought the British were supposed to be reserved, polite, civil, and shy when they were abroad."

"American propaganda," Alfred said.

She sipped her wine while he poked among the oysters. It was only her second glass, and it would be her last. The British began to sing a barracks song, the refrain off key.

"Try one," he said.

She smiled and shook her head. The sight of the oyster with its green collar almost made her ill; her stomach began to turn. She put her hands on her belly, looking out the window and concentrating on things in the distance, a water tower and beyond it a jet's contrail. It was coming on to dusk.

"They're good now but a month ago they weren't. They were fat and mealy, like chewing glue. No one on earth likes a fat and mealy oyster. They're disgusting. They're corrupt."

"How interesting," she said absently, watching the contrail. The jet was moving east to west and she wondered whether it was bound for the British Isles or North America. Well, it would be the British Isles because planes did not leave for North America in the late afternoon. She had been in Europe a year and had never left Paris except for Normandy, and she had always wanted to visit the Tate in London.

"There's a hierarchy," Alfred said. "It's important to know the differences among oysters, the belons, the claires, and the speciales. There are other varieties but those are the important ones. The belons are the aristocrats, beautifully shaped, thin, indolent to a fault. They have an unusual color. They're the color of — what's that shop in Place Vendôme? The one where a pair of silk trousers costs as much as a Peugeot?"

"Armani?"

"Armani gray. They're the color of Signor Armani's silk trousers."

She laughed at that, imagining someone served silk on the half-shell, or a woman clad in oysters with green collars. Alfred held up a belon for her inspection and she turned from the window to look at it and him. Her stomach was quiet again.

"They come in different sizes. The larger they are, the more they cost. The French think more is better."

"And you don't?"

He shook his head firmly. "Never. That's why I prefer the papillons. They're the size of your thumb and taste like the purest iceberg. They're crisp, workmanlike oysters without pretense. They're premodern. Steely." He thought a moment, wondering how much farther he could take this. He wanted to take it far away from malicious California and the anxieties of Chicago. He loved her but he was not interested in learning more about the men she had known or the woman, Nicole. It was not difficult imagining Georgia in a *ménage à trois,* always an appealing idea until a crisis of some kind that obliged the parties to choose up sides, with someone always left out. Still, she had come out of it wonderfully; one day she walked away. When the arrangement became inconvenient she decided to leave it, and was as good as her word. He did not understand completely why she wanted to give him the woof and warp of her romantic life, which was not more ecstatic or disappointing or chaotic or strenuous than most romantic lives. One was often attracted to the wrong person, especially in a society that did not value equilibrium and looked always to a sunnier future, prosperity just around the corner, peace at hand, love walking in. Americans heard train whistles in the night and experienced something like rapture, believing the trains were bound for a gorgeous wide-open terminal, the free gateway to paradise. Europeans imagined a concentration camp.

He watched her now, so pale, her chin in her hand, staring out the window.

"Daydreaming?" he said. He touched her cheek.

She shook her head.

"More wine?"

She covered her glass with her hand, smiling at him. Then she resumed staring out the window.

He was afraid he was losing her. There was so much that divided them, so much in their histories and the way they looked at things, what they worried about and what they took for granted. Was there a house that could contain them? He wondered if she was thinking now about politics, the balm that took your mind off things, as if it were a kind of recreational drug that induced democratic hallucinations. This was a harmless enough thought in North America. But politics was a knife at your throat or a hand in your wallet, or a fat thumb turning the pages of your passport and an invitation to assist the authorities with their inquiries, whatever those inquiries might be. Politics was humanity's skin and you necessarily lived within it while pressing against it, testing limits; and the skin never stretched very far. Probably Americans were devoted to the idea of transfiguration; but when you were finished with that, all you had altered was the outward appearance. The blood inside was the same, rancid, sweet, or something in between. And the heart, that was the same, too. And you used it to stay alive. You used it sparingly, always keeping something in reserve.

But they were a wonderful people. They'd do anything, believing they could dominate life; and if life dominated them instead, they either denied it or decided to make the best of it. He wanted her to begin thinking of the future, and to do that she had to incorporate the past. She had to unify it. The past was not a series of episodes but all one episode. The past was seamless. You carried it around with you like a limp or bad eyesight or a fat wallet or a talent for the piano. Georgia knew what she could be but not what she was.

And me, he thought.

With me, it's the other way around.

But she was right about one thing: nobody cared. Why should they? And if they did care, what difference would it make? The point was to avoid the fat thumb in your passport or the hand in your wallet, and when you could no longer avoid it you succumbed to it and trusted to luck or the grace of God. You didn't trust the authorities, though. He wanted to make her see that. She was very intelligent about her work, but had allowed herself to be manhandled in life. She was willful and careless and did not take care of herself. She did not look well; a bright flush on her cheeks and little beads of perspiration on her forehead. It was hot in the buffet car, but at least the British were quieter now.

She would be better if she ate something and did not drink so much wine, though she was better about that now. He watched her raise her glass and put it down again.

He said, "If papillons were an item of clothing they'd be a fine pair of shoes. Belons would be a powdered wig." He smiled benignly and put an oyster on her plate, setting it down softly as if it were fragile and might break.

And she returned it.

He said, "Are you all right?"

She said, "I'm passable. I'm a little tired."

"It was walking on the beach in the rain."

"No doubt," she said.

"There's a flu going around," he said.

"It's not the flu."

"I hope to God it's not the flu you had the night we met, when you went into rue Blaise to join the demonstration. The night it was raining and you were so sick for so long."

The express was going very fast now. Suddenly they were rocketing through a station, moving so swiftly she could not read the name of the town.

He said glumly, "We're out of Normandy and into the Île-de-France. That was Mantes-la-Jolie."

"Where your lawyer was that day," she said.

"Supposedly."

"Mantes-la-Jolie is where they have the trouble with immigrants."

"Where the immigrants have trouble with the authorities," he said.

"The French say the immigrants refuse to fit in."

"The authorities make it impossible."

"They refuse to become French."

"The French don't want them."

"What does it mean, to be French?"

"It means that you don't like immigrants." He looked at his watch. "It's only thirty minutes to Paris."

She said after a moment, "I've had a good time with you."

He said, "So have I."

"You were good to listen."

"Everyone's life is a novel."

She said, "Everyone's?"

He gestured out the window. "Even the immigrants'."

She said, "Maybe theirs most of all."

"I like being with you in the here-and-now." He reached across the table and took her hand, which was clammy to the touch. "The other things." He shrugged, and did not finish the sentence.

"Well," she began.

"You and no other," he said.

"There are always others," she said.

He said, "You misunderstand me."

She smiled. "Probably."

He said, "It's not important."

"We can do this again," she said. "Next time, we'll stay in the here-and-now."

He looked out the window and did not reply.

"At the end of the month," she said.

He sighed. "You've forgotten. At the end of the month I'll be gone."

She said, "I have not forgotten. You said you would talk to the lawyer first."

"The lawyer has nothing to say to me."

"You should hear him out."

"It's useless," he said.

"There are ways and means," she replied, not knowing what she meant when she said it, only that when people were in legal difficulty they consulted a lawyer. And if the lawyer was capable, he won a postponement and the case went on and on until there was a settlement or someone died.

"I'm going to Auvergne. That's the end of it."

She sat quietly, toying with her wine, and then took a sip. She saw him watching her, so she took another.

"I will be sorry to leave you."

"Not Paris?"

"I can come back to Paris."

"And when you come back I'll be there, maybe. Maybe not."

"It's not the same."

"No, it would not be the same."

And she was correct about that; it would not be the same. Apart, they would change and find it difficult to reunite. He did not think they would survive separation, and the thought filled him with dread. She would move farther into her work, become lost in it; and that would be sufficient. And he — he had been independent for so long it would be natural to continue, and that too was sufficient. At a point in the future she would find it necessary to move on and he would also. That was the way of things generally.

He said, "Perhaps you will come visit me."

"When I finish my work," she said.

He was working on his last oyster, cutting the muscle, squeezing lemon, holding it at eye level, taking it down naked, chewing. He looked mournfully at her across the table. "That will be quite a while, I'm afraid."

"No, I'm very close now."

"Really?"

"Yes, really."

"And when you finish —"

"I'll start something else. It's time for me to begin a new series. I can feel that. A new theme."

"Do you know what it will be?"

"Intimations," she said, smiling a little. "I have intimations."

"And you won't tell —"

"It's bad luck," she said.

He hesitated a moment and then said, "I'm sorry."

"It's not your fault," she said with a sly smile.

"Of course it's my fault," he said. "The stupid papers. They're *my* papers and they're the cause of all this —"

But she was not thinking about his papers. She thought to say, "And your wife."

"Ex-wife. It's because of the wretched papers that she's a problem. She's not a problem otherwise. I could take care of her if I was not." He paused and lowered his voice. "Illegal."

"Not quite in order," she said, smiling broadly. "It's one of those things about you that I find attractive. Did your wife know?"

"It's not attractive," he said.

"Different, then," she said, still smiling.

"I am not the only one," he said defensively.

"You're the only one I know," she said.

He looked away, exasperated.

"How were you able to get married with no papers?"

"It's not difficult getting married. It's difficult getting unmarried."

"You're still married then?"

"A piece of paper, that's all it is. I renounced it."

"Did she?"

"I don't know what she did. That other one came to live with her and they're married. These are bureaucratic things, matters for the authorities."

She said, "What a tangle."

He made a dismissive gesture.

"Still, it doesn't really matter, does it?"

"Why should it?"

She poured the last of the wine, only a few drops.

"Only a few minutes more," he said.

She said tentatively, "I still worry about money."

"I told you," he said. "You should not worry. I have money. I save the tips. I save most of my salary. People like me always have money, a little here and a little there. I have enough. I have money for what you call the emergencies. I have lived this way for a very long time. Some of the money is in gold coins, napoleons. My father taught me that trick. Of course gold has been losing its value lately but it will rise again. It always has." Alfred replaced the empty shell on the bed of ice and wiped his hands on the napkin. "And I can surely find work as a musician at one or another of the hotels or if I am lucky at a restaurant that draws the Americans and Japanese. And it is cheap in Auvergne."

"You're a very self-sufficient musician."

"I've had to be," he said.

"I know that."

"There isn't another way. You live with your bags packed and something set aside for emergencies. You worry about the police and live in anonymity. You avoid public disturbances. You do not call attention to yourself. And believe me, there are worse ways to live. You don't worry about nationality, a homeland to defend or denounce. And you get used to it and it becomes your nature and you get on in that way, day to day."

"I know that, too."

"And it won't change."

"Probably not," she said.

"You learn to look after yourself."

She stared at him, nodding slowly. It had grown dark outside and she could see his reflection in the window, the reflection making him seem much younger; and he was speaking with a youthful intensity.

"And you too are independent."

"Yes," she said.

"You and your work. A closed circle."

"So far," she said.

"It's hard to imagine another way to be."

"Very hard," she agreed.

"Yet we have managed, you and I."

"Quite well," she said.

"If we part now, that's the end of it."

"It doesn't have to be."

"But it will be," he said. "You believe it, too."

"I suppose I do," she said.

"We are too self-sufficient for our own good," he said with a smile.

"Our failing," she said.

"If I am there and you are here —" He did not finish the

sentence. He was aware of people moving around him, gathering their belongings from the overhead racks, making plans for the night ahead.

"We can't know for sure," she said.

"You must come with me."

She watched him run an imaginary scale with his left hand. He was proposing a one-handed life. The one she had was one-handed but she was used to it, and there was now this enormous new thing. She moved uncomfortably, wanting to shift the conversation to neutral ground; there were too many sudden changes, and she did not know how to describe them to him. Now the train was losing speed. They were in the Paris suburbs, crossing the river, the water glittering, barges strung along the quays. She turned her head and high on the horizon was bulbous Sacré-Coeur, creamy and absurd on Montmartre. Gare St.-Lazare was only minutes away, and she wondered if Alfred would object to a taxi. She did not want to face the Métro. "Auvergne," she said with a ghost of a smile. "What would I do in Auvergne?"

He nodded, not arguing.

"Later," she said.

"Only a few minutes more," he said.

"A taxi," she said.

"The Métro's quicker."

Her stomach did another turn and she closed her eyes, holding on.

"Georgia? What's wrong?"

"It's the heat," she said. "I'm fine, really."

But she looked dreadful. She was suddenly gray, leaning back in her chair. Her face had lost all color. He remembered the night he had helped her up the stairs and into her room, her body burning with fever. At first he thought she was drunk, then saw that she was ill. She said something to him and at once he knew she was an American, from the slang expression she used, thanking him. She said, Thanks a bunch. And inside her apartment, an unmade bed, an easel with a canvas covered with burlap, and empty bottles of Calvados lined up along the wall. So she was a middle-aged American woman who painted and drank. But when she looked up at him he saw that she was not old, but young; and not plain, but lovely. When her eyes closed she looked like a young girl. But the bottles worried him and the apartment was in disarray, and freezing. Of course artists made their own queer rules, but why were they attracted to squalor and drink? She was very sick that time. He never walked up the stairs without re-membering her huddled there, crumpled and stiff. She opened her eyes now and smiled weakly and he knew it was ended be-tween them. They were destined to make separate journeys, and that meant he would be alone again, as would she. Probably it was for the best.

She said, "Alfred."

He said, "Only a few minutes more, we can get something in the station —"

She took a deep breath and held up her hand.

He waited for her to speak to him.

"Alfred, I'm pregnant," she said.

They took a taxi to rue Blaise, Alfred solicitous, carrying his luggage and hers, insisting she lean on him. They went to his apartment, which was always warmer. He made a cup of tea and brought it to her in bed. She slept for an hour and when she woke she felt fine. The upset was gone, vanished as if it had never existed. She sat up in bed and saw him across from her, sitting in his chair near the window. A book was open in his lap but he was not reading it.

"Are you feeling better?"

"Much better."

"Dear Georgia," he began.

"The doctor warned me there might be sickness."

"How long have you known?"

"Since last week."

"You had a test?"

"Yes, Alfred. I had a test. It was painless, and it was definite."

"But you didn't tell me."

"That's right."

"Why not?"

She was silent a moment.

"I had every right to know at once."

"You know how we are in America. We take our rights seriously. Anyhow, it was my business before it was yours."

"I don't understand."

"It doesn't matter."

"It's wonderful news. It matters a great deal." He rose from the chair, put the book down, and sat on the edge of the bed, kissing her lightly. "You must not keep things from me."

She smiled at that.

"One thing's settled," he said grimly. "There must be no argument about it. We will leave here together."

"We will?"

"Of course," he said. "We are going to have a child."

"You and I and the child in Auvergne."

"We will lease a suitable house."

"You with your false papers and me and the child, living in a farmhouse in Auvergne. And in a year somewhere else. The next year, some other place, perhaps another country even."

"This won't be necessary."

"We could find a mountain range to cross, the Pyrenees into Spain or the Alps into Italy or Switzerland or the Vosges into Germany. You, me, and the child. Let's hope it's a healthy boy with a taste for the out-of-doors. And whatever possessions we have, my art supplies and so forth, and of course the money that you've saved for the emergencies. This would surely qualify as an emergency. How heavy is your gold? The Vosges have mountain trails especially maintained for clandestine winter crossings and the Germans are hospitable to refugees. They have special laws and many pleasant internment camps. We can be guest workers, like the Turks. A guest worker who can play Fats Waller would be unique."

"There are ways and means," he said.

"*Which* ways?" she said. "*Which* means?"

"They would not interfere with an American woman and her husband."

"So now it's marriage," she said.

"Naturally," he said.

"But you're already married," she said.

"They don't know that," he said. "What is it but a piece of paper?"

"Alfred," she began.

"It's what I've always wanted," he said.

And she burst out laughing. Life with Alfred would be droll indeed. She wondered if he had any idea what he was getting into; and then she decided he probably had a better idea than she did. But she remembered now that one of the Impressionists had gone to Auvergne for the hot springs and had painted spectacular landscapes, living there happily to great age, painting in the morning and hiking in the mountains in the afternoon. She could not remember if he had a family. She looked at Alfred and posed a last question, not that she thought it was necessary, and not that she thought she would get a straight answer to it, but she had natural suspicions. Who wouldn't?

"Perhaps." She looked at him evenly. "Perhaps America."

"Not America," he said. "I could never live in America."

"You could come with me. I would arrange it with the Imm. and Natz. You, the child's father. I could get you a passport."

"I am a European. I can't live in America. In America there is no equilibrium."

"As opposed to here?"

"Auvergne is the most ancient part of France, and the most stable."

"America —"

"Don't make me go to America," he said. "It would be impossible for me."

"Well," she said. "That's good. That's lucky, because it's impossible for me, too."

"Why did you ask me?"

"I thought perhaps you wanted to go to America. So many

do. And now I find that you don't. That you want to stay right here."

"And why did you say we would have to cross mountain ranges?"

"I was joking."

"We won't have to cross mountain ranges, I promise. We'll be safe."

"Don't count on it, Alfred."

"So it's settled then," he said.

She rose from the bed and told him to wait a minute while she went next door. She returned with a bottle of Calvados and poured a measure into her teacup and stood drinking it while she looked into rue Blaise. Her general was in deep shadows, on his eternal reconnaissance. She touched her forehead to the window glass, looking at the statue in the park on the street that she knew so well. *L'heure de maman* indeed.

"One other thing," he said.

"What's that?" She was still looking at the statue and now she threw open the window and leaned out, breathing deeply. From his tone of voice she knew that he was about to issue instructions of some kind.

"You have to stop that."

"Stop what?"

"Drinking," he said. "It's bad for you, bad for the child. And Calvados is worst of all; it raises your blood pressure. It disturbs the metabolism. The child will be swimming in alcohol. Surely you know this is not the way to behave. As behavior, it's self-destructive. You are not twenty-one years old. You are a sensible woman who must obey the natural conventions of good health. You are carrying a child. Even Frenchwomen are careful during pregnancy. The Americans have conducted many studies on the matter. And you must stop that also." While he was talking she had lit a cigarette, her first since they had left the buffet car. She blew a thick smoke ring into the night, leaning forward, watching the smoke ring collapse in the breeze and rush away. She was looking for the young musician who played Schubert in the evenings, but there was no one in the street, and even the lamps seemed dim. It was not so late; where could the people be? Then she saw movement in the park; one figure and then another detached itself from the shadows. Warmed by the Calvados, she imagined these figures to be her own creations, friends from this life and from previous lives. They were her subjects, saints and selves, all the figments of her imagination. They gathered around the general's statue, bidding her farewell, wishing her bon chance. All of them were smiling, sorry to see her go — but didn't she think ambition had got the better of her, attempting to bring a twice-dead object to life? Shouldn't the general be allowed to advance in peace? What were you *thinking*, Georgie? She waved back at them and blew a last smoke ring, turning then to listen to Alfred.

"Tobacco is a disgusting habit that should be outlawed. And someday it will be."

"Alfred," she said.

"These are ordinary precautions," he said.

"I'll go to Auvergne with you."

"Yes, this is wonderful."

"I'll have the child in Auvergne."

"And a wonderful child she'll be."

"And we'll live there happily."

"Very happily," he said.

"I'll paint, you'll play the piano."

"And we'll have our child."

"We'll settle the matter of your ex-wife. One way or another."

"Yes," he said.

"So listen," she said.

"I'm listening."

"Never tell me what to do or how to behave."

"But," he began. "*Mais c'est pas logique, Georgie.*"

"Never, Alfred. I don't like it." All her old truculence had returned in a surge, and she was forming objections even before he was finished. I do not respond well to logic, Alfred. I do not respond at all to instructions. Shut up, Alfred. Fuck off, Alfred. Who do you think you are, anyway? And just as suddenly the objections evaporated and she was defenseless, understanding that she was no longer alone and that he was not her enemy.

She said, "Logical, is it?"

He said, "Yes."

"All right," she said. "For you, Alfred."

"Not for me," he said. "For you and our baby."

She looked him in the eye and raised her teacup. "Our health," she said.

HARRY

GEORGIA WHYTE had told me this story in bits and pieces over a half-dozen dinners at the brasserie near the Musée d'Orsay. I always looked forward to seeing her, though what she said usually put me on edge. She held nothing back and her candor seemed to invite a confession from me in return; but I never gave one. Whatever confessions I had I saved for my novels. Her story reminded me of my own early ambition, my hopes for myself and my work. There is no reason why I should have compared lives — we worked in different mediums with different results — but weighing and measuring is basic to the artistic life. We live in a competitive environment whether we want to or not; there is no such thing as invisible writing or invisible drawing. She attempted to make a coherent whole of her life, and listening to her, I was forced to make an accounting of mine — debits and credits, goals met and goals defaulted. This was not entirely to my disadvantage, for I had gone much, much further than I'd expected when I started out. And it could be said also that Georgia and I had started from the same place, with the same desire.

But the novels I wrote were not the novels I intended to write. In my dreams I wanted to write about the North Shore, delivering the plain truth about the Brownes and Harold Barrimore and my brother Dean and audacious girls like Georgia Whyte, and what set them apart. This world has changed since F. Scott Fitzgerald was alive, and I thought I needed to cross an ocean to write about the romance of a summer night at a country club in Winnetka. I knew more stories than I could ever tell, stories from the North Shore, stories from Mackinac and Michigan Avenue, stories of breakdown and recovery, and how people defended themselves against the world. And they are in my mind still because, instead of writing about America, I wrote about Paris, so lush and accessible, so graceful and finished, loaded with lore. Winnetka was my clumsy uncle, and the Brownes and Harold and Dean and Georgia — distant cousins, far from home.

My novels are travelogues disguised as detective stories. Pease is Baedeker. They are written to formula with occasional digressions, and it is always the digressions that earn the praise. Comparisons with Beckett, comparisons with Sagan. It was my good fortune that the novels were successful from the beginning, and I spared no effort to make them so, the competitive environment, et cetera. One arrondissement led to another and the arrondissements led to a television series; and I became the sole proprietor of a profitable industry.

Georgia's story reminded me how far I had wandered from my original path. The path I had taken was not shameful, but it was not original either. And it had nothing to do with romance, of a summer night in Winnetka or any other night. She had broken her pick but I thought that somehow she had got the better of the bargain. I had skipped forward a step at a time. She had taken one step backward for each step forward but her concentration had been absolute, all the steps meticulously scrutinized. She knew where she had been, and she knew where she was; she seemed to know the *merit* of what she had done. Georgia proposed to divide human motive into ambition and love, an equation I never accepted. I think she was in pursuit of virtue, and that was her ambition; she preferred to call it love.

I would see her once or twice a month, and in the early fall I noticed she was drinking less. Her focus seemed now to be on the future, she and Alfred somewhere in the French countryside. Our last dinner together was almost sedate, one carafe of wine instead of six, and she was no longer smoking between mouthfuls. We were trading travel stories when she suddenly looked at her watch and excused herself to make a telephone call, explaining that Alfred would be worried about her and she needed to reach him anyway before he left for the club. It was his last night there and she had bought him a new shirt for the occasion. She wanted him to wear it, and the black onyx studs that had belonged to her grandfather. I watched her lean comfortably on the zinc bar, half-covering the mouthpiece against the noise in the restaurant. She said very little but seemed to be listening attentively. Once she turned to me and winked, making a duck's bill with the fingers of her free hand. Quack, quack, quack, Alfred talking. Then I heard her laugh gaily.

When she returned to our table she was smiling broadly, saying that Alfred was grateful for the shirt and studs but was concerned that she had fallen in with bad company and would be out all night.

She said, "He worries too much."

"Didn't you tell him how reliable I am?"

"I told him who you are, an old friend from America. But he thinks you're a bad influence. He has this slight problem with my drinking."

"So you told me. He'll get over it. It looks like he'll have to."

"And naturally he's worried about the baby," she said slyly.

"Naturally," I said. I knew that she would begin to talk about babies, so I caught the eye of the waiter and pointed at the empty carafe. I needed fortification because babies were not in my repertoire.

"It's so great," she said.

"Fabulous," I said.

"So he worries more than ever. He's a worrier, my Alfred. It's sweet, really. Him worrying. And what do I drink? About two glasses of wine a night, sometimes less. And very occasionally a Calvados before I go to bed." She sighed. "My new regime."

"Does it worry you?"

"No, it never has. I used to drink with my father."

"Yes," I said. "You told me. In his study. Amid the books and Sidney Bechet."

"Scotch," she said, as if that explained something.

"Alfred probably doesn't approve of spirits."

"My father loved the taste of Scotch. He said Scotch gave the world a different tilt. Drinking Scotch, he looked at things askance. He said it was sometimes helpful to look at things indirectly. "So," she said brightly, "despite his fine example, I'm practicing moderation."

The waiter took the empty carafe and replaced it with a full one. She shook her head when I offered her a glass, but I filled my own to the brim and took a long pull.

"It's a pain, watching someone else drink. You finish that and we'll call it a night."

"Anything you say."

"I don't mind drinking alone but I hate watching someone else drink."

"I'll be quick," he said.

"Take your time. I don't want to be a bully about it."

After a moment, I said, "Are you really pregnant?"

"Why would I joke about it? You don't sound very enthusiastic."

"Of course I'm enthusiastic," I lied. "Congratulations."

"I'm going to Auvergne with Alfred to have the baby."

"It's a wonderful place for babies," I said, filling my glass again. I thought she was headed for disaster, a Chicago girl so far from home with a man who had never had one, a man who even by her account was a loser par excellence. I could not see them together in Auvergne or anywhere else. And the child would interfere with her work. However, she had not asked my opinion. I said to myself, Don't be so quick to judge. I said to Georgia that she was taking on a lot. I wished her very good luck and let me know if there's anything I can do, you'll love Auvergne, and French medicine is first-rate, really. And in the end I could not resist.

"What about your work?"

"What about it?"

"The baby." I smiled, awaiting her reaction. "The pram-in-the-hallway-is-the-enemy-of-art."

"So they say," she said. "But I always thought the enemy was indifference."

We were alone in the restaurant now. There was only a single waiter yawning at the caisse, and at last even his patience was exhausted and he began turning off the lights. Georgia looked at me and rolled her eyes, making the duck's bill gesture again, only this time she was laughing at herself. She rose and said something to the waiter, who moved off behind the bar, returning with a bottle of thirty-year-old Calvados.

My treat, she said.

You've been a good friend.

Very good luck to you, too.

Just save me a little sip.

So I can toast the pram in the hallway.

The Calvados finished beautifully. I called for the bill, paid it, laid a very large tip on top of the service, and struggled to my feet. I helped her with her coat and the waiter bowed us out, and presently we were standing in rue de Lille in a soft drizzle that was more mist than rain.

She hooked her arm through mine and leaned close to say something, but I wasn't paying attention. I was thinking of the number of times I had left restaurants late at night, with my wife or with friends, and somehow I could always remember the laughter left behind at the table. We were always animated, deciding whether to go home or to a café or to someone's apartment for a nightcap. Keep the night alive! Our voices echoed in the empty street and if we were too loud someone would call down,

Arretez!

Silence!

Respect those who sleep!

Behind us the lights of the restaurant would go off, one by one. Wherever we were in Paris, if we raised our eyes we would see a landmark, Sacré Coeur or the Eiffel Tower or the dome of Bonaparte's tomb or the rooftops of the Louvre or the Tour Montparnasse. And then we would huddle together, whispering like schoolchildren, not wanting the evening to end. There were a thousand possibilities and it was necessary to consider each one, understanding all the while that there was no place on earth that you would rather be, and no one else you wanted to be there with. A cab would ease up to the curb, pausing, the driver looking hopefully our way; and we would wave him on because our minds were not made up, owing to the many possibilities for adventure. And it seemed that more often than not there would be rain in the air, bringing a clean, sweet smell to Paris at midnight, an invitation to treat the city as a film set and explore it on foot. I had been doing this for many years and I knew from experience that most evenings ended thoughtfully, as if to balance the hilarity of the table. But those nights were not this night. I was dispirited that Georgia was leaving Paris; her life intrigued me and I was sorry that I would be unable to follow it. I knew that once she left Paris for Auvergne our friendship would collapse. Alfred believed me a bad influence. Of course I believed that she had been seduced against her will. She thought she could make a European life with Alfred, disappearing into provincial France as Gauguin had disappeared into the Society Islands. This was romantic nonsense, even for a Chicago Bohemian. She thought she could leave life behind as you leave laughter at a table; and then I realized that idea was mine, not hers, and that she was leaving nothing behind.

She had her work and Alfred and now she would have a child, too.

But she had been a good friend to me, and I hated seeing her go.

"Equilibrium," I said aloud.

Georgia said, "What?"

"Nothing," I said.

You said, 'Equilibrium.' That's what Alfred says America lacks."

"Does it? I hadn't noticed."

"That's what he says."

"What the hell does Alfred know about America? Has he ever been there?"

"Alfred's very intelligent," she said, bristling a little. "And no, he's never been. And he doesn't want to go."

"Don't you want him to see Chicago?"

She looked at me strangely and said. "No. Why would I want him to see Chicago?"

I realized suddenly how tight I was. I had no business advising her on her life or making judgments about the man who was the father of her child. I muttered something about equilibrium in the heartland, making a joke of it.

"You don't like Alfred, do you?"

"I don't know Alfred," I said.

"But you suspect him."

"Of what?"

"I don't know. Gold digging?"

"Are you rich? You didn't used to be rich."

"I'm richer than he is."

"He sounds fine," I said.

"He's a gentleman," she said and I knew then that any protest I might make would have no effect. Gentlemanliness was a trump card.

"I'm sure," I said.

"Come on," she said. "Let's not stand around. I want to see the river."

So we walked slowly down rue de Lille and across the plaza of the Musée d'Orsay. I looked through the windows to see if *Les*

Romains de la Décadence was visible, but it was not. A night guard seated on a stool stared at me incuriously, and then I realized he was asleep. We crossed the street at the light and leaned against the concrete barrier to look at the houseboats, lined up like toys along the quay on the Right Bank. Most were dark but a few had their interior lights lit and I imagined riotous parties within.

I began to laugh, it was all so familiar. I explained to Georgia that years ago I had spent weeks walking up and down the quay watching the activity aboard the boats, researching my first book, *Inspector Pease in the First Arrondissement.* I did not have a plot or characters but I knew I would find them once I knew about life belowdecks, where the galley was in relation to the saloon, where everyone slept, the view from the portholes, and the motion of the boat on the river. There was a particularly handsome barge of Dutch registry. The owners had drinks on the deck each night at six and were happy to invite us aboard. They showed us around and described riverine life and then it was a simple matter to contrive a boat tied up across from the Musée d'Orsay, the boat occupied by an American college student and his high-born French lover, the lover's low-life brother, a thriving drug trade, an ugly murder, and gallant Inspector Pease to solve it all in three hundred pages.

Georgia nudged me and said, "Who died?"

"The college boy."

"Why him?"

"He was an innocent abroad, too much money and too little sense. He was in over his head."

"Poor American college boy. And the lover?"

"Smart as a snake," I said. "She was a countess. Her family had survived seven centuries of French misrule. She was a connoisseur of other people's weaknesses and the American boy had a basketful and she exploited every one."

"He doesn't sound very heroic."

"He was dumb as a post."

"What happened to him?"

"It was grisly. You don't want to know."

"Tell me anyway."

"They tied him to an anchor and threw him overboard into the Seine."

"Because he was so dumb?"

"Because he'd outlived his usefulness. He had his revenge, though. The body worked free and came to the surface. By then Pease knew he was dead and knew the lover and her no-account brother had killed him, but since there was no body, there was no crime. Pease is on the foredeck conducting a brilliant interrogation when they hear a noise, the boy's head scraping against the hull. They look over the side and there he is, face up, an eel around his neck. That's the last sentence of the book. Justice done, and seen to be done."

"And it all happened right over there?" Georgia pointed across the river to the Tuileries, and the barges lashed to the quay below. She threw out a low, sarcastic whistle, grinning. Upriver we could see the summit of Notre Dame. The river glittered with yellow light from the streetlamps and the floodlights used to illuminate the great buildings. The sky was clear now and a bright half moon was rising over the Louvre.

She said, "Why did your wife leave you?"

I had been thinking of her just then. We had stood at this spot many times, researching *Inspector Pease in the First Arrondissement,* and in fact it was Ellen who had had the idea of the houseboat in the Seine, and the eel necklace in the last sentence. She discovered so much river lore, she was going to write a guidebook to the quays, but she never did. Our love affair began in the First Arrondissement, and we were married on the day the book was published.

Georgia said, "Forget it. It's not my business."

I thought, What the hell. I said, "She said she couldn't stand it anymore."

"Couldn't stand you?"

"France," I said. "And me too, I suppose. But mostly France."

"It's not so difficult here."

I looked at her and raised my eyebrows.

"What's so difficult about France, Harry? And anyway, she'd been here so long, married to you —"

I stared across the river at the boats. Of course the Dutch boat was long gone, returned to Delft. Ellen and I had made friends with the owners and used to stop by on Sunday afternoons for lunch on the deck, sitting on canvas chairs under an awning and watching the river traffic, and being watched in turn by Sunday strollers on the quay. Thinking about the long afternoons aboard the boat made me heartsick. I said, "It would have been the same anywhere in Europe. She kept knocking on the door and finally realized she'd never be admitted in the way she wanted to be admitted, as an equal, that she was an American outsider and would always be an American outsider." I explained that Ellen came from a very small town where everyone knew each other and all she thought she had to do was make an effort, learn the language and become acquainted with the culture and throw smart dinner parties, and she'd be accepted, as she always had been in her hometown. But it didn't work that way in France except at the very highest levels, where money made the introductions, and even then it was mostly an illusion. She hated being an outsider. She called it "spectating." And one day she looked up and said, It's been twenty years. That's enough. She decided to go home alone, since I wouldn't go home with her.

Georgia was silent a moment. Then she asked, "What did Ellen do?"

"Helped me with research," I said. "She hated the Tenth Arrondissement. That's the most recent Pease. I liked it but she didn't. She thought there were too many Arabs and she hated going there to collect lore. She said it was like going to Oakland. She loved the First and the Second and of course the Eighth, Seventh, and Sixth. She had friends in those arrondissements. Maybe that was it, the Tenth Arrondissement was the straw that broke her back."

"Maybe it did," Georgia said. "But that's not what I was asking. I mean, what did she do for *herself*. Other than helping you with your Pease. Did she have her own work?"

"She romanced the French," I said, and Georgia nodded, smiling tightly, figuring that she knew all she needed to know. It was foolish to argue with her. If she wanted to believe that work or a career was a specific for desperate homesickness, that was her privilege. But Ellen wouldn't have agreed. She greatly admired the Frenchwomen she knew. None of them worked. They loved not working. Not working was the sine qua non of the well-lived life. Why would anyone work if she didn't have to?

But there was something else that I wanted to say, and I was careful now to choose my words. I was at that point in the evening where I could formulate the first sentence but not the sentences that would follow. I said, "Still, we got along better than most. We believed in the same things, mainly. We had fun in the same ways. We liked the same jokes. We were better off than the mixed marriages, Americans married to French or English married to French or Americans, any of several combinations." I had lost my way and tried now to recoup. "And it was hell being with them because they fought all day long and into the evening, no holds barred."

"And why was that?"

"They didn't believe in the same things."

"Like what?"

"Virtue," I said.

She looked at me suspiciously.

"Politics," I said. I didn't want to talk to her about virtue.

"Politics? Who cares about politics anymore?"

"You damn well care about it when your security depends on it." I was aware that I was speaking in what my former wife called my Swiss franc voice, a blowhard currency of last resort. "The exchange rate. NATO. Terrorism." I backed up again. "When it's all around you and you and your mate have different definitions of it. At the end of the evening the Europeans are talking about American stupidity and the Americans are talking about European cowardice. You don't know what fun it is until you've seen a man and his wife go at each other on that firing range. *Boom boom!* Because it's obvious they're not talking about nations. They're talking about each other."

She was silent a moment.

"Too bad you didn't read *Inspector Pease in the Seventh Arrondissement;* it's all laid out. It's fully explained. A diplomat is murdered and everyone assumes it's an espionage affair. But it isn't. It's a crime of passion. The diplomat's wife has heard one too many supercilious remarks and smashes his head with an iron poker. While he sleeps."

"That's ridiculous," she said slowly.

"American wife, French husband." I sought to deliver the coup de grâce. "After a while, they couldn't even agree on Impressionists. They didn't agree on *food.*"

"What about drink?" she asked belligerently. "Did they agree about drink?"

"And someone always ended face up in the soup with an eel around his neck. Or her neck."

She muttered something caustic and leaned forward, watching a long barge ghost upriver, its engines silent. Its wake was lost in the glitter of the water, and when it passed under Pont Royale you could believe it had never existed at all, or existed in your imagination only.

She said suddenly, "Let's have a nightcap."

"Too late," I said.

"Be a sport," she said urgently. "It's only a few steps. We can walk."

"Georgia, it's late. I'll see you home."

"It's a place I know you'll like. It's in the Sixth Arrondissement. Isn't that one of your wife's favorites, an upscale arrondissement?" She hooked her arm through mine and we walked up the quay. Georgia navigated, I was so unsteady. She was whistling under her breath. At this hour the city was very quiet, the sidewalk deserted except for a few lone strollers. The moon was high over Notre Dame and I reflected again how coincidental life was. You went to the Musée d'Orsay and discovered a magpie, the magpie led you to Madame Canoville, and Madame Canoville to *Les Romains de la Décadence;* and you encountered a woman you had not seen in many years, and she told you her story, holding nothing back, telling it because it was there to be told and you were there to listen to it.

We crossed the street and walked up Quai Voltaire to Quai Malaquais, and then into rue de Seine. From the restless silence of the river we entered a different city. Back of the quays the streets were lively, the cafés full, and the streets noisy with carousing tourists and unruly students from the Latin Quarter. There was music and the hum of conversation, everyone animated, even the ragged panhandlers. We were jostled this way and that, Georgia laughing, taking it all in stride, pausing here and there to look into gallery windows. She said she lived nearby but had never gone into rue de Seine late at night because that was her working time; and this was probably the last time she would see it. I suppose I've missed a lot, she said, but you have to live in a way that suits you.

We stepped off the sidewalk and into the street, hurrying now. Cars were stalled and honking, drivers leaning out of windows and making irritable gestures. Students were moving back and forth between the cars, tapping on hoods and generally making good-natured nuisances of themselves. Georgia pointed to a house and said that was where Molière had lived, rehearsing his plays in the parlor. She gestured around us and said, Doesn't it remind you of Rush Street in the old days? And while I was trying to remember Rush Street in the old days, she turned abruptly into a narrow alley. It was a kind of oasis. Behind us we could hear the students and the movement of traffic, and very close by the sound of a piano.

"It's here," she said, leading me down a short flight of steps past a sign that said MEMBERS ONLY and through a heavy door into a cabaret. We stood in the vestibule while our eyes adjusted to the darkness. There was a long bar on one side of the room and a tiny dance floor and tables around the dance floor. The place was filled with smoke but wasn't crowded, the atmosphere suggestive of a New York nightclub of the nineteen fifties. Four men in tuxedos lounged at one of the tables, and I took them to be musicians since the bandstand was empty, a saxophone on one chair and a bass leaning against the wall and a guitar in its case next to the pianist.

"Alfred," she said.

But I knew that. A customer was humming something into Alfred's ear and at the same time extracting a bank note from his wallet and putting it carefully on the piano, Alfred nodding politely while he listened and ran little aimless riffs with his right hand. Then the customer patted Alfred on the back and moved off, returning to one of the front tables, where he sat alone.

Alfred's tuxedo was threadbare, all right. The serge had a dull sheen. But his white shirt with the black studs gave him a worldly appearance, dapper enough so that you forgot about the tuxedo. He bent now to his work, moving easily through one of the standard American show tunes. He put some blues into it, trying to give the customer his money's worth. The customer was nodding and tapping his foot, evidently satisfied. From the look on his face, the tune meant something intensely personal and very tragic. When Alfred swung out of it and into "Bye-Bye Blackbird," the customer clapped and yelled, Bravo! No one else in the restaurant was paying any attention. The off-duty musicians ostentatiously studied their knuckles.

Georgia gave the doorman some money and he escorted us to the bar, where she ordered Perrier. I took Calvados. Alfred had not seen us but we had a good view of him, an expressionless middle-aged European with a swarthy complexion and black hair combed straight back. His was a face you would lose in any crowd except in America, where he would stand out because of his composure. He had the bearing of a civil servant, indifferent to his surroundings, and oblivious of the buzz of conversation and the tinkle of cocktail glasses. He played with all the emotion of a typist, head slightly bent, back straight, feet levered above the pedals, fingers striding purposefully. There was no score in front of him and I noticed that the bank note had disappeared.

Alfred's technique called attention to the music, and as I watched him he seemed to fade and be replaced by the tune he was making. He disappeared into his material.

"Isn't he a wonderful technician?" Georgia said.

I nodded. She was right about that.

"This is the first time I've heard him play."

"You ought to tell him we're here," I said.

"He'll see us," she said. "It's a surprise."

"That's good," I said. "If he's the sort of man who likes surprises."

Alfred had moved into a brisk version of "I've Got a Feeling I'm Falling," though from his demeanor it could have been a Bach fugue.

"Do you like his left hand?"

"I don't know," I said. "I suppose I do. Is there something particular about it?"

"It's weak," she said.

"It is?"

"Yes, can't you hear?"

I looked at her. Georgia's expression had gone soft as a kitten's. The weakness of Alfred's left hand seemed to have some tremendous significance for her, like Beethoven's deafness or Toulouse-Lautrec's dwarfism. She had taken a pen and an envelope from her purse and was sketching Alfred at the piano, giving him the force and dignity of Arthur Rubinstein.

"He talks about it all the time. It bothers him."

"Of course," I said. I had no idea what she was talking about.

"It's a difficulty when he's playing Fats Waller."

"The customers seem to like it," I said hopefully, but as I looked around I saw that this was not strictly true. The crowd was thinning out and the musicians were talking loudly among themselves. No one was listening to Alfred but us, yet he seemed not to notice or care. Then I heard a familiar song that I could not identify and looked up to see Alfred staring directly at Georgia and grinning broadly. So far as I could tell, it was his first smile of the night. She blew him a kiss and he moved his shoulders in acknowledgment and began to play very loudly, allegro, his body swaying with the rhythm. Georgia laughed, touching my arm, turning to the barman to signal for more Calvados.

"I love him so," she said.

Alfred was using the piano's full register, winding down now with great crescendos.

"Doesn't he play wonderfully?"

"Yes," I said.

"And he doesn't play for himself. He plays for *them.*"

"What's the song?" I said.

"You don't recognize it?" She laughed again and clinked glasses.

My eyesight was beginning to blur and a headache to gather in the center of my skull, but I swallowed anyway. Georgia leaned close to me and whispered something, but I didn't hear what it was. She still had the dreamy look on her face, listening to Alfred. The musicians at the front table were beginning to stir, so I guessed that Alfred's intermission was about to end and their set to begin. He was in the third or fourth verse of whatever song he was playing, the crowd strangely quiet now because he was so athletic, arms pumping and feet tapping to the rhythm. It might have been Fats himself at the piano. Even the musicians were attentive. Georgia could not take her eyes off him, giving little throaty cries whenever he made a particularly deft riff.

"My Alfred," she said. "He's playing for me," she said and it occurred to me at that moment that there were at least three Alfreds at the piano, the crowd's, mine, and Georgia's. None of these Alfreds would recognize the others, and all of them were off center, since they were by necessity observed from the outside in. Alfred would have quite a different view of himself; and then again, perhaps he wouldn't. Perhaps he was one of those who saw himself as others saw him. Or as Georgia did. He had ended in a crashing of chords and was now taking applause. Even the musicians were clapping. Alfred sat at the piano smiling shyly.

I slipped off the bar stool.

"He'll be here in a minute," she said.

"I'm going," I said.

"You can't go before you meet him. All I've told you about him."

"I like your version. He might spoil it."

She said, "Fuck you, Harry," in a tone of voice that hinted she agreed with me.

Alfred was talking to the musicians, nodding at us. The leader had picked up his saxophone and was fussing with the valves; then he looked up and smiled appreciatively at Georgia.

"I wish you great good luck," I said.

"But you won't stay to meet him."

"No," I said. I could feel the electricity between them and believed that my presence was unnecessary. But I had no choice because suddenly he was at her side, kissing her warmly, placing his hand lightly on her stomach, turning to shake hands with me.

"This is Harry," Georgia said. "But he has to leave."

"I am pleased to meet you," Alfred said.

"Harry's my friend from Chicago," Georgia said. "The one I haven't seen in years and years and years and years and years."

He looked at her closely, thinking she was tight. His eyebrows lifted fractionally, but he smiled gamely.

"Congratulations," I said.

"Good-bye," Alfred said.

The band struck up the song Alfred had played. Alfred turned from me now, standing to one side, beaming. I left them like that, holding hands while the band played — it was "Georgia on My Mind." The barman brought two glasses of Calvados and they toasted each other. I suppose he allowed her to have a glass after work; or she insisted and he had to agree. She showed him the sketch she had made and he blushed — or seemed to. She folded the sketch and put it in his pocket. The band played on to an indifferent audience. She reached for her glass, lifting it high, taking the Calvados all the way down, and I had the feeling that was not the last glass Georgia Whyte would drink late at night, drinking to give the world a different tilt and a more human face, her Alfred stiff and disapproving at her side.

I used them both as minor characters in *Inspector Pease in the Twelfth Arrondissement,* a novel that centered on the Gare de Lyon. Alfred was a Bulgarian gunrunner and Georgia his hard-drinking American girlfriend. At the end of the book the Bulgarian dies and the girl goes home to America. I suppose I thought that was what would happen to Alfred and Georgia; that or something like it. Alfred would drift away and Georgia would continue her grazing.

Then they slipped from my mind as I wrote *Inspector Pease in the Thirteenth Arrondissement.* France had acquired a nervous tempo as things began to break down in Europe. I set to work researching the Fourteenth Arrondissement, though I could not seem to get my hands around the material. I could not seem to get my hands around anything. I wanted to write something about the Franco-German alliance, much in the news then; I did not see how such an alliance could hold. They were opposites that could never attract and I imagine that in the back of my mind I was thinking of Alfred and Georgia.

I was going with a woman who worked in the Louvre and she gave me the idea of a plot involving a stolen masterpiece. The masterpiece was German, brought to France by smugglers. Carefully presented, the plot had allegorical possibilities. Anna supplied me with wonderful lore about the art business. I was attempting to contrive a story with French and German art experts, a shady American buyer, and, of course, Pease. But I couldn't get it going and wondered if I had exhausted Pease, and Paris as well; I began to worry that I was working a played-out mine. Of course I always felt that way in the early stages of a book.

I was well behind schedule when Anna brought me to dinner one night in Montparnasse, the apartment of friends who had an extensive art collection. That was all they did, collect, and Anna gave me to understand that they were not particular how they

went about it, or whose aid they enlisted. A painting's provenance was less important than its potential, and provenance anyway was a matter of perspective. Hélène and Roland had time
and a great deal of money and cost was never an issue if they
wanted something badly enough. They traveled everywhere in
Europe and Asia, always searching for the lost or unidentified or
potential masterpiece.

Perhaps they were a little bit roguish, Anna said. But they
were also serious people. Roland, particularly, had an excellent
eye and a photographic memory. Hélène was the negotiator.
Really, they were very agreeable in small doses. Collecting was
all they cared about and they were amazingly eclectic, almost
promiscuous: Chinese porcelain, pre-Columbian pottery, Impressionist landscapes, German altarpieces, Moghul whatnot.

And everything is for sale, Anna said.

There were two other couples for dinner, a journalist and his
wife and a banker and his mistress. Anna told them that I was
a writer of *policiers,* well known in America and a cult figure in
France. But they knew that already.

"I've seen you on television," the journalist's wife said.

"Synergy," the journalist said.

"You mean tie-in," the wife said. "The Americans call it *le
tie-in.*"

"Is the series in America, too?" the journalist asked.

"Late night," I said.

"Dubbed or subtitles?"

"Dubbed," I said.

"I'm writing a novel," the journalist said. "Maybe —"

"Of course," I said.

"— when I wrap it up you can give me some tips on how it's
done, names. The people you have to suck up to and so forth
and so on, and what you can expect. It's a natural for television.
The tie-in, you see."

"It's set in Luxembourg," the wife said.

I nodded. Luxembourg.

"If I can get it into the right hands —"

"Yes," I said.

"It's a natural," he said.

"Everyone admires your skill, Monsieur Forrest."

And Georges was now charging 150 francs for my first editions, I thought but did not say.

Over Champagne the conversation moved quickly to the *scandale du jour,* a cabinet minister accused of extortion. The cabinet minister had many complicated relationships in and out of government and it was certain he was not acting alone. Everyone knew the minister or one or another of his entourage, so the conversation was lively but difficult to enter if you did not have some fresh fact or rumor to add, and I had none; the journalist retailed some choice details. I had not followed the scandal and did not know the minister. These affairs are a dime a carload and I had no more heart for them than I had for my work. So I half listened and allowed my eyes to wander.

Anna had not been wrong. I identified a Cham pot and a Goya drawing from the *Horrors of War* series, the drawing strangely benign despite its subject, and a complicated landscape that looked like Corot or Millet. Various small objects were visible on mantelpieces and tables, the whole conceived with the sort of taste that's called exquisite and — I suppose the word is *aplomb.* I was filing things away in my memory, which objects were next to which, where the Cham pot was in relation to the Goya, and the scheme that bound it all together. I imagined the organizing principle to be nothing less than ownership of anything that suited the collectors' fancy, so I concentrated hard because I wanted to remember it all, placing the room in my memory as you would place a snapshot in an album.

I was particularly drawn to an exacting portrait that seemed to be of the modern era, at any event of the twentieth century. I thought its strenuous spirit was out of place in this room. It reminded me vaguely of Max Beckmann's *Arrangement in Black and White,* the self-portrait in a tuxedo, the young artist standing truculently before a window, his hand on his hip, a cigarette smoldering in his fingers. This portrait showed a middle-aged man in profile, standing rigidly in a field, a low mountain in the background. He was wearing a tuxedo, very out of place in the rural surroundings. His face was not clearly visible but there was high tension in the way he stood, his left hand resting in a black box. The picture seemed to step up to the surreal, salute, then back away. It was turbulent, and filled with mystery.

I was aware of a sudden silence in the room.

"I'm afraid we're boring our American friend," Hélène said.

"It's the portrait," Roland said.

"Go ahead," Hélène said. "Take a closer look."

"The artist is a countryman of yours," Roland added.

And when he said that I knew it was a picture of Georgia Whyte's. As I moved closer, it became obvious that the middle-aged man in the tuxedo was Alfred and the black box not a black box at all but the edge of a piano. I knew it was Alfred because of the way he stood and held his head. He seemed made of granite. And in the background, emerging from a wood at the base of the mountain, was a lithe female figure, nude, obviously Georgia. Looking at it, I was tremendously moved. I suppose in a way it was like encountering an old friend, and remembering in that moment how fond you had been of each other; you would embrace at once. I searched for the obvious confirmation, and in a moment found it: in the lower left-hand corner, in letters no bigger than the type on this page, were her initials: GW.

"She lives in Auvergne," Hélène said.

"Her French is not so good," Roland said. "But the one she is with is fluent enough. He makes all the decisions anyway."

I started to say that I knew her, that she was an old friend, that we had known each other in Chicago and later in Paris, and that it was extremely unlikely that anyone would make Georgia Whyte's decisions for her, least of all Alfred. But I sensed a strain in the room and said none of these things. I remembered what Anna had volunteered about the collectors being a little bit roguish.

"Do you like it?" Hélène asked.

"It's a wonderful piece," I said.

"Yes," she agreed. "It is. Strangers come into our house and notice the Goya and the Corot at once. They admire the porcelain and the *objets*. But this is the picture they ask about, where we acquired it and how. It has a very unusual quality, don't you agree?"

"Stunning," I said.

"The artist is extremely difficult," Roland said.

"She's eccentric," Hélène said flatly.

"She and her friend," Roland said.

"We met them quite by chance," Hélène said. "By accident in Mont Dore. We go there for the hiking and also there are antiques to be found if you know where to look and don't mind paying."

"It's peasant country," Roland said disagreeably. "Vulgar. Most of them are still in the Middle Ages."

"This piece," I began.

"She was difficult about it," Roland said.

"She didn't want us to have it," Hélène said.

"But when we want something we usually get it. If we want it badly enough we will fight for it." Roland smiled thinly.

I wanted desperately to know how much they had paid but did not want to ask directly. I hoped that Georgia had soaked them. I hoped she had soaked them good. They were the sort of people who deserved soaking. I tried to imagine how Pease would go about it in an interrogation. I said off-handedly, "The price would be high, naturally." And then I added, as I thought Pease would do — nothing ventured, nothing gained, in for a penny, in for a pound, back them up a little — "Georgia Whyte is much admired in America."

In the surprised silence that followed, Roland said silkily, "So you know her work then?"

"No," I said. "Strangely, I don't." Then I looked at him directly. "But I know her."

"Ah," he said, the sound someone makes when a dark suspicion is confirmed.

"Not well, I'm afraid."

"The black box?" he said.

"It's a piano."

"A piano," he said. "Of course."

"We had never heard of her," Hélène said, "and she refused to discuss any aspect of the canvas."

"It was all by accident," Roland said, and then laughed sharply, signaling the novelty of what he was about to say. "We wanted it because we *liked* it."

"At first she wouldn't let us have it," Hélène said.

"That oaf she was with —"

"Alfred is her husband," I said.

"— acted in our behalf."

You son of a bitch, I thought, looking at the picture. I wondered what had happened to Georgia that she would let Alfred conduct her business affairs. I had trouble believing it, and then suddenly I didn't. I waited for them to continue.

My back was to them. I heard the rattle of ice when Roland took the Champagne from the bucket and refilled glasses. There was a moment of desultory small talk, the journalist and his wife recalling a long-ago weekend in Auvergne.

"They wanted too much for it," Hélène said.

"So we had to bargain with him."

"She was impossible."

"But when we want something —" Roland brought his fists together, then bent them as if he were breaking a pencil.

"She tried to pretend she didn't care if she sold it or not."

"They talked among themselves, it was hard to follow them. They were speaking rapidly in English. She kept saying, If you insist. Fifty Large. Not one cent less than Fifty Large. And she was smiling when she said it and he was smiling, too. What does 'Fifty Large' mean?"

I laughed out loud. "It means fifty thousand dollars. Or francs. Depending."

Roland colored and muttered something.

Hélène looked at him and shook her head. Then, to me: "We paid seventy-five thousand francs."

"His commission," I said lightly. I gestured at the portrait. "That's him, you know."

"The oaf?"

"Alfred," I said. "Her husband. He's a musician. Hence, the piano."

Roland stepped up beside me, peering at the picture. I guessed that I had brought unwelcome news, for he was scowling now as he looked at Alfred, virtually a guest in his living room. "That one insisted that we wait a day, and if we still wanted it, then we could have it. But it seemed to be a joke between them. They had a long conversation about it, and that was when she laughed and said Fifty Large." Roland hesitated, then added in a low voice, "I think she is cleverer than she looks. And he is, too."

"I didn't know it was him," Hélène said. "Put a tuxedo on a man and he's a different man."

"Lately the picture has become an irritant," Roland said.

"It's disturbing," I said.

"Still —" Hélène paused.

"I don't know how serious she is," Roland said.

"She has no reputation in Europe," Hélène said.

"We could fix that," Roland said.

Hélène turned to me. "We like it less now than we did. The picture does not hang well. Do you see what I mean?"

I said, "What does she call it?"

"Artists," Hélène said scornfully. "They make titles to suit themselves, not the owner of the picture. She calls this *Indivisible Deux*. But in Roman numerals, like the kings of France."

"That woman is impossible," Roland said.

"As you say," Hélène said. "We could fix it. What is a reputation except the gossip of experts?"

"But is it worth our while?" Roland put in.

"It's worth our while to recoup what we gave away," Hélène said.

"Probably it wouldn't be," I said smoothly. "It takes time and effort to manufacture a reputation. And it can be costly, and even then —" I shrugged doubtfully, explaining that Georgia Whyte was a recluse, famously stubborn, private, and neurotic. She was unpleasant about her work. She was sullen generally. She had no interest in money but valued her pictures far in excess of their market value, or any value. She was just an American Bohemian from Chicago. Also, I concluded, she drank heavily.

I was still looking at the picture, Alfred aloof in his tuxedo, his left hand on the piano, Georgia emerging from the wood. There was an erotic charge to it that was entirely unexpected; that was the turbulence I had seen earlier. It seemed to me a tremendously personal picture, instantly recognizable as Georgia Whyte's work; it was as recognizable as a Vermeer. Yet I had never seen anything she had done. I had only heard descriptions in her own words, and these were bound to be unreliable. Suddenly I knew that I must have *Indivisible II,* that owning it would help to revive my own heart; and I knew that I would have it only on loan, no matter how much I paid. I felt better than I had in months, the cloud over my spirit dissolving as I looked at Georgia's picture. I had no doubt that Roland and Hélène would give it up; only the price remained to be negotiated. And whatever they asked, I could afford.

I had one last question as we moved into the dining room, with its glittering chandelier and formal portraits of Roland and Hélène, flanked left and right by wee Matisse sketches.

"I haven't seen her in a while and I'm not sure I'd recognize her," I said to Hélène as we took our places. "But I am often in Auvergne."

She looked at me strangely.

"So perhaps I'll look her up."

"She shows at a little gallery near the church in Mont Dore. You can't miss it. And you will find her in the market on Saturdays."

"And her appearance?"

"I suppose she's younger than I am. Perhaps she does not take care of herself as she should but she's attractive in an American way. She dresses without chic. She wears her hair carelessly. She is like any ordinary American housewife. You will notice her easily enough because she is always followed by her husband, and he is dressed in a dark suit and carries a straw basket. They stand out in a crowd, those two. And they have a little boy, who I must say is quite adorable."

"Her husband," I began.

"Never leaves her side," Hélène said.

"And he negotiates for her?"

"Fiercely," Hélène said. "As I have told you. Indiscreetly."

So far, so good, I thought. I wanted to believe that she and Alfred had succeeded. I wanted to believe that whatever Georgia was looking for she had found in Auvergne: consolation, a way to live, a new objectivity even. But I had one more question, hoping for one answer but dreading the other. "Would you say she is happy?"

"Happy?" Hélène said with a laugh. "What is happy?"

The opposite from you, I wanted to say but didn't. I thought suddenly of Monet's heroic magpie on a fence rail in the winter sunshine, the magpie no longer poised for flight but at rest.

"I'll tell you this," Hélène said. "She has no ambition, that one."

I nodded sympathetically.

"Instead, she is an egoist. Heartless."

"Heartless," I said.

"We would have gone to a hundred," Hélène said.

"A formidable price," I said.

"She's indifferent," Hélène said. "She's a cold one. I know girls like her. They are on every continent, taking themselves seriously, saying they do not have to play by the rules. They make me laugh, so wrapped up in themselves, loving themselves and saying they love their work. They believe they do not have to conform. They believe that the world will run to their clock, and that they need not be cooperative. And you are quite wrong, Monsieur Forrest. You of all people, it surprises me. She does not value her work. If she valued her work, she would want to see it sold and would make an effort. Loving is valuing, Monsieur

Forrest. Love *is* ambition, don't you see?" Hélène's voice had risen, and now she shook her head angrily. "But yes," she said. "Yes, I would say she is happy enough. Why wouldn't she be happy? She's a fool."

I waited a moment before replying.

"Good," I said mildly. "I'm happy to hear it. She deserves it, whether you think she is chic or not. I'll look her up when I'm in Auvergne."

"Do that," Hélène said. "An old friend. Surely she'll be glad to see you."

"And perhaps at a later time we can talk about your picture. As it no longer amuses you."

"Of course. An appointment is easily arranged." She looked at me with a bright malicious smile. She knew that I wanted the picture and would do anything to get it. Hélène was a connoisseur of desire and acquisition and knew all the symptoms.

"But first, I'll see what she has in the gallery."

"There are only one or two pieces," Hélène said. "Inferior things, unpriced. You must negotiate your own price, and she'll probably take anything you offer, since you're a friend from Chicago. But I daresay your experience will be similar to ours. Out of sentiment you'll pay too much for the picture and then discover that you can't live with it, because it won't hang. And nobody can. It asks too much. It's hers and will always be hers. It isn't intended for anyone else. That's her little joke on the world."

Hélène paused then, all mischief. "But you'd better hurry because I have the suspicion that they're moving on to somewhere else, perhaps to another region of our remote countryside, some place you've never heard of. They are like Gypsies, those two. They are afloat in our world. They will never settle. They will never be content. And there is something not quite right about him." Hélène sipped her wine, leaned close to me, and confessed, "She made the strangest remark when Roland insisted about the picture, saying that he did not wish to wait. He wished to buy it *then,* that moment. She said — almost bitterly, I thought, certainly rudely — 'I am not an entertainer.' Whatever could she mean?"

I looked at the ceiling. "I'm afraid she doesn't care for people like you, Hélène."

"Ridiculous," Hélène said. "Without people like me, she would cease to exist. She would be *kaput.*"

"As you say, artists suit themselves."

"The world would be better off if there were no artists, only art."

"A devout thought," I said.

Hélène turned then, and the table turned with her. Conversation was general but I did not contribute. Hélène was ignorant and undependable but probably she was right about Georgia's joke on the world. Everyone had a private joke. The private joke was the sword we defended ourselves with. Georgia had her own rules, and it was true that they were different from the world's rules. There were very many voices available to a human being and you chose the one that suited you. You chose the one you could live with and that pleased you, hoping that it would please the world as well; and if it did, you were a success. I of all people understood this.

Through the dining room doorway I could see Georgia's picture. At a distance it seemed to lose some of its turbulence; it acquired the equilibrium of its surroundings. Of course I was viewing it through candlelight, and the laughter at the table was loud. My glass was empty and a servant refilled it. I wondered if *Indivisible II* was a picture for the long haul or only a momentary thing, an infatuation. From this distance, nude Georgia could barely be seen, and of course her initials were invisible. Only Alfred was front and center. The picture seemed to recede as I looked at it, and then I wondered if it would always stand as a rebuke, a kind of aesthetic reprimand.

I turned back to the glittering table — in anger, I thought, but shame quickly took its place. How little we know of desire, and how crudely we define satisfaction. In judging, how convenient it is to slip truth's noose, and let the lie live a little longer. I heard Hélène's laughter; someone was telling a joke. I imagined Georgia and Alfred and the baby in flight, on the run here or there in provincial France. They would come upon a village in Ardèche or Dordogne, some place safely out of the way. It was Saturday afternoon and they were returning home from the market, Georgia in her American jeans and Alfred in his black suit, their little boy at their side. Only a few hours of daylight remained, and Georgia wanted to get back to her canvas. She would be explaining the canvas to Alfred, who would be nodding as if he understood. And then she would laugh, making some private gesture, bending to kiss her son.

I pulled for them, wanting them to succeed, and then I felt a sudden rush of despair because I saw the future. I feared that for the rest of my life I would be seeing Georgia Whyte's work in unexpected places. I'd look up and there she'd be, staring at me accusingly from the window of some out-of-the-way gallery or Left Bank living room, the near North Side or Winnetka even, the artist herself all but invisible, disappeared into her portrait as Alfred disappeared into his music, but her work potent, heroic, mountainous in its unrest —

Oh, what a life!